# WHAT GOES *UP*

★ "Katie Kennedy has invented a young cast so sympathetic and disarmingly funny that even science-indifferent readers will resolve to understand the laws of physics and other geeky topics of conversation that come up alongside more typical teen concerns." —*Shelf Awareness*, starred review

"A funny, introspective story." —*School Library Connection*

"Likable characters and laugh-out-loud dialogue will make this a winning choice for reluctant readers and science-fiction fans alike." —*Kirkus Reviews*

"An original and funny adventure." —*SLJ*

"Smart science, plenty of action, and no small amount of snarky banter round out an exciting and poignant read." —*Publishers Weekly*

# LEARNING TO SWEAR IN AMERICA

An Indies Introduce Pick
An Indie Next Pick
A *USA Today* "Happy Ever After" Must Read Romance

★ "Pitch-perfect. This novel is made to savor—readers will want to catch every nuance of Kennedy's multidimensional characters." —*Publishers Weekly*, starred review

★ "The balance of wit, romance, danger, and one huge philosophical and ethical dilemma is brilliantly managed here. . . . A nail-biting climax with a cinematic aftermath and an even more nail-biting resolution round out this thoroughly entertaining sci-fi disaster, romance, action/adventure mashup." —*BCCB*, starred review

"An end-of-the-world romp that will prompt readers to think and to laugh." —*Kirkus Reviews*

"Kennedy's snappy depiction of the multifaceted, whip-smart teens and the crackling dialogue . . . is an entertaining, genre-bending mix of quirky romance and realistic sci-fi, with some thought-provoking questions about adulthood." —*Booklist*

Books by Katie Kennedy

*Learning to Swear in America*
*What Goes Up*

# WHAT GOES
## *UP*

## KATIE KENNEDY

**BLOOMSBURY**
NEW YORK  LONDON  OXFORD  NEW DELHI  SYDNEY

BLOOMSBURY YA
Bloomsbury Publishing Inc., part of Bloomsbury Publishing Plc
1385 Broadway, New York, NY 10018

BLOOMSBURY and the Diana logo are trademarks of Bloomsbury Publishing Plc

First published in the United States of America in July 2017 by Bloomsbury Children's Books
Paperback published in July 2018 by Bloomsbury YA

Bloomsbury books may be purchased for business or promotional use. For information on bulk
purchases please contact Macmillan Corporate and Premium Sales Department at
specialmarkets@macmillan.com

ISBN 978-1-61963-914-0 (paperback)

The Library of Congress has cataloged the hardcover edition as follows:
Names: Kennedy, Katie, author.
Title: What goes up / by Katie Kennedy.
Description: New York : Bloomsbury, 2017.
Summary: Teenagers Rosa and Eddie, trainees in a top-secret space exploration and research
program, must thwart the aliens' Earth-destroying mission by stealing their spacecraft and
traveling extra-dimensionally to an alternate Earth.
Identifiers: LCCN 2016037882 (print) • LCCN 2016050234 (e-book)
ISBN 978-1-61963-912-6 (hardcover) • ISBN 978-1-61963-913-3 (e-book)
Subjects: | CYAC: Science fiction. | Adventure and adventurers—Fiction. | Human-alien
encounters—Fiction. | Survival—Fiction. | BISAC: JUVENILE FICTION/Science Fiction. |
JUVENILE FICTION/Humorous Stories. | JUVENILE FICTION/Action & Adventure/
Survival Stories.
Classification: LCC PZ7.1.K505 Wh 2017 (print) | LCC PZ7.1.K505 (e-book) | DDC [Fic]—dc23
LC record available at https://lccn.loc.gov/2016037882

Book design by Colleen Andrews
Typeset by Westchester Publishing Services
Printed and bound in the U.S.A. by Berryville Graphics Inc., Berryville, Virginia
2 4 6 8 10 9 7 5 3 1

All papers used by Bloomsbury Publishing Plc are natural, recyclable products
made from wood grown in well-managed forests. The manufacturing processes
conform to the environmental regulations of the country of origin.

To find out more about our authors and books visit www.bloomsbury.com and sign up for our newsletters.

*For Mary Beth McFarland,*
*my first friend*

# WHAT GOES
## *UP*

# CHAPTER ONE

NASA stored the future in a hangar in Iowa. Rosa Hayashi's future, anyway. The tryouts for a position with the Interworlds Agency would take two days, but they started now. Rosa stepped into the hangar and didn't wait for her eyes to adjust. She found a seat and bounced a pencil on her leg while she waited for the future to catch up with her.

There were two hundred chairs with swing-up writing surfaces, all but one occupied by people just done with their junior year of high school. Enough legs were jackhammering to remove a stretch of highway. Finally a woman walked to the front of the room. Everything about her was sleek and measured and controlled.

"I'm Friesta Bauer," she said. She didn't have a mic on, and didn't need one. "You are all here because of your stellar qualities, but we're looking for people with interstellar ability." A few people chuckled.

Just then a big blond kid slipped into the doorway, his uncertainty outlined against the sky. He managed to be rumpled and clean-cut at the same time—*like a hobo in a fifties movie*, Rosa thought. He stepped in and stood against the wall, but everyone was looking at him and there were two red laser points on his chest from Friesta Bauer's eyes. He sighed and began searching for the only empty seat. It was in the middle of a row, of course.

No one shifted over for him.

He began the bump-and-apologize tour down the row, and was halfway to the empty chair when Ms. Bauer called out, "Do you know where you are?" The kid kept his head down but nodded.

"This is a place that requires excellence in a wide range of special skills. *Punctuality* is not a particularly advanced skill. I have half a mind just to cut you now."

The kid plowed on toward his seat, his face twisted in misery.

"You have interrupted me," Ms. Bauer barked. "Do you know who I *am*?"

"No," he said. He looked up at her. "Do you know who *I* am?"

"No," Ms. Bauer said.

"Good." He sank into his seat as laughter rose up around him. Ms. Bauer gave him a wry smile and a long look, but then she went on.

"Everyone here has survived a rigorous preliminary exam administered through your high schools, but you'll find our tests are beyond what a high school can conduct. You're applying for one of the most elite jobs in the world. We're looking for specific skills—extreme skills—and we're not telling you what they are."

She looked at a guy down the row from Rosa. He had a sweep

of dark hair and was fingering his phone. His case had his name spelled in gold block letters that Rosa could see without squinting: *BRAD*. "A reminder that you have all signed a gag order regarding the testing process and IA facilities. The only place you can take photographs is in the cafeteria." She pursed her lips slightly. "We're not afraid of aliens coming across pictures of our meat loaf. It would only make them fear us."

They laughed, and the guy with the hair—Brad—slipped his phone back in his pocket.

"So—a reminder of who we are and what we do. The Interworlds Agency is under NASA. When they proved that the universe is infinite, IA was created to deal with the implications." She gave them a sober look. "In an infinite universe, every possible combination of atoms will occur more than once. Which means that many habitable planets are out there—most of them very different from ours, no doubt—but some of them harboring intelligent life."

She looked at them over a clipboard.

"That means there are aliens."

Rosa felt a little thrill run up her spine.

"Contact with them will require traditional exploration—travel in spacecraft," Ms. Bauer went on. "NASA's working assumption has been that this will be a lengthy process." She looked around the room. "That's true unless a more advanced civilization is looking for us."

Two hundred kids shifted in their seats.

"IA's mission is to explore, assess, engage, and protect. We are Earth's sentries. Given the mission," she said, "and the magnitude of the task, our testing procedures are not excessive. This isn't a normal job application because it isn't a normal job."

She tapped her clipboard against her leg.

"We want to add a third team to IA's roster. We haven't taken a new team in several years, but have decided it's prudent to prepare for alien interaction sooner than we'd expected."

Rosa exchanged an uneasy glance with the girl next to her.

Friesta Bauer's gaze swept the room. "When the day comes that we encounter intelligent life from another planet, our IA teams will be Earth's first line of defense. The military will take its cue from us. There are two people per team. *Two people.* That means you have to be better than excellent. We make no guarantee that we'll take a new team on—but if we do, there are two hundred of you, so you have a zero point five percent chance of being selected." She smiled faintly. "Congratulations. In the multiple worlds' business, those are good odds. If you are selected, you will receive a free education—your last year of high school and your college will be here. It will be rigorous, and it will make you highly employable in aerospace-related businesses, should you decide that IA is not for you."

She tucked her clipboard under her arm and rubbed her hands together. "You may consider yourself applicants, but we consider you contestants. This is a competition, and we began evaluating you when you entered the compound."

There was a rustle at that, and the blond guy slumped down but Rosa sat up straighter. She'd hugged both her parents goodbye, and her dad had cupped her head with his hand and kissed her forehead. "We're so proud of you," her mom had said. "No matter how the testing goes." Then her dad had whispered, so just the two of them could hear it, "But win, anyway." Had they been watching that?

Two aides stepped forward, holding stacks of tests. "Your first exam today is mathematics," Ms. Bauer announced. "Followed by physics, and then some more . . . idiosyncratic tests. There are bottles of water in the back of the room, and we'll give you lunch.

"You have two hours for this exam."

The aides passed Scantron sheets, scrap paper, exam booklets, and sharpened pencils down the aisles. When they were done, Friesta Bauer said, "These preliminary exams are to weed out anyone who's here because of an irregularity with the test at their high school." She stared hard at the blond kid, then gave the rest of the room a frosty smile. "We will be making the first cuts at the end of the day. You may open your booklets."

The first problem was $3 + 5$. Rosa stared at it for a moment, wondering if there was a trick. She chose (B) 8, and moved on to a calculus question. Twice more there were first grade questions and she read them both three times, just to be sure. She checked her watch, but she was okay on time. She felt good about the math section until she realized that everybody in the place probably felt good about it, too.

Rosa had checked all her work when Ms. Bauer called, "Pencils down," and they got a break. She didn't need to go to the bathroom but she did, anyway. No point taking any chances. There were eight guys standing outside their bathroom, and about thirty girls ahead of Rosa. They had proven that the universe is infinite and contains an infinite number of planets—an infinite number of Earths—but they still couldn't put enough women's bathrooms in public buildings.

When the break was over, Ms. Bauer led them to an adjacent building, to a room with banks of computers separated by partitions. "Take a seat," she called, moving to the front of the room. "By the way, some of you have terrific pedigrees."

Rosa straightened, in case Ms. Bauer was going to mention her. In case people were going to look.

"Among you are the offspring of a Fields Medal winner, two astronauts, a chemistry Nobel laureate, a Gauss Prize winner, a Maxwell Medal winner, and the heads of the National Oceanic and Atmospheric Administration and the Los Alamos National Lab." That last one was Rosa. And then Ms. Bauer read their names and made them wave to everybody. The guy who came in late was a row ahead of Rosa. He turned and looked at her, and not in a particularly friendly way. The way Rosa saw it, the only reason Ms. Bauer would single out the science legacy kids was to up the pressure on them. And she did not actually need that.

"The physics exam is fifteen questions long. You have two hours. In order to take the exam, you first have to find it. Go." She hit a stopwatch.

Rosa stared at her, and then at the people around her, half of whom were still standing. All of them had wide eyes as they scrambled for seats. Most people were frantically booting up their computers, ready to scan files for the exam. The big guy ahead of her stood on his chair, glancing over the room's perimeter. Smart—what if this exam was also in paper booklets, stacked somewhere in the back? They'd all be messing with their computers, wasting precious test time. She watched his eyes while she booted up, and when his blond head sank below the partition she gave the computer her full attention.

It wasn't difficult to find the exam, as it turned out—it was on the hard drive. The file name was the date and the formula for pressure. Fifteen questions, two hours—eight minutes per question, including checking her work. There was no scrap paper, but there was a notepad feature on the computer, and a calculator, too. She allowed herself six minutes for each question.

Which was fine until she finished the fifteenth problem and saw that the scroll bar wasn't all the way to the bottom of the screen, so she scrolled down and discovered five more problems. Hard problems. Was the exam really twenty problems long? Was it a test to see if they noticed the scroll bar's position? Or was it to see if they could obey orders—were they only supposed to do fifteen problems because that's how long Ms. Bauer had said the test was?

Rosa worked the last five problems as fast as she could, trusting that her earlier work was correct as it stood. When Ms. Bauer called, "Time!" Rosa was done, but barely. She wasn't used to close scrapes—nobody here was—and she didn't like them. "The cafeteria is on the ground floor," Ms. Bauer said. She was very calm. It was incredibly irritating. "You have half an hour."

The lunch room was blue and silver and decorated with giant posters of photos taken by the Hubble telescope. Rosa got a vegetarian pilaf and a cup of fruit, and hesitated for a moment at the end of the line. Because of course everybody had spread out, and there was no empty table. She started walking, slowly, so she

didn't look awkward. She was passing a group of guys when one of
them caught her eye and motioned her over, and she was grateful
to slink in opposite him. "I'm Ellis," he said, and actually stuck his
hand out to shake. Seriously? At lunch? She gave him the quick-
est handshake she thought she could get away with.

"Rosa."

The other guys introduced themselves. One of them put his
phone on hover and grinned as it snapped a group photo of them.
"Upload to my social media sites," he said as it returned to his
hand. He smiled sheepishly. "Gotta make some people jealous."

As soon as Rosa took a bite, Ellis spoke again.

"So, where are you from?"

She looked up. Of course he was talking to her. She chewed
slowly, but he kept his eyes on her. "New Mexico."

"But where are you *from*?"

"A pleasant ranch house on Bayo Canyon?"

"Like, what are you?" he asked.

"Dude," one of the others said. "She's from New Mexico."

"*What* am I?" She wanted to say, *Smarter than you*, or *Not
a jerk*. Instead she sighed loudly and said, "I'm an American of
French and Japanese descent."

"Wow," Ellis said. "Good combo." She flushed. "Which half is
which?"

Rosa stared at him. "My left side is French."

One of the guys snorted appreciatively. Ellis scowled.

"What do you think will be on the 'idiosyncratic' exams?" the
other guy said. "That can mean anything."

They started talking about the exams, and she only half listened. Across the cafeteria the late guy was snarfing down a cheeseburger. He was listening to the kids he was sitting with, but wasn't talking. And—seriously? He was eating the fries some girl didn't finish.

Rosa glanced up and for the first time noticed discreet camera domes on the ceiling. She straightened involuntarily, although it probably wasn't going to be her posture that got her kicked out.

Were they watching, even now?

# CHAPTER TWO

Eddie had a pretty huge lunch, once you counted finishing the food of everybody around him, but he hadn't had breakfast. Didn't have dinner last night, either—he was still hitching out here. He'd slept in the bus station in town, then walked to the compound that morning. So he was still chewing french fries when the IA aides came to take them back to the hangar. He'd hoped they would get to try a flight simulator, but no luck. While they were gone somebody had cleared out the desks, and in their places were two hundred copier-paper boxes in even rows.

"Stand behind a box," Ms. Bauer called.

Which box might matter. It might matter a lot. Eddie took a position behind a box near the front. If they had to take anything up to show her, he'd get there before the stiffs in the back.

"This is partly a physical task," she said. Eddie rolled his shoulders. Rosa gripped the crossbody strap of the coral bag she was wearing. "When I tell you to, you're going to take the lid off your box. There's an item in it that you need to assemble, and you're on a tight timeline."

Eddie exchanged a glance with the guy next to him, a small, nerdy-looking black kid. He gave Eddie a half smile, and Eddie gave him a half shrug. They were only giving things by halves today. When you have a half percent chance, you don't give away more than you have to. Even in smiles.

"You'll receive one point for each part of the item you finish, and each unfinished part will cost you two points. When you're done, or when the whistle blows, return your item to the box and sit down." She looked out over them. "Your task is to complete the item in your box—to put it together. Is that clear?"

It was clear.

"Go!" she shouted.

Eddie pulled the box lid up with both hands and stared inside. It was a strand of Christmas lights, very long, incredibly tangled. All the sockets were empty; the bottom was filled with loose bulbs—the tiny, white kind. He pulled the string out hand over hand, the way you'd pull entrails from a shark. Bulbs cascaded off it, most falling back into the box.

Eddie grabbed bulbs two at a time and fell into a rhythm, screwing one in with each hand. The guy next to him was untangling his whole string before he started. He saw Eddie looking.

"It'll be harder to untangle when the bulbs are in," he said.

Which was true, but that wasn't part of their task. The IA woman—Bauer—had said to put it together. Untangling wasn't part of putting it together.

Eddie hoped.

He worked on one knee, filling the exposed sockets first. When he hit the plug he worked his way back along the wire, poking a finger under tight loops, feeling for empty places. He pulled the green wires into looser loops so he could get to the sockets but didn't take time to pull the plug through.

And . . . he was done. He dumped the tangle of lights into the box. It flopped over the edge like a dead octopus. The kid beside him kept working. His wires were lying in an orderly coil, but only half the bulbs were in. He'd wind up with a negative score.

The whistle blew.

"Leave them," Ms. Bauer said, standing up from her desk. "Follow me."

They trailed her out of the hangar and across a tarmac toward the building they'd taken the physics test in. The sun felt good on Eddie's arms, and a breeze ruffled the sleeves of his T-shirt. Ms. Bauer led them into a corridor and stopped between two doors, shouting to be heard down the hall.

"It's the same setup inside both rooms—it doesn't matter which one you go in. There's an Agency official in each room who will tell you what to do next." She nodded to the first two kids, and they looked at each other and then one pulled the big silver handle on the left door, and the other the one on the right. After maybe thirty seconds Ms. Bauer looked through the glass panels on the doors, nodded to someone inside, and sent the next people in. The line was long, but it was moving fast. The people at the front were craning to see through the glass, and that's exactly what Eddie was going to do, too. Speed must be an issue with this test.

Even a hint of what to expect could make the difference—because this was a competition he had to win.

When he got to the front of the line he peered in, but there was a panel set up to block the view. Then Ms. Bauer motioned a girl into the left room and sent Eddie through the right door. A man stepped out from behind the screen. He wore an IA ID badge on his lapel.

"Step around, please."

Eddie did. There was a box, about a foot square, on a table like you see in church basements. That was all that was in the room: the table, the screen, the man, the box.

"There's a scorpion inside the box," the man said. Eddie tried to look cool but knew his eyes popped. There was a rubber cuff at the opening in the box—no seeing past it. "If you're stung, you'll receive medical care." He lowered his head slightly and held Eddie's gaze. "Put one hand in the box, and keep it there for ten seconds."

Eddie thought of Schrödinger's cat, in a box with poison. You didn't know if the cat got into the poison and died until you opened the box. Schrödinger said the cat was both alive and dead—and he was right. On one world it would be alive; on one it would be dead. Maybe the scorpion was dead. The man hadn't said it was a live scorpion.

Right then Eddie heard scrabbling from inside.

"You have two seconds to put a hand in the box."

Eddie stared at him. Then he grabbed the man's wrist and pushed his hand in the box. The man's eyes flared wide with surprise and his mouth opened, but he didn't struggle. Eddie held his wrist tight, anyway. "Time," the guy said, and pulled his hand out.

"You used a big beetle, didn't you?" Eddie said. "There isn't really a scorpion in the box."

"Oh," the man said, "there is . . ." He looked at Eddie's adhesive name tag. ". . . Eddie Toivonen."

Then he pointed to the far door.

# CHAPTER THREE

Rosa sat with everyone else in a banked lecture hall beyond the scorpion room, rubbing her left hand on her shorts. She wasn't hurt, but the scorpion had brushed against her—hard, scaly like a roach, and now she couldn't stop squirming. She didn't see anyone who'd been injured, but she didn't see anybody who looked happy, either.

Ms. Bauer walked forward, and she was almost smiling. "You'll break into two groups for the next tests, just to make them manageable. Split yourselves into even groups." No one moved. She clapped her hands together and barked, "You're supposed to be smart. Can you count to one hundred?"

They jumped up and pulled apart like a cell dividing. Eddie's group wound up with an extra person, and they all seemed to decide that Eddie was the spare. Several people pointed him across the room, and, face impassive, he joined Rosa's group.

A man led the first group away. Friesta Bauer stood in front of the group containing Eddie and Rosa. "You probably have a little restless energy after the last test," she said. They laughed nervously. "So, time to play outside."

She led them out behind the hangar to a field with a zipline—the tall takeoff tower, the lower landing platform, and the cable strung between them. Rosa's stomach jumped off the tower and landed in her ankles.

The kid with the sweep of dark hair—Brad—ran his hands over his temples. "Looks like we don't have to get on that thing," he whispered. "Thank goodness."

Rosa nodded, but her focus was on a guy standing in the middle of the field. He held a box containing a bunch of remote controls like the type for video games. "Take one, and then line up. Give yourselves about a yard on either side."

Ellis from lunch was in the group, and when Rosa reached for a remote control her hand touched his and he smirked. She slipped beyond Eddie so she wouldn't have to see him. On the ground ten yards ahead of them was a line of foot-long toy helicopters. Thirty yards beyond that were plant stands topped by yellow cylinders with blue lids.

"You're going to play with blocks," Friesta Bauer said when they'd lined up. "Your goal is to put a block in the container directly across from you. If you put your block in a different container, you will fail the exercise. If you fail to get a block in the container, you will fail the exercise. You may not talk. Got that?"

They all nodded. She walked across the path, dropping blocks beyond the helicopters. They were red and oddly shaped—more complicated than triangles, but too far away to get a good visual. Rosa examined the remote while she finished, and wondered if it would operate the helicopter in front of her, or a different one. Because they took remotes at random, and each would have to be programmed for a specific helicopter. Anybody who didn't realize that was going to operate one helicopter while looking at another.

Ms. Bauer had dropped all the blocks and stood now at the far side of the field, beyond the zipline cable.

The first thing Rosa had to do was determine which helicopter her remote was operating.

Friesta Bauer held up a stopwatch and shouted, "Go!"

Rosa pulled the joystick up and toward her, scanning to see which helicopter would fly the opposite direction from all the others. But two helicopters were coming toward them, so she nudged it left. Two swooped left. Had they rigged it so that each person controlled more than one? She tapped the control up, so the helicopter would rise—she didn't dare move it right; unless the other toy moved right, too, she would crash them. Besides, it was a good idea to gain height, because all around them helicopters were crashing and people were swearing and then going suddenly silent as they remembered they couldn't talk.

Two helicopters rose.

Beside her, Eddie hissed under his breath. Rosa looked at him, an eyebrow raised. She held her control so he could see it and moved her helicopter a little to the left. One helicopter moved. Ah—mystery solved. He'd been thinking along the same lines that she had, and now she knew which was hers. Around them people were untangling rotary blades and the pincers on the bottom of the choppers to lift the block. All without talking.

Rosa descended carefully over her block. Eddie swooped down for his, opened the pincer perfectly, and was off with it, headed for the container. She suspected he had more remote control experience than she did. Rosa hovered over her target, wallowing in the air, until she figured out how to get a grip on it. But she got airborne again and was off to the container before anyone else was untangled.

And—ha!—Eddie couldn't get his block in the opening. She hovered over the container, carefully centering her block, and lowered it. She could see the red against the blue lid—this must be why they used different colors. But it wasn't going in. She moved the block around on the lid, in case the hole was off-center. Seemed like the kind of thing they'd do.

Maybe the block was a complex shape and she was holding it wrong. What if she had it on its side? It would never go through. Eddie wasn't having any more success than she was. Everybody else had their helicopters sorted out by now and were swooping into their containers. *Crap.* She'd squandered her advantage.

Rosa flew the helicopter straight back to her and made it hover in front of her face so she could look closely at the block's shape. It was a star—it wouldn't go in on its side, but her pincers were holding it upright. Why wouldn't it go in?

Eddie took a good look at it, too, which wasn't fair—it was Rosa's idea to examine the block, and he hadn't lost any time because of it. She sent her helicopter swooping back toward her container. Blondie's hovered, pincers empty, trying to pry his lid off. She glanced down the row of cylinders—no one was getting a block to go in.

Rosa wished she could talk to him. Instead, she left her block on the floor and flew her helicopter over to his cylinder, angling to avoid his rotors. He looked sharply sideways at her. Rosa concentrated on getting her pincer to grip the edge of his lid. Ms. Bauer stood at the far side of the field, watching them, and she didn't want to risk disqualification by communication—she didn't dare nod to the kid, so she held her control out in front of her, her thumb on the lift toggle. He held his control beside hers, and together they lifted the helicopters. His lid came off.

He could have retrieved his block and won, but he swept over and helped Rosa get her lid off. When they dropped their blocks in their respective cylinders, they plunked at almost the same time. Did he beat her? Even if he did, *she* was the one who figured out the test. It was an exercise in cooperation—the only way to get the lid off was to use two helicopters. If they scored fairly, she would come in first.

But Rosa didn't trust these people to be fair.

# CHAPTER FOUR

Friesta Bauer led them into a cavernous building and called, "Listen up. There are four more tests this afternoon. You'll move through them as fast as you can. You start by running across this rope net," she said, gesturing behind her. The thing was immense. "When you reach the other side, there's a card game."

They shifted at that. Seriously? Cards?

"The instructions are on the sign at the table as you sit down. Read them, and play the game until the dealer tells you you're done. Then follow the arrows to the glass elevators and get in. When you exit the elevator, there will be one more test. That'll be it for the day."

Eddie didn't like the mention of the elevator—Ms. Bauer made it sound like one of the tests. And the only thing you can do with an elevator is stop the stupid thing and make people sweat it out— see how they interact in close quarters, and if they're claustrophobic. This could go badly for him.

"First twenty!" They shuffled into position. "Go!"

He ran forward and jumped onto the rope net so that he landed about three feet in from the edge. It creaked and dipped beneath him, coarse under his fingers as he pulled himself forward. The net stretched horizontally maybe fifty yards. The open spaces were large—plenty of opportunity for a leg to fall through. He crawled forward. Eddie was pretty sure he was in better shape than most of these kids, and his size gave him a reach advantage, but a smaller guy scrambled past, the ropes barely sagging beneath him.

Eddie had to win.

He grabbed for the ropes, imagining his basketball coach in his face, blowing his whistle, pushing, pushing. He passed the skinny kid, leaving the ropes swaying in his wake. He reached the far side of the net and swung to the ground in first place, which meant he had his pick of the twenty card tables. Eddie ran for the one closest to the sign to the elevators. It would save him a step running to his claustrophobic doom.

His dealer was an older guy with a ponytail and one earring. He stared impassively as Eddie picked up the white sign that was lying facedown on the table.

*You have responded to a hostage situation. Twenty civilians are trapped in a diner. You have no backup, no weapons, and no way to change this situation. However, the perpetrator will let you play a game of 21 for each hostage's life. If you get a score of eighteen to twenty-one, he releases the hostage. If you go over twenty-one, he shoots him/her on the spot. You have five minutes.*

*What even the heck?* A timer dinged. Eddie looked up to see the dealer holding up a photo of a young woman in a blue shirt. She was smiling at the camera like she was in love with whoever was holding it. The dealer slipped him two cards off the top of the deck: a ten and a five. Eddie needed at least an eighteen or the bad guy would shoot her. He tapped the table. It was kind of a stupid scenario, really. You had to play for everybody, and if you went over you went over—he was going to kill them, anyway, so you really didn't have anything to lose.

The dealer slid him a third card facedown. Eddie flipped it over—an eight. Well, he lost that one. Sorry, pretty lady in blue. The dealer flipped up another photo—not the next hostage, but a photo of the woman crumpled on the floor, a bullet hole in the soft hair that framed her face. One hand was splayed across the floor as though she'd died reaching for the chair leg before her. *Son of a bitch.* She was a real person, a real hostage. Somebody really shot her.

*Son of a bitch.*

Eddie stared up at the dealer, hating him. The dealer looked at him blankly and raised an eyebrow. *Ready for the next?* his expression said.

They were using photos of a real shooting at a real diner. Real people. Which meant he had to have a photo like that to show for all twenty. Because Eddie could go over twenty-one on any hand. Which meant the earnest young man whose picture he flipped up was already dead. Eddie stared at him for a moment, and suddenly, desperately, wanted to hit twenty-one, even though he knew he couldn't save him. The guy could have been him.

The cards were a three and a four. Eddie tapped the table, and the dealer slipped him another card. A five. Twelve. Eddie tapped again—a ten. *Son of a bitch*. The dealer pulled a photo out and there was the guy on his back, his legs tucked under him, a giant red rip through the front of his white shirt, blood pooled below him and onto a copy of *The Hitchhiker's Guide to the Galaxy*. He never got to finish it.

The dealer flipped out a photo of an old woman standing outside holding a basket of tulip bulbs in one hand, a trowel in the other. Beaming. Eddie looked up at the dealer.

"Stop this," he hissed.

"No talking," he said. "If you speak again, you're disqualified."

Eddie rethought his strategy, but there was no getting around it. He had to play for every hostage, and just hope he would win a few—for his own sake. There was no helping them.

The dealer slipped him two nines and Eddie stopped—an eighteen. He'd saved the old woman. The dealer didn't show him the second photo, but he knew it was there. Next up was a little girl standing in front of a Christmas tree. All Eddie could do was spare himself seeing the next photo.

But he didn't.

In all, he saved the old woman and two more hostages—three of twenty. When the dealer flipped up the last photo of a man crumpled inside a door, Eddie stood, unsure if there was more, but the dealer jutted his chin toward the sign to the elevators and Eddie took off running, glad to get away from the photographs.

*Creeps.* Why had they done that to them? Eddie's armpits were clammy by the time he raced around the corner and stumbled to a stop in front of a row of four glass elevators. A redheaded guy was already there, and a moment later Rosa and another guy ran over. Four people, four elevators. Go time?

Friesta Bauer pressed a button, and all four elevators opened. "Enter." They stepped in, Eddie half a step behind the others because he took an extra lungful of air before crossing the threshold. They stood facing her, the glass doors open.

"This is a simple test. State your best observation of the physical laws in play around you while you're in the elevator. When you've said something accurate and meaningful, the elevator stops." She pushed a button, and the doors closed soundlessly. He couldn't see through the top or bottom, but the rest was a seamless glass oval, unbroken save for the handrail that ran around the inside. There was nothing worse than being trapped in a glass elevator, he thought.

"By the way," her voice sounded through a speaker on the ceiling, "try to stop the elevator quickly. There is a bottom."

Then the elevators began to free-fall. *Holy crap, there is something worse than being trapped in an elevator.* Eddie threw his hands up against the doors, trying to pry them open. *It's glass. Break the glass and you free-fall through the shaft.*

He had to say something about nature or some crap like that. Rosa's elevator creaked to a halt. He shot past it. "The humidity in my pants has increased significantly," he shouted. It didn't stop. "Um, for a liquid in free fall, surface tension, viscosity, and inertia are the relevant forces!" His elevator plunged on, but the redheaded guy's stopped. "The behavior of the liquid will depend on the contact angle with the container, which in this case is my pants," Eddie shouted. The glass under his palms vibrated as the elevator shuddered to a stop.

The elevator descended at a normal pace for maybe a floor, then the doors opened. Had he been that close to the bottom? He stepped into a corridor. A young guy in an Interworlds Agency shirt motioned him into an empty room.

"The others will be here in a minute," he said. They sat for a couple of minutes, the guy drumming his fingers on his thigh. "Did they tell you about the whiteboard?"

Eddie shook his head.

"They wrote down what you guys said in the elevator, so the judges can read it. There's some kind of scoring system." Eddie flushed. "Hey." The guy stood. "Do you mind if I take you on out there? When everybody's ready, they'll take you to another room." He glanced over his shoulder. "I'm kinda supposed to be somewhere else."

"Yeah," Eddie said. "Okay."

The guy led him out of the room and around the corner to a whiteboard. "They'll come out down there. Just fall in with them when they come by, okay?"

Eddie nodded, distracted by what was on the board. Each of their names was on a sticky note, and below it what they'd said. They'd written it word for word. Some kid named Ellis said, "Holy shit! Gravity! Gravity! There's no gravity in free fall! No gravity! Oh god I'm going to die no gravity." Eddie smirked. That made him feel a little better.

Under the note that said "Paul," someone had written, "Um um um. So in zero-g a free falling body can have tidal effects but possibly not in an elevator. Um, the inertial frame, um, shit, it takes two thousand three hundred newtons to crush the human skull. Let me out!" Eddie wanted to laugh, but the note with his name was over two references to humidity in his pants.

The last note said "Rosa"—Chopper Girl had a name. While plunging to her probable death she apparently had said, "Uh, uh, the geometry of space-time is Minkowskian—special relativity applies to free fall." So yeah, she won their round.

Then Eddie realized something. The guy had pointed to where the others would come out, and it was farther down the hall. They weren't going to pass the board. He scanned quickly for cameras—none. Some jerk could switch the sticky notes, and suddenly he would be the one who'd mentioned Minkowski. Why hadn't they thought of this? Somebody could totally steal that girl's thought.

He could.

She was one of the kids that Bauer pointed out—a science princess. She did it to tell them they already knew who was going to win. The pedigree kids. The ones who went to prep schools during the school year and expensive camps in the summer. She was saying that even though he had a chance, he didn't have a chance.

He could give himself a shot, right here. But he was not a thief.

Eddie crossed his arms and leaned against the wall. He didn't have to hope he looked tough—he knew he did. He'd guard the board until somebody came along, and then he was going to point out the problem to them. Because a place like this? He wasn't going to be the only contestant desperate for a spot with the Interworlds Agency.

A couple of minutes later an IA official appeared at the end of the hall and motioned him over. He just nodded while Eddie pointed out their security flaw, and then led him into a room and left. Chopper Girl—Rosa—was the only other person in the room. She waved at the chairs.

"Figure it out yet?"

"What's that?" Eddie said, sitting next to her.

"The final test. It was whether we'd cheat at the board."

He stared at her. *Oh, man. Of course they knew what they were doing. Of course they did.* He sat down and laced his fingers behind his neck.

"You okay?" She hesitated. "You didn't cheat, did you?"

"No, I didn't cheat!" He barked it at her.

Her breath caught and the color rose in her cheeks.

*Well, too bad.* Why would she assume he'd cheat? Why did everyone?

"Um, sorry," she said. "But maybe you're a little oversensitive?"

He snorted. "There are two hundred applicants, and every one of you is the top of some fancy-ass science school. Except for me."

"You're salutatorian of a fancy-ass science school?" she asked, a faint smile on her lips.

"No. I'm from Oolitic, Indiana. I go to a public high school—and it's not even in my town."

"Oh my god! I'm so sorry." She grimaced. "Sorry for how that sounded, too."

"Don't be."

"So are you, like, self-taught?"

He hesitated. "I live with my grandmother. She was an engineer. Never got promoted the way she should have. Women back then, you know." She nodded. "But the stuff she could tell you." He shook his head. "She kept me home from second grade once because I asked her why when I rode my bike to the ice cream stand my legs were sore the next day, but my heart wasn't. She explained that cardiac muscle can't go into anaerobic respiration, but I wanted to know why."

"So why is it?" Rosa asked.

"The percent of mitochondria in a skeletal muscle cell is one to three percent. In cardiac muscle, it's thirty to thirty-five percent."

"Wow. No wonder it doesn't go into anaerobic."

"I know, right?" He realized he was leaning toward her and shifted back in his seat. "Anyway, Grandma taught me most of what I know, or made me find it out myself. We built a rocket in the backyard once, and when we shot it off, it fell sideways and chased the neighbor's cows around the field."

She laughed.

"Then we had to climb in and get the rocket so the neighbor wouldn't know why his cows were spooked." He rubbed his thumbnail on his jeans, making a sawing sound. "Sorry I'm telling you all this."

She looked startled. "Don't be. Who knows, we might wind up working together."

He shook his head. "No, I think I ruined my chances earlier, on the scorpion test."

"That was just to see if we put in our dominant hand without thinking. It had to be, don't you think? A lot of these are just to see what we do under pressure."

"I didn't put in either of my hands."

"You froze?" she asked, frowning slightly.

"No. I put in the instructor's hand."

Her eyes popped comically wide. "You didn't!"

He nodded, then laughed. "I'm screwed, but no way you are. The Minkowskian space-time answer—that was genius." She flushed. "And you thought to work together on the chopper blocks. Cooperation would never have occurred to me."

The door opened and a kid came in. Rosa twisted her legs away. Eddie wasn't sure what was going on, but he scooted his chair out a little, just letting the guy know he was there.

"What do you think the last test will be?" he said.

"It's whether you cheated at the board, Ellis," Rosa said. "The guy who brought me in told me."

He went white. "What do you mean?"

She arched an eyebrow. "Did you switch the sticky notes with our names?"

Ellis stared at her for a second, then dropped his head to his chest.

# CHAPTER FIVE

They were back where it had started, two hundred kids in a hangar. Friesta Bauer was up front, but now Rosa was sitting next to Eddie. She was sorry he wouldn't be staying—there was something comfortingly solid about him.

"So, we come to today's cuts," Ms. Bauer said.

"Wow," Rosa whispered. "She doesn't go in for small talk." Eddie nodded.

"You all scored in the top tenth of the top percentile on the math test, compared to a national average. Seventy-nine of you failed to complete the physics exam. You didn't make good use of your time." The extra five questions. That didn't really seem fair.

"Those were just general screening tests. We expected these results. Failure to finish the physics exam only hurt you if you got a questionable result on another test. Which brings us," she said, glancing at her clipboard, "to the Christmas lights. She stared out at them. "People, there was no need to untangle the lights. Were you asked to untangle them?"

She waited, as though anyone was going to answer.

"No, you weren't. It was a waste of your time. This was about priorities and decision making." Fourteen people finished with negative scores. Another twenty people who didn't notice the scroll bar on the physics test finished with scores under two hundred. Those people will be cut." She glanced back at her clipboard. "Now, the scorpion results were very interesting."

Everyone squirmed except Eddie, who slumped fractionally. Rosa felt bad for him, but after what he did, she was surprised they hadn't cut him loose right then. Or arrested him.

"You were told to put a hand in a box with a scorpion—its tail was clipped, by the way." Nervous laughter from the contestants. "If you froze under pressure and put in your dominant hand— well, we're not the right place for you. We cut another seventeen people based on the scorpion test. Thank you for participating today. Your parents have been called and are waiting for you." She motioned to the door and read the names of all the people who'd been cut so far. Rosa hoped Ellis would be one of them, but no such luck. No one moved for a moment, then a girl got up and moved to the door without looking at anyone, and the others who were cut followed her out. The room was quiet.

"We got an unusual result from an eighteenth person," Ms. Bauer went on. Eddie slumped farther, and his shoulder bumped Rosa's. "One contestant, Eddie Toivonen, chose the attendant's hand, and put *it* in the box." There was an audible gasp from the crowd. "Eddie, stand up, please." He took a breath and rose. "Well done." He stood there for a moment, looking confused.

"Which brings us to the helicopter test," she said. Eddie slowly sank back onto his chair.

"Am I supposed to leave?" he whispered.

"I don't think so," Rosa said, and gave him a big smile.

"Sixty-seven people never did get the block in the canister. Eight of those wrecked their helicopters because they never figured out which one they were controlling. The other fifty-nine kept mashing the block into the lid of the canister, even though it didn't have an opening."

Rosa turned and looked at Eddie, eyes wide. "I thought it was off-center," she whispered.

He nodded.

"The opening was in the back of the canister," Ms. Bauer said. "Five of those sixty-seven people were eliminated by the scorpion test. The remaining sixty-two may leave now: Amy Stone, Maryanne Billings, Donald Jeffrey Tardall . . ." People started filing out. There were suddenly a lot more empty seats.

"The net was simply designed to frustrate you, to set you up for the next tests. However, one person was completely unable to negotiate it, became stuck, and didn't try to extricate herself. Britney Peterson, you've been cut."

Rosa slunk a little lower in her seat. Britney Peterson had to be a top-notch student. All she'd done was get stuck in a rope and cry about it. This was humiliating. Britney seemed to think so, too, because she was in their row and was sniffling as she pushed past, rushing for the door.

"The card game gave us some interesting results. The strategy was obvious—you had to take chances to reclaim the hostages. There was no other option. But once you realized they were real people, and saw graphic evidence of what happened if you didn't win their release, twenty-nine of you refused to play, or became so cautious that you didn't get a chance to play for all the hostages. How did that help them?"

"Like anybody's going to answer," Rosa whispered.

The woman looked over. Had her voice carried that much? There weren't as many people in the hangar now—less ambient sound to cover the whisper. She gripped her purse tighter.

"The point is, fifteen of you were so clouded by emotion that you failed to do the logical thing, even when your course of action was obvious. Those fifteen people are dismissed."

Again the names, the hesitation, then the shuffling for the exit.

"Which brings us to the elevator," she said.

A general groan rose from the room.

"There were two parts to this test—the first was making some observation of free fall while under stress—that is, while in free fall. There were any number of things you could have said." She looked up. "'Oh, shit' turned out to be the most common."

The contestants laughed nervously.

"Twenty-one people became completely tongue-tied and said nothing whatsoever. We had to stop their elevators. Two people recited the alphabet . . ."

Eddie snorted.

". . . which, while accurate, was not relevant. One person declared his love for Jenna Lindeman . . ."

Rosa winced. This was just humiliating.

"... which, while interesting to whoever Jenna is, has nothing to do with us." She read the list of people who were dismissed. When she called Eric Barger's name, she added, "Give Jenna our best." There was a little ripple of laughter.

"This is going to be terrible when it gets to me," Eddie said.

"What did you say? They hadn't put the sticky notes up on the board yet when I went past it. The guy just told me what they were doing." Rosa didn't say it was because she was the best. But she thought it.

"Um."

She kept looking at him. She wasn't letting him off that easily.

"I discussed states of matter."

"Well, that doesn't sound ..."

"Shh," he said.

"The rest of you referred to various natural laws that were vaguely relevant, usually interspersed with swearing," Ms. Bauer said. "The second part of the test was to see if you would cheat. We made it easy for you to claim someone else's thoughts as your own, and waited to see if you would do it." She scanned our faces. "Seven of you did. You have been cut."

Across the room Ellis rose. "That's not fair!" He turned and pointed over rows of empty seats toward Eddie. "That guy cheated with the scorpion!"

Eddie got very still. It was a coiled kind of quiet. Ms. Bauer gave Ellis a hard stare, and he dropped his hand but kept standing.

"We asked him to choose a hand," she said, her voice clipped, "and he chose the one of the person who'd put him in that situation. Where one hundred ninety-nine of you saw only two options—dominant or nondominant hand—Eddie saw a third way. We consider that to be excellent aggressive thinking under pressure. You, on the other hand, were standing in a hallway, looking over your shoulder, deciding whether to claim Miss Hayashi's thoughts as your own, knowing that she risked disqualification if your words were attributed to her." She flipped the pages on her clipboard. "Let's see what *you* said. 'Holy shit! Gravity! Gravity! There's no gravity in free fall! No gravity! Oh god I'm going to die no gravity.'" She looked up and the laughter stopped. "The people we select will be a *team*. They'll have to work together. Trust each other. She read the names of the people who cheated, and they had to get up and walk out in front of everyone.

"That would actually kill me," Rosa whispered.

"Based on the rankings, several of you will probably be eliminated by the first test tomorrow," she said. "But that's it for today. There are forty of you left. Rosa Hayashi and Eddie Toivonen, please stand."

They glanced at each other, and then stood. "These are our current leaders. Unless one of you can find a way to unseat them in tomorrow's tests, Rosa and Eddie will be our new trainees." She nodded to them, then turned and walked out of the hangar, her heels clicking on the floor.

Everyone was looking at them, and Rosa had the feeling she was the least popular kid in the room.

"Wow," Eddie whispered. "She just painted a target on our backs." They sank back down in unison, and one of the IA guys who'd been helping with the tests stepped forward.

"I'll take you to your dorm for the night. There's a pool table in the basement. Breakfast tomorrow is at seven thirty. You know where the cafeteria is—someone will drop by there at eight and show you where to go." He beckoned and they all lined up, shuffling forward as he handed out keys.

"Rosa Hayashi?" She nodded. "Room 331. Girls are on the third floor, boys on the second. Your bags are already in your room." A smile played at the corner of his mouth. "Two suitcases—you were planning to stay?"

She took the key. Of course she planned on winning—they all did. The suitcases had nothing to do with that. She just didn't travel light.

"I had a duffel," Eddie said quietly to the guy.

"Yeah, we got it," he said.

Eddie nodded, relieved. It had taken longer to walk out to the IA facility than he'd expected, and he hadn't had time to check in. He'd just dumped the duffel outside the hangar and hoped for the best. When they all had keys, the guy led them across a courtyard to a three-story cement building with a sign out front: Bohr Hall.

"Your key gets you into the building, onto your floor, and into your room. Dinner's ready for you. You're welcome to explore the compound, but be in your rooms by ten." He opened the door and they filed out.

Rosa was in the lead—along with a kid who stuck somebody else's hand into a box with a scorpion.

# CHAPTER SIX

Dinner was free and unlimited, so Eddie loaded his plate with macaroni and cheese and mashed potatoes and maybe a pound of bacon and two pieces of cherry pie. By the time he got through the line, there seemed to be a guys' table and a girls' table. Fine with him. He slid his tray onto the end of the guys', across from a skinny kid with a shock of mousy hair and a face like a bone chip. He looked like he was designed to slip into crevices. In a previous life he might have been a railroad spike, or a piton.

Eddie picked up a couple slices of bacon and ate them together. *My god, that's good stuff, all salty and fatty and crisp.*

"People should exchange bacon at weddings," he said. "Who gives a crap about rings? But if you're willing to share your bacon—that marriage is gonna last."

"If our test tomorrow morning involves cholesterol," the skinny guy said, "you're going to wash out."

"Worth it," Eddie said around a mouthful of food.

The kid grinned and extended his hand. "Trevor Clayborn."

Eddie wiped his hand on his napkin and shook. "Eddie Toivonen."

"You going to study this evening?" he said.

"No," Eddie said. "I know this stuff. You think I don't?"

Trevor put his hands up. "A couple of us are going to work together after dinner, if you want to join us."

Eddie took a drink of root beer to cover his hesitation. He'd intended to study, but he could do it on his own. "Thanks, but I'm good."

They spent the rest of dinner talking about the crazy things IA had done to them that day, and speculating on what they might do tomorrow. Guessing was pointless and they all knew it, but it passed the time.

Eddie went back to his room. He couldn't concentrate and didn't know what to study, anyway. How did you prepare for people who made you fly remote control helicopters?

So he wandered around the IA compound looking for a basketball hoop. It was a perfect night—the air still held a hint of warmth and carried the smells of the surrounding fields. Early summer in corn country, and full of possibilities. He found a rec building, but it was locked. The equipment these people must have, and they didn't have an accessible basket? NASA needed to prioritize better.

He went back to the dorm. The place had a no-frills bunker feel, a stairwell with a locked door at each end of the hallway, and bathrooms in the middle. It was a small building and most of the rooms were full. A few guys stood in doorways, talking quietly, but most of the doors were shut. Trevor's door was open and he was alone, sitting at the desk. His study partners had gone.

"How did you even prep for tomorrow?" Eddie said, on the off chance he hadn't been entirely polite earlier.

Trevor smiled. "We just reviewed formulas for a while—anything we could think of." Eddie nodded. It was as good a strategy as any. "I'm just reading a novel now." He lifted the book as proof. "What did you do?"

Eddie twisted his mouth ruefully. "Mostly look for a basketball court, but the rec center was locked. On another world, I could have gotten in," he said. "Hey, let's develop the means of interworld travel and go there."

"Sounds good. But what if it has weird diseases or something?"

"What? Another Earth?"

"Yeah," Trevor said.

Eddie shrugged. "I dunno. Maybe they'll have weird antibiotics to go with them."

"Would you still do it? If you knew there were weird diseases?"

"Probably." But Eddie knew he would. There was nothing he wouldn't risk, nothing he wouldn't do to get on here. He had to get a job, one way or another. And right now it was either exploring the cosmos for the Interworlds Agency or handing people fries back in Oolitic.

Well, not in Oolitic. They didn't have a fast-food place—you had to go to Bedford for that. *God, that's depressing.*

"I'm in third," Trevor said.

"What?"

"They taped the standings to the bathroom mirror."

"Yeah? What did you say in the elevator?"

Trevor flushed. "I talked about gravitational acceleration. I punctuated my discussion by beating on the doors."

Eddie laughed, and it turned into a yawn. He gave Trevor's door frame a double fist tap. "I gotta get to bed. It was a long day."

"Yeah."

Eddie unlocked his room, grabbed his toothbrush, and walked down the hall, brushing. By the time he got to the bathroom, he'd be ready to spit. A few guys watched him from doorways and open rooms, and it wasn't entirely friendly. Ms. Bauer had really stuck a bull's-eye on his back, announcing that he was in line for one of the spots. He spat and peed, and when he got to his room he flipped his dead bolt.

Eddie stripped down to his boxers. Then he set his phone alarm and lay on his back in bed, hands folded behind his head, and thought about things. He wished his grandma could see him now.

It was past midnight when he dreamed that he was back in Oolitic, working at a drive-through, and a fire truck pulled up to the window. He wasn't fast enough with the order and the driver blared the siren in his face, and what even the heck, because those guys are usually okay. Then he sat up in bed and the wail didn't stop. Doors banged open in the hall, and people shouted.

A fire, in the middle of the night, on a night they all needed sleep. What were the chances? Eddie jumped up and felt the door—cool. And then he thought about his own question. What *were* the chances? He picked up the trash can, and when he opened the door he led with it. Just in case some melonhead in the hall was waiting for him.

It didn't connect—no one was lying in wait for him, and he felt like an idiot running down the hall carrying a trash can.

"Holy crap!" Trevor shouted at him as he ran by in astronaut pajamas. Trevor was never going to live those things down.

Eddie thought about yelling that they should do a head count. Could anyone sleep through this? Somebody might have brought earplugs or a white noise machine—it wasn't out of the question. And there weren't any adults around. But another danger struck him as a lot more likely.

A guy was standing at the far end of the hall, shouting and waving everyone away toward the other end. Eddie ran at him.

"Other way!" he shouted. "Fire's in the stairwell! Exit the other way!"

"No," Eddie said.

The guy stared at him for a second as Eddie ran the last yards toward him, gripping a trash can. He took a step forward to block the door.

"You have to exit the other way."

Pretty calm, really, for a guy with a fire at his back. Eddie reached for the handle with his left hand and brought the trash can up with his right. The guy went for his hand, which meant that technically he walked into the blow. He pulled back, hands over his nose, swearing, and Eddie ran into the stairwell—which was going to be a major mistake if it was filled with flames.

The door handle was cool, though, and the stairwell was clear. For a moment Eddie thought he'd miscalculated and trash-canned an innocent do-gooder. He had to check, though—Ms. Bauer had told everyone that if they wanted a spot, they had to eliminate him or Rosa. Some people would do that with a dirty trick in the night. Eddie was six-two and one-ninety. If they were smart, they'd aim for Rosa. And everyone here was smart.

Then he heard scuffling on the floor below. Eddie swung down the steps, fingers playing on the rolled edge of the trash can. Rosa was in the first floor stairwell, and there were two guys there—one of whom had her arms pinned together and was hoisting her over his shoulder. Eddie could see the white spots on her wrists where his fingers pressed in. Rosa was kicking like crazy. The guy at the bottom of the stairs plastered himself against the door, avoiding her heels. The one holding her turned to carry her up the stairs and saw Eddie on the landing, and his face darkened.

"Put her down."

"She hurt her ankle. I'm helping her."

"Eddie!" Rosa screamed.

Eddie was going to reason with him, to point out that eliminating her probably didn't get them much closer to securing a spot. It seemed like the safest thing to do for everybody.

Then she screamed his name again, and the guy put his hand on her neck.

Eddie vaulted down the stairs and brought the can up and smashed him full in the face—he couldn't get his hands in front of him in time. The second the guy loosened his grip, Rosa twisted free, landed on the stairs, and shot past him, heading up. Eddie could kick this guy's ass, or follow Rosa. He really wanted to kick his ass.

He followed Rosa.

She was fumbling with her key on the third floor landing

when she heard him and looked, panicked, over her shoulder. The
key scraped in and she jerked the door open. Eddie hesitated in
the hall.

"I'd like to hide out in your room for a little while," he said.
"That okay?"

"We have to get out," she said. "There's . . ." She looked at
him. "There's no fire, is there?"

He shook his head.

"God, those jerks. Do we have to go out and get counted?"

"I don't see why," he said. "I think we should sit tight till the
firefighters come through to clear the building. And I think we
should stick together."

She unlocked her room door and stood in her door frame, staring him dead in the eye. "Am I safer with you than without you?"

He met her eye. "Yes," he said, and he meant it. "Yes, you are."

She thought about it for a moment, then motioned him in and
locked the door behind her.

# CHAPTER SEVEN

Rosa pulled her comforter off the bed and wrapped it around her, then sat on her desk chair with her legs curled up. Eddie sat on the floor with his back against her closet door.

"They were going to throw me down the stairs and say I tripped evacuating."

"God," Eddie said. "I'm so sorry."

They sat in silence.

"Knock knock," Eddie said.

She looked at him, an eyebrow raised. Finally she said, "Who's there?"

"Betty."

"Betty who?"

"Betty gets kicked out tonight."

She gave a soft snort. "Yeah. Both of them."

"There were three," Eddie said. "One was guarding the door."

"Three people were willing to do that?" she said. "Wow."

Eddie shivered. The day had been warm but now it was cool, and the floor was institutional tile. He was only wearing a pair of boxer shorts.

"You okay?" he asked.

She shook her head. "I had the best qualifying score in New Mexico. That may not sound all that impressive, but Los Alamos is in New Mexico."

"The National Lab," he said.

"Yeah. A lot of kids there are groomed for something like this since they were born. I'm one of them." She thought about her and Eddie being one-two for the trainee spots. She'd seen what he said in the free fall elevator. She knew she was the "one" in the one-two, though she didn't say it.

"I had a childhood devoted to memorizing the molecular weight of strontium," she said.

He tilted his head at her.

"When my parents were decorating my nursery, Dad painted the value of the cosmological constant around the top of the wall."

Eddie laughed. "Good man."

"Mom was *so mad*, and hired a decorator to paint pixies peeking through all those zeros. They laugh about it now."

He grinned.

She leaned forward. "I was born for this kind of thing. I'm really, really good at it. And then some Neanderthal grabs me in a stairwell. *That's* the cosmological constant—if you're female, it doesn't matter what you do, or how good you are at it—some jerk comes along and it all feels like nothing."

Eddie didn't say anything.

"Some jerk *will* come along," Rosa whispered.

"It's the Jerk Diffusion Principle," Eddie said. "Newton first proposed it."

She took a tissue from the box on her desk and wiped her nose.

"Because jerks repel everyone, even each other, every organization winds up with one. You know when you call customer service someplace and you get an officious pimple of a bureaucrat? That's their jerk. Because normal people don't like to answer the phone, right?"

She looked at the tissue balled in her hand.

"Knock knock," Eddie said.

She sighed, but she looked up.

"Who's there?"

"Carol."

"Carol who?"

"Carol lot about that blanket? Because I'd really like to wrap up in it."

He waited. She gave him a wry smile but didn't move toward the bed.

"Knock knock."

She rolled her eyes. "Who's there?"

"Juan."

"Juan who?"

"Juan way or another, I'm going to sweet-talk you into letting me use that blanket."

She pressed her eyes shut and shook her head, but she was smiling. Then she stood up, pulled the blanket off the bed, and dumped it on his head.

"Oooh, I get it," he said. "You wanted to keep ogling my manly physique."

"Oh, please."

"If you insist." Eddie curled his arms in classic biceps pose.

Rosa sat back in the chair and started to cry.

"Oh god," Eddie said. "I'm sorry."

She flipped a corner of the comforter over her head.

"I don't know what I did."

"It's not about you!" She pulled the comforter back down and screamed at him, "It's not about you! It's about *me*."

He nodded and stayed still. He was a big guy in the room of a small girl who'd just been attacked. Was it possible that knock-knock jokes weren't adequate to the situation? He wrapped tight in the blanket but he left his legs free. The door was locked, but he wanted to be able to get to his feet fast if he had to.

When Rosa was done crying, she wiped her face on the inside of the comforter. "Why do you tell knock-knock jokes?"

"Because I have a sophisticated comedic sensibility."

She lifted one corner of the comforter and gave him a baleful stare. Her skin was blotchy. "I don't think you know any other jokes."

Eddie drew up, mock offended. "Of course I do. Hey, why did the wise men have ashes on their feet?"

"The wise men? Like at Christmas?"

He nodded.

"I don't know."

"Because they came from afar."

She cocked her head, and then she got it. "From a fire? Oh my god, that's horrible. That's a horrible, horrible joke."

"That's why I usually confine myself to knock knocks."

Footfalls and voices started to fill the hall.

"They must have given the all clear," Rosa said.

He nodded. "You want me to get out before anybody sees me here, or wait a while longer?"

She hesitated. "Um, it would probably be best if you went back to your own room." She smiled an apology.

"Yeah," he said. "I should report those guys." He stood and gave the blanket an appreciative sniff. "Girl." He grinned and pitched it back onto her bed. He threw the dead bolt, peeked into the hall, then stopped with his hand on the edge of the door. "Lock it, okay?" She nodded. He touched his index finger to his forehead and left.

Rosa locked the door behind him, then turned off the light and got back into bed. She straightened the blanket and pulled it over her, then gave it a little sniff. "Boy," she said. And she smiled.

# CHAPTER EIGHT

Rosa wore red to breakfast because it's a power color, and she didn't want them to think she was afraid. She got a veggie omelet and cranberry juice and sat beside a couple of girls.

"Hey, I heard you got attacked in the night," one of them said. She was an African American girl with huge dark eyes and a sleeveless shirt that showed off toned arms. "You okay?"

Rosa nodded. "Yeah, they were trying to move up." She cut a piece of her omelet with the side of her fork. "I'm okay."

"What do you think we'll do today?" the other girl said. She was a white girl who didn't wear makeup.

"I don't know," the sleeveless girl said. "But I'll bet it's crazy."

They chatted a little but mostly ate. Eddie came in halfway through breakfast, wearing untied shoes. His socks were sticking out of his pocket, and he put them on while he shuffled through the line. He looked over at Rosa. She flushed and pretended not to see him. She turned to the sleeveless girl, then regretted it and looked back. He'd already found a seat by himself.

At eight o'clock a guy in an Interworlds Agency shirt poked his head into the cafeteria and motioned to them. They followed him to a conference room set up with rows of chairs facing a podium with a rolled-up screen. Ms. Bauer stood at the podium. They shuffled in. Rosa sat between Toned Arms and No Makeup. She looked around for the goons, even though she was sure they were gone.

"Good morning," Ms. Bauer said. "Yesterday I mentioned that there was another test today. That was a little misleading—you've already had that test. Three of your number failed, in spectacular fashion."

She looked at Rosa, and Rosa's cheeks grew hot.

"You may have heard that three prospective trainees assaulted Miss Hayashi last night. Those people have been expelled from the compound, and their parents—and the police—have been notified. I would like to apologize to Miss Hayashi, and also to Mr. Toivonen."

Rosa snuck a look at Eddie.

"We singled you out to see if anyone would try to sabotage you. Usually people confine themselves to stealing your clothes so that you miss breakfast."

*Yeah, well, that wasn't what they did this year.*

"We did have cameras in place in case something more serious happened, and we would have intervened if Mr. Toivonen hadn't beaten us to it." She smiled faintly.

*Hell,* Rosa thought. *I have to be the victim, and he gets to be the hero.*

"Unfortunately, more of you were eliminated yesterday than we announced. We simply wanted a bigger crowd in the dorm last night, so we could watch the social dynamics."

No Makeup shifted in her seat. She had been on the bubble— in danger of being cut.

"At this point, eight people are left in the competition. Would the following people please stay in the room? Thank you to the rest of you for your participation. I wish you well in your future endeavors."

She called Rosa's name, and Eddie's, and apparently Toned Arms's, because she stayed seated, too. The others filed out quietly, and Arms stuck her fist out and Rosa bumped it.

Ms. Bauer lowered the screen. "There's something I want you to watch," she said. They groaned as the picture came up—it was a guy Rosa didn't know, filmed yesterday in a falling elevator— one of the eight who were left. The clip rolled. The camera was inside the elevator, but you could tell when it started to fall—the kid's eyes flew wide and his arms went out. Then he sucked in a breath and snapped into focus, and his mouth started moving. "The sound is off," Ms. Bauer said, "for your privacy." They laughed.

She ran the footage for each of them. Rosa's was the shortest, which made her proud. Eddie's was the longest, which surprised her since he was in the second spot.

"What do you notice about each of these?" Ms. Bauer said. They sat in silence.

"Um . . ." Trevor raised his hand.

"Go ahead."

"Everybody adjusted really quickly. Nobody took more than a second to start talking."

"Exactly!" She jabbed a finger at them. "Eddie took the longest. Why was that?"

They glanced around at one another. All Rosa could think of was, *He's the stupidest?* Not something to say out loud.

"I'm the stupidest?" Eddie said. They all laughed.

Ms. Bauer smiled. "Your math and physics tests belie that." She looked at them. "What did Eddie do that none of the rest of you did?"

"Almost die?" Trevor said.

She smiled again. Definitely nicer than yesterday. "Watch one more time." She played the clip.

"Um, he was more active," Toned Arms said. "Physically. He moved around more."

"That's right," Ms. Bauer said. "Eddie, what were you trying to do?"

"Find a way to stop the elevator," he said. They laughed.

"Eddie never quit. You almost all beat on the doors, but he was the only one who touched every wall, the floor, and the ceiling." She looked at him. "You tried to pull a railing off, we presume to try to pry the doors open."

"No," he said. "I thought I might pop the ceiling off with it, and get on top of the car. You know, so I could jump to something on the side if I couldn't stop it with words."

"Did you really think we'd let you crash?" she said.

"No. But I didn't want to die if I was wrong."

She clucked her tongue. "Such interesting results for Eddie. Every test, his were a little different." She tapped her clipboard. "Who was the one person who never touched the elevator?"

Rosa hadn't even thought about it until then. "It was me," she said.

Ms. Bauer nodded. "Why? You're the only one who didn't touch the doors."

"It was an ineffective strategy," Rosa said. "The test was to stop it with a relevant discussion of natural laws relating to free fall, so that's what I did."

"Fascinating," Ms. Bauer said. Rosa tried not to squirm. "You focused completely on the task at hand without regard to the physical peril. You almost completely divorced your mind and body." She looked across the room. "And Eddie didn't trust us, and multitasked. He got the job done with words—but barely." She smiled. "And in a rather entertaining fashion."

His flush rose through the roots of his blond hair.

"So. Our team has pored over your test results. Some of your challenges had no single right answer. The helicopters, for example—we intended for you to think that the hole might not be in the top of the canister. Some of you discovered that, but Eddie thought to remove the lid, and Rosa figured out that with two helicopters working together, it could actually be accomplished. We've compiled profiles of your strengths and weaknesses based on a number of factors, including observing you in social interactions in hallways and at meals."

Rosa sat up straighter.

"There's one more test this morning, then we'll have a brief recess while our panel discusses you." She walked to the door. "Follow me."

They went down a hallway, turned, and entered a gym. She motioned them to the bleachers and they sat. There was a wrestling mat behind her.

"Seriously?" Toned Arms whispered to Rosa. "In case we ever have to wrestle a tentacled alien?" She flared her eyes in comic horror.

"Your final test is fighting," Ms. Bauer said. Rosa sucked in her breath. "It will go until one participant is unable to continue or we stop it. We'll take one pair at a time. The rest of you will wait outside until it's done."

"You can take her," Eddie whispered. He was sitting behind Rosa, and his knee bumped her back as he leaned forward.

Rosa nodded, but she was sure he was wrong. Toned Arms was the only other girl left, but she was tall and rangy and Rosa was small boned. Arms had an advantage in height, weight, and reach. And she hadn't been roughed up last night. Physically, Rosa was okay. Mentally—she didn't know.

Eddie leaned forward again and whispered in her ear. "Knock knock."

Rosa smiled.

"Who's there?" she said.

"Interrupting cow."

"Interrup—"

"Moo!" he whispered triumphantly.

She twisted to roll her eyes at him, but she gave him a smile. A good one.

"We're taking the pairs according to rankings," Ms. Bauer said. "The first pair is Rosa Hayashi and Eddie Toivonen."

Rosa froze. Because—seriously? Eddie could smash Arms. She bet he could beat any of the boys. She figured this had to be a gut check for her. That they thought everything was easier for her because of her dad—that she was soft. That she hadn't earned it. It was the only explanation that occurred to her.

"Rosa and Eddie, on the mat. The rest of you, please wait in the hall."

The others filed out quietly. No one met Rosa's eye. Arms was sizing up the other guys. Behind her, Eddie stood. Rosa stayed seated. When the door closed behind the others, he spoke.

"Look, this is crazy. I'm not going to hit her."

"To the mat, Mr. Toivonen."

"It doesn't make any sense," he said. "Punching ability can't be necessary to work for the Interworlds Agency."

"And how would you know what's necessary?" she said coldly.

"Because I've seen some of the fat old physicists who work for you, and they can barely punch a time clock."

For a second Ms. Bauer looked like she was going to smile, but all she said was, "To the mat."

"No."

"If you refuse, you will be disqualified and *eliminated from the competition*. Do you understand that? I'm giving you both five seconds to get down here."

Rosa thought about the previous night, how Eddie had sat in her room in a pair of boxers. He was heavily muscled for a seventeen-year-old. In another five years he'd be one of those guys with a chest like a slab, but he already had a body that had seen serious gym time. *Or maybe,* she thought, *he lifted lots of feed sacks. Maybe Indiana was a big ruralnasium.*

He stepped past her and walked down to the mat. Rosa stood and followed him. She felt light and a little dizzy, as though her brain was getting ready to be crushed—a preconcussion.

"This makes no sense," Eddie said.

"I am not interested in your opinion of our challenges."

He leaned forward, angry, invading her space. "You invite the brightest high school students in the country to go through all this testing, and when you've found the best ones you mash their brains to pulp? That's counterproductive. It's *illogical.*"

"There's no biting or gouging," Ms. Bauer said. "Don't attack each other's eyes or necks. Kicking is fine."

"How is this scored?" Rosa said. "Is it number of touches or something?"

"No, it's a straightforward fight. We have cameras above in case our panel needs to deliberate on who the winner is." She looked at Rosa. "I don't think that will be necessary in this case."

"This is just wrong," Eddie said. "You put her in danger last night, and you did it *deliberately,* to draw out the vermin. You owe her better than this."

"You'll have a break after three minutes," Ms. Bauer said. "I'll blow a whistle and you'll have one minute of recovery time before the next round. At any point when I blow the whistle, you stop *immediately.* Do you understand that?" She came toward them. "You need to wear these electrodes."

"You're going to electrocute us, too?" Eddie's voice was openly hostile. That didn't make Rosa feel any better, because friendly Eddie was a little intimidating. Angry Eddie was really scary.

"No. They evaluate your brain waves."

*Oh my god.* Was it worth it? Could she get hurt so badly here that she couldn't do something else—be a pharmacist, or teach physics at some college?

"If I forfeit the match, will I still rank in the top two?" Rosa asked. Eddie's look brightened.

"No, you'll be sent home. Failure to complete any challenge is an automatic disqualification."

"Hey, do you know judo?" Eddie asked.

"That's racist," Rosa said. "Because I'm Japanese you assume I know martial arts?"

"No," he said. "But I do assume it's your only chance."

"Oh." She shook her head. No martial arts.

Ms. Bauer put electrodes on their scalps. They were thin leads, not the round type.

"What do these even sync with?" Eddie said, looking around for a monitor.

"My phone," Ms. Bauer said.

Rosa tried to focus. What advantage did she have over Eddie in physical fighting?

"Hey, Eddie? Can you stand the sight of blood?"

"Um, yeah."

"Well, heck. I thought maybe you'd faint when you saw my blood and I'd win."

He screwed his mouth into an almost-smile.

"My backup strategy is to move around a lot. I saw what you ate for breakfast—you're not going to be able to move."

"This isn't a stand-up comedy competition, right?" he asked Ms. Bauer.

"No," she said crisply. "Also, Eddie, the judges wanted me to stress to you that this is a physical fight. No calculus at ten paces or anything like that. This battle you fight with your body."

She pulled a whistle out of her pocket. She was going to blow it. Rosa was going to die.

She blew the whistle.

Eddie stood there, looking at Rosa's jawline, avoiding her eyes. She had a small jaw—delicate, people called it.

"We'll send you home, Eddie," Ms. Bauer said softly. "What are you going to do in Oolitic for the rest of your life?"

He balled a fist. He bounced it off the side of his leg in frustration. His eyes were wet as he turned away.

"I'm not hitting her. This is just wrong."

"Are you that sure your moral compass points north, Eddie?"

He looked at Rosa's jaw again, and didn't answer as he stepped to the edge of the ring.

"Eddie!" Rosa called. She stuck her hand out and willed him back with her eyes. He hesitated, then returned and shook her hand. Rosa didn't let go. He pulled gently, then stood and looked at her warily. She flipped her thumb over the top of his, not touching it.

His eyes lit up.

"One, two, three...," she said, and they started to thumb wrestle. She pinned his thumb once, but he got her three times before Ms. Bauer blew the whistle.

"Very creative," Ms. Bauer said, gently pulling the electrodes from her hair.

"We fought with our bodies," Rosa said.

"Yes," Ms. Bauer said. "You did." She pulled the electrodes off Eddie's scalp.

"No brain damage," he said, grinning and giving Rosa a high five.

"That's not what they were for," Ms. Bauer said. "They sense decision making. Eddie, if you'd decided to hit her, a light would have gone on and I would have attempted to blow the whistle before you actually swung."

"Attempted?" Rosa said.

"It was a calculated risk."

"What even the heck?" Eddie said. "You didn't want me to hit her?"

"Of course not!" Ms. Bauer said, looking at him as though he were insane. "Look, your test results are unusual. We're not entirely sure what to make of you."

"So you designed this test especially for me, to see if I'm psycho?"

"Basically," she said. He shook his head and started to speak. "Some of them were," she said, cutting him off. "The boys you fought off last night?" She raised her eyebrows, daring them to contradict her. They couldn't.

"Thanks for not smashing me," Rosa said.

He smiled. "Thanks for thinking of thumb wrestling." He turned to the official. "I'm guessing she wins this one?"

"Hands down," Rosa said. "See what I did there?"

"Ruined thumb-related humor for me?"

"Thinking it up was more important than actually winning a thumb-wrestling contest," Ms. Bauer admitted.

Rosa threw her arms in the air and danced in a circle. "The winner—Ro-o-o-o-o-sa Hay-y-y-y-ashi!"

Ms. Bauer smiled. She texted on her phone for a minute.

Eddie ducked down and tapped his shoulders, and Rosa sat on them and he ran her in circles around the mat. She threw her fists in the air and clasped her hands together, and he hummed the theme from *Rocky*.

Then the far door opened and the thin-faced kid—Trevor—walked in, looking deeply unsure of what he was seeing, and behind him Brad, the guy with the dark hair.

"You're alive?" Trevor asked Rosa.

"How is that possible?" Brad said.

"She won," Eddie said, kneeling so Rosa could slide off his shoulders. He didn't offer an explanation, and they both laughed at the guys' expressions.

"So," Ms. Bauer said, pocketing her phone. "Eddie, Rosa, this is Trevor Clayborn. He came in third." Trevor groaned. "And this is Brad Quatro." Brad lifted a hand. "He was fourth. You know that we only planned to accept one team—two trainees—but we've decided to take on an extra team." She smiled at the two guys. "Trevor, Brad, you're in."

Eddie gave them both a high five, then said, "Wait—this is because you're still not sure of me, isn't it?"

"Frankly, yes," Ms. Bauer said. "Think of it as having understudies."

Eddie was silent for a moment. "If I get a sore throat, you have to do stuff for me."

Brad snorted.

"Absolutely," Trevor said. "But I get to keep the bouquets at the end."

"I think you will find," Ms. Bauer said, "that you won't be getting bouquets."

They had no idea then what was out there in the dark, and coming their way.

# CHAPTER NINE

Eddie thought they'd live in the dorm, but an IA guy took the four of them to a small apartment building by the rec center and gave them each a key.

"We're going to let you call your families to give them the news," the guy said, grinning. "So you get to hear their reactions yourselves. Remember not to discuss the exams." They nodded. "Have them send your stuff. Your apartments are furnished, but you'll need your clothes, whatever."

"Are we confined to campus?" Brad asked.

"You're all underage," the guy said. "So, yeah."

"Oh, that does *not* work," Rosa said.

The guy put a hand up. "You can talk to your instructor about it."

Rosa arched her eyebrows. It was pretty effective. The guy put up his other hand. "I'm just supposed to get you settled. You meet your instructor at lunch, and he'll take you from there. So," he said, "mailboxes on the first floor, laundry in the basement. A couple of staff people live here, too, so you won't be rattling around by yourselves." He turned to go.

"You mentioned lunch?" Eddie said.

The guy pointed. "You can go ahead to the cafeteria. Your instructor will find you there."

They lugged their bags in. The guys' rooms were clustered at the end of the first floor hall, and Rosa was on the second floor. She had two huge suitcases, but she made it fine up the stairs. The guys could hear her rumbling down the floor above them.

Eddie's apartment faced the front of the building. A small living room, with a bedroom to the right and kitchen and bathroom to the left. Basic furniture and a TV on the wall. Good enough— home sweet home. He tossed his duffel onto the bed and started a list of things he was going to need.

A few minutes later he met Trevor, Brad, and Rosa out front, and they walked to the cafeteria together.

"My dad took my call at work," Rosa said, beaming. "He never does that."

"Was he happy?" Trevor asked.

"He shouted 'Woo-hoo!' even though he was in a meeting." Trevor gave her a high five. "Mom could only talk for a second, but she was thrilled, too. What about you guys?"

"My dad claimed he's going to put up a notice in every building he owns," Brad said. "Which means half of Manhattan will know about it by tonight." He beamed.

"My parents took the day off so they could wait for news," Trevor said.

"That's great," Eddie said.

"Yeah. Well, they're both on call, but they were home. They said they were proud of me." He gave a cheesy grin and pointed his thumbs at his chest.

"What did your grandma say?" Rosa asked.

"She was speechless," Eddie said. Technically that was true, since he hadn't called her. And then they were at the cafeteria.

It was like a new kid's first-day nightmare. The trainees didn't know anybody else, but everyone else knew exactly who they were. Eddie slid a fiberglass tray down the railing and got an open-faced roast beef sandwich, the kind with mashed potatoes and gravy dumped right on top. When he fumbled for his wallet at the register, the cashier said, "Trainees get their food free," and waved them through.

"Oh," Rosa said. "You do *not* know what you're doing."

"All this fancy equipment, and it's their cafeteria that will bankrupt them," Trevor said.

"Hysterical," Eddie said, and reached back to snag a big plastic-wrapped cookie since it was free.

The windows went floor to ceiling, and they sat by the side, looking out toward their little apartment building.

"We have apartments," Trevor said. "We are adults. That's almost scarier than the weird stuff they're doing to us."

They'd finished lunch and Rosa was sucking down a little bowl of grapes when a trim black guy in khakis walked over. He'd shaved his head but you could still see the baldness line.

"I'm Reg Davis," he said, shaking their hands. "Your instructor.

Welcome aboard." He sat across from Trevor. "You gonna eat that dill pickle?"

"No," Trevor said. "That's why I put it in quarantine."

Reg Davis snagged it from the edge of Trevor's plate and bit the end off with a snap. He closed his eyes. "I'm hoping we find a planet out there that's filled with dill pickles."

Rosa and Eddie exchanged a glance.

"Um, that would be this planet, really," she said.

He took another crunch. "Good point." He had a faint drawl— he was from somewhere in the South. He pulled a napkin out of the dispenser and dejuiced the corners of his mouth. "I'm going easy on you this afternoon—we'll be in the classroom doing cosmology basics, just to make sure everybody's on the same page. I haven't instructed newbies before," he said. Eddie caught Trevor's eye. This was hopeful. Substitute teacher dynamic?

"You probably shouldn't tell us that, Mr. Davis," Rosa said.

"Damn it, Reginald!" He grinned at them. "Don't worry. You're going to be the best-trained babies IA's ever had, because my career depends on it. You will not let me down." He snapped the last bit of pickle in half, chewed, then popped the end into his mouth. "Follow me."

They slid their trays into the rack by the kitchen and followed him toward the door. A couple of cosmologists sitting near the exit flapped their arms and quacked.

"Your vocabulary's improving," Reg said affably. "You learn to cock-a-doodle-doo and they'll promote you." The guys cracked up. Rosa caught Brad's eye and raised an eyebrow, but he just shrugged.

"They were insinuating," Reg said as he led them down an angled sidewalk, "that I am a mama duck and you are my ducklings."

"Yeah," Brad said. "We got that."

"Excellent!" Reg said. "You're brighter than I thought."

He ushered them into a brick building and settled them in a small meeting room, then started a presentation giving an overview of the universe, how it's infinite, and the math proving it. He stopped a couple of times to make sure they were following.

Trevor, Brad, and Rosa had gotten this in prep classes for the IA tryouts. Eddie learned it at his grandma's kitchen table while she fried eggs and tossed questions at him over her shoulder, waving the spatula in a vaguely threatening manner when he messed up. He knew this stuff as well as they did—but he also appreciated the review.

"We'd planned to have you work some with Team 1 and Team 2," Reg finally said, laying his laser pointer in the whiteboard tray. "Things have come up that have limited their availability, but I'll make sure you meet them at some point."

Reg gave them problems to work out—calculating the interference of states that differ in a macroscopic number of degrees of freedom. He didn't offer calculators. They were leaning forward, pencils scratching along the legal pads he'd dropped in front of them, when something hit Eddie in the back of the head.

He rose and turned, his peripheral vision catching a Ping-Pong ball bounce off across the carpet. Reg stood there, leaning against the wall, tossing another ball in the air.

"What even the heck?" Eddie said.

"Why are you standing up? You done with that problem?" Brad snorted.

Eddie stared at Reg, then swiveled to look at the others. They snapped back to their work. "You got a job to do, you don't get distracted by a little thing like a Ping-Pong ball," Reg said. And then Eddie understood.

He sat back down and continued to work while Reg tossed balls at his head. Reg moved around to the other side of the table, stood behind Brad, and started bouncing the balls off Eddie's face. It didn't hurt, but it still made him want to hit Reg. Brad saved him. One of the balls hit the end of Eddie's nose, careened off the table, and hit him again. Brad snorted a laugh, then tucked his head down, but not fast enough.

"Is that funny, Mr. Quatro?"

To his credit Brad said, "Yes, sir."

"You know what? That boy's hair is like a toothbrush. I believe it is *abrading* NASA equipment." Reg had a way of dragging out words that emphasized them somehow. And he began to pitch the balls at Brad. By the time they'd moved to the last problem, he was slinging them at all the trainees in unpredictable sequences, and they were coming in pretty hard. He was aiming at their torsos. The balls didn't hurt, but they made concentration incredibly difficult.

"All right," Reg said when they turned their tablets over, first

Rosa, then the guys. "That was slower than it should have been, but I know you were up in the night." Rosa flushed. "I've got some releases for your parents to sign," he said, handing them out, "so that I have permission to lob Ping-Pong balls at your heads." He grinned. "By the way, I enjoyed my first day as mama duck."

Eddie gave him a little snort. It conveyed a lot of meaning.

"If they're coming in person to bring your stuff, have them sign then. If not, mail it to them. You can't figure out how to get a stamp, see me. I am your resource person for all things."

"My grandma already signed," Eddie said, holding the papers out to Reg.

"Yeah, that was for the tryouts and to cover an initial period. This covers everything—in case we shoot you off into space," he said, swooping his arm upward.

"Could that actually happen?" Rosa asked. Her eyes were bright.

"No," Reg said. "Almost nobody gets to go."

"You ever been?" Eddie asked.

"Yeah."

Trevor heard the wistful note. "You want to go back," he said.

"Sweet Betsy Ross, yes," Reg said. "But I will content myself with torturing you for now." He grinned. "I've got homework for you." He motioned them to the door, and they walked out with him. "You ever heard of the Gordian knot?"

The guys shook their heads. "It was an ancient thing. Some knot that nobody could untie?" Rosa said.

"You know the details?" Reg asked. She shook her head.

"Good. Don't look them up. You do, and it violates my very strict code of honor, which would make me switch to golf balls."

Eddie grinned, in spite of himself.

"Gordius founded a city in Phrygia," Reg said.

"Where's that?" Trevor said.

"Oh, hell, I don't know. I'm a scientist," Reg said. "He made this huge, intricate knot tying his cart to a pole, and said whoever could untie it would rule Asia."

"World domination?" Trevor said. "You have my attention."

"For years people came from all over to try, but nobody could untie it."

"Was it too tight?" Brad asked. "Did he shrink the rope after he tied it?"

"No," Reg said, regarding him, "but you're thinking along the right lines. They thought he'd woven the ends together, buried somewhere deep in the knot, so that it had no end."

Rosa frowned. "You can't untie it if you can't find the end."

"Precisely," Reg said, opening the door and ushering them outside. "You know who undid the Gordian knot?" They waited. "It was Alexander the Great."

"And he ruled Asia!" Rosa said.

"Your assignment for tomorrow is to decide what you would do if you were Alexander. You arrive in town and find out about this puzzle. How would you approach the Gordian knot?"

"Like, what would our strategy be?" Eddie asked. "To find the end, or whatever?"

"Yeah. Just a few sentences is enough," Reg said. "No looking it up. This is a thought piece." He started to walk away, then turned back. "Eat a light breakfast tomorrow. You're going to learn to fly."

They stared at one another. Reg Davis walked away, whistling.

After dinner Eddie went back to his apartment, laid the release on his dresser, and curled on his bed. He didn't do the homework and he didn't practice calculating the energy in inflaton fields. He felt like hell, and fell asleep in his clothes. When the knock on the door came, he looked at his phone. It was 1:17 a.m.

# CHAPTER TEN

Eddie's light was on, and when he came to the door he was still dressed, but Rosa thought he looked like he'd been asleep.

"What's going on?"

"I need to get off campus," Rosa whispered. "Help me?"

"Um, maybe this is something to take up with Reg?"

"No. I can't. I just . . . I need to get to town."

"Boyfriend?"

She snorted. That would be the first thing he thought of. "No." He stood there with his hand resting on the door frame. Not really a glad-to-see-you-Rosa posture. "Do you know if there are Agency cars somewhere? There must be, right?"

He took his hand off the door. "You can't just drive off campus. The checkpoint's guarded. Jeez, you try something like this, they might kick you out."

"'Jeez'?" Trevor said, stepping into the hall. "Somebody sounds like a Hoosier farm boy."

"Thank you," Eddie said with great dignity. He moved aside. "Let's not wake anybody else up."

They went into his apartment. Rosa had brought white twinkle lights and already had them strung over her curtain rod. She was using sheets from home, had set out a couple of photo collages and a throw pillow, and had some pretty pens on the desk. It wasn't much—but Eddie's apartment was sterile. Trevor must have thought so, too, because he said, "Dude, you could operate in this place."

"You woke me up to criticize my decorating?"

"Possibly," Trevor said. "Why did we wake him, Rosa?"

We. *Crap.* Rosa really, really didn't want to talk to Eddie about this. But Trevor, too? She stood with her back to the door. She couldn't say anything. She had lost the power of speech.

"She wants to go into town," Eddie said.

"Boyfriend?" Trevor said.

"No," Rosa said. "I need to get something. From a store." They looked at her. *Guys are idiots.* "Tonight."

They exchanged a glance. "Like, shoes?" Trevor said. Rosa bit her upper lip.

"You guys just won entrance to a prestigious training program. Think about it."

They did. It was slow and painful to watch. Then Eddie's head came up, but his eyes focused on her neck. Yeah, he'd figured it out.

"Uh, do you need unmentionable things?"

"Yes."

"What's unmentionable?" Trevor said.

"Trevor, there's a reason you came in third," Rosa said. It wasn't nice, but damn.

He looked back and forth between them. "Somebody is going to have to mention the unmentionable if I'm going to get it."

"Um, she needs accessories for her lady parts," Eddie said.

"Oh my god," Rosa said.

"I didn't know they came with accessories." Then Trevor's eyes widened and he said, "Oh!" Rosa nodded. "I thought he meant like eyeliner, or a little hat."

Eddie shifted abruptly. "You can't go to town in the middle of the night. Just ask Reg in the morning."

"I can't wait till the morning, and I can't ask Reg. Ever."

"I can sort of understand that," Trevor said.

"Yeah, but ask a woman. One of them would have something you could borrow, right?"

"There aren't any women here overnight. I already looked. I've been working on this for an hour."

"There are no women?"

"*No.* I called everyplace—even the guard booth—and I tried to get into buildings to see if there was a dispenser. This whole stupid place"—and this is where her voice cracked with frustration—"has the most advanced technology in the world. Do you know we could hijack a craft and go to *Mars*? But after five p.m., it does not have access to one single tampon dispenser!"

Eddie and Trevor winced, and it wasn't because of the injustice of it. It was because she'd said the word.

"IA isn't all it's cracked up to be," Rosa said, wiping her eyes with her fingertips.

"Yeah," Eddie said. "I knew there'd be a string attached." He grinned, pleased with himself.

"I kind of hate you," she said.

"Oh, come on. I'm just trying to lighten the mood. I'm the menstrual minstrel."

"If I didn't need your help, I would totally kill you," she said.

"If you didn't need our help, I wouldn't be taking comedic chances," Eddie said.

"Um, couldn't you have foreseen this?" Trevor said. "Just saying."

"I'm a little early, okay? Do you want to know all about it?"

"Oh god, no," Trevor said.

"I can't tell Reg because he'll think I should have planned ahead, too. And what if they kick me out because of this?"

"They wouldn't kick you out because you didn't bring your accessories," Trevor said.

Rosa leaned forward. "Oh yeah? They kicked people out because they untangled Christmas tree lights! Today they threw Ping-Pong balls at us. Everything is a test with these people." She looked around for a tissue box, but of course Eddie didn't have one. She wiped her nose on her knuckle. "They took two new teams," she said quietly. "How long do you think that's going to last?"

They were silent for a moment. "They might keep both," Eddie said. "I suppose you could lose your spot, but not for this."

"They could say I displayed lack of foresight for mishandling something you guys didn't have to handle at all."

"You know, that kind of *isn't* fair," Trevor said.

Eddie stretched. "If we all go, they can't kick anybody out if they catch us. You in, Trev?"

Trevor hesitated. "I guess they couldn't make Brad a team all by himself." He stuck his fist out and Eddie bumped it, and they held their fists there, waiting for Rosa. She squeezed her eyes shut for a moment, then bopped their knuckles. They might be dense, but they didn't have to help her. They were being decent—that was worth a fist bump.

They left through Eddie's bedroom window so they didn't risk waking the guys down the hall. They stuck to shadows when they could, working their way through the IA compound, walking casually when they had to cover an open stretch of ground.

"They've got to have security cameras all over," Eddie whispered.

"Yeah, but that doesn't mean they're watching them," Trevor said.

They made their way to the fence that ringed the compound.

"Electric," Rosa said.

"Looks like it." Eddie dropped to the ground. "Stay low."

He pushed forward. The lowest line was a foot off the ground so nocturnal rodents could scamper through without constantly setting off alarms or shorting out the wire. Eddie was a solid guy, and Rosa thought his shoulders might brush as he pulled himself under, but he made it to the other side, rolled over, and grinned at them. Trevor was a couple of inches shorter than Eddie and thirty pounds lighter, and Rosa was small, so she flattened herself and slipped through at the same time as Trevor.

They were halfway under when the fence sizzled and Trevor

yelped, and then his arm flailed and hit the top of Rosa's head and she pressed herself into the soft earth, resisting the urge to roll. Eddie grabbed Trevor's arms and pulled him through, and Rosa swam on the ground till her legs were clear.

"I'm burned!" Trevor said. "I scorched my ass!"

Eddie stooped and peered at him. It was a waning crescent moon, but there was plenty of light from the compound. "It singed your jeans. You're okay."

"Let's get out of here," Rosa whispered. "This could have caught some guard's eye."

"Uh-oh," Eddie said, grinning. "Tampon-gate."

Rosa ignored him. They walked quickly away from the fence, Trevor fingering the seat of his jeans.

"Are my underpants showing?"

"Tighty-whities," Eddie said.

"Crap."

They walked an hour to the town. It had expanded with the influx of agency workers and their families when they built the IA facility. It wasn't huge, but it would have an all-night grocery.

"It's a big sky," Eddie said, exposing his Adam's apple to the stars.

"Infinite," Rosa said.

"I understand it in theory," Trevor said. "With enough space, every possible configuration of molecules will repeat. That means that somewhere out there is another Earth just like ours."

"Every possible combination," Rosa said.

They looked out at the stars, bright and beckoning.

"Somewhere there's an Earth that never had Mozart," Trevor said.

"Somewhere there's an Earth where Hitler won," Eddie said.

"Oh my god, you guys. What is wrong with you?" They kept walking. In the distance, car lights strobed the road. They ducked down, but it turned somewhere south of them, so they trudged on. "Somewhere," Rosa said, "there's a world that had Mozart, but not Hitler."

"It's not this one," Eddie said. Rosa looked at the side of his face, but he didn't say anything more.

They could see the blue light of a gas station at the edge of town for a mile before they got to it.

"This should work," Rosa said. "I'll be out in a minute." *In other words, do not come in with me.*

"No," Eddie said. "I passed a pharmacy when I came here. It's better."

"We've already walked like three miles," Trevor said. "And I have a severely burned ass."

Rosa snorted.

"I have a hot ass, too," Eddie said, "but without the acrid smell of burning flesh."

Rosa started forward, and Eddie caught her arm.

"No, let's go to the pharmacy. It's only a few blocks down."

She looked at his hand on her arm, and he dropped it but didn't change his body posture.

"Um, why?" she said.

He hesitated. "I want to get something, too."

"Bandages for my smoldering buttocks?" Trevor said.

"Yes. That's it."

She shrugged. What did it matter? They were going to be exhausted the next day, anyway. She turned and waved a lead-on hand, and he rewarded her with an almost-smile. The air was perfect. The heat of the day was gone, and it was quiet in town. A few cars came by but none slowed, and twice they saw glowing eyes low to the ground—a possum? An armadillo? She wondered if they had those in Iowa—but nothing came toward them.

They reached the pharmacy. It was painfully well lit, and they blinked as they walked in, the door shushing aside for them. An older guy with a comb-over looked up, stashed his magazine under the counter, and watched them without comment as they split down separate aisles.

Rosa got back first and paid for a box of tampons and a bag of pads, and had used the bathroom before the guys checked out. Trevor brought up two rolls of gauze, adhesive tape, a thermometer, and a box of disinfectant wipes.

"Seriously?" she said.

"Do you wish to examine each other's purchases?"

She did not.

Eddie came up a minute later, holding a two-liter pop bottle by its neck with one hand and carrying a houseplant with the other. He didn't look at them.

He paid and they walked out, leaving the cashier to go back to his magazine.

Eddie opened the root beer as they hit the edge of town, took a long pull, and handed it to Rosa. She took a little swig.

"It pairs nicely with the stars," she said, handing the bottle to Trevor.

"That's what I thought," Eddie said.

"Eddie?" Rosa said. "You could have bought root beer at the gas station." He didn't say anything. "Which means we walked another half mile so you could get a plant."

He kept walking.

"Miss the farm?" Trevor said.

"You people realize I don't actually live on a farm, right?" He took the bottle back and took another draw on it, then Rosa carried it so he could cradle his little pothos in its four-inch pot. "Well, not a working farm." They walked down the road in silence, drinking the root beer, looking at the dark sky, Eddie's big hand wrapped around the green plastic pot.

Their brains were on standby, lulled by the rhythm of their strides down the long road, when Eddie spoke.

"You ever think about how alone we are?"

They looked at him.

"The universe is expanding faster than the speed of light, carrying galaxies away with it. The beginning of the universe— the Big Bang—separated matter at astonishing speed. The very first action in life—birth—is an act of separation." Rosa and Trevor exchanged a glance. "By the laws of physics, we are getting farther and farther apart, and always will. The universe just gets colder and lonelier every second, and there's nothing we can do about it."

Rosa stared at his plant, its tendrils swinging as he walked.

"Hey, Eddie?" Trevor said. "You okay?"

He turned to look at them. "The universe is two degrees above absolute zero. We don't feel it because we're so close to the sun."

"And also because if we were at two degrees Kelvin, we wouldn't feel anything," Trevor said, then, "Sorry."

"It's not true that the universe is pushing everything away," Rosa said. "Asteroids hit the Earth. Galaxies can collide."

"Um, Rosa?" Trevor said. "Those things are catastrophes."

"Oh," she said. "Right."

"So we are doomed from the start—from the creation of the universe—to be profoundly alone," Eddie said. "And whenever we do touch, it's a disaster."

They walked in silence for another mile.

"No," Rosa said. Trevor raised an eyebrow at her, but Eddie kept staring down the road. "You're not alone. The universe is infinite, and by those same laws of physics, we know that there are other Earths out there, and on some of them there are other Eddies."

"Poor bastards," he said.

"Yeah, being smart and good-looking is a real shame," she said, then wished she hadn't said the good-looking part. She thought of something. "You know, maybe you're the only you left."

"What?" Eddie said.

"Yeah," Trevor said. "Maybe you're dead on all the other Earths. It would explain why you feel so alone. Maybe you are."

"So there's an infinite number of Earths with an infinite number of Eddies, and every single one of the idiots has gotten himself killed?"

"It would be a statistical outlier," Rosa admitted.

"Like flipping a coin," Trevor said. "You do it infinity times, once it'll be heads every time. Somebody is going to die on every Earth."

"So everywhere I'm either dead or alone? You guys have a future in motivational speaking."

Rosa bit her lip. "But maybe that's why you're lonely," she said. "Maybe most of you are missing."

They didn't talk after that, just walked in silence down the road, looking up at the stars, and beyond them, into the two-degree universe.

# CHAPTER ELEVEN

Reg smiled at Eddie and Trevor as they sat down.

"You look like crap," Eddie whispered to Trevor.

"Why, thank you," he whispered back. "You look like donkey diarrhea."

Eddie nodded. It's what he felt like. Brad shushed them. An actual shush. Eddie was trying to figure out a response to that when Rosa came in, a minute late. She was wearing a blue skirt and white top she'd obviously ironed, expertly blended eye shadow, and her hair was up. She looked tired but pulled together. Eddie had no idea how she'd managed that.

"Thank you for joining us, Miss Hayashi," Reg said.

"You're very welcome," Rosa said, taking a seat.

Reg gave an exaggerated sigh. "So tell me what you have regarding the Gordian knot. What should Alexander's approach have been?"

*Holy crap,* Eddie thought. *I never did that.* He hadn't done the assignment the previous night, and forgot about it during Tampon-gate.

Trevor flipped open his notebook and looked at his page. "There's no way to untie a knot without finding the end. So I think Alexander should mark the rope as he went along, so he could tell if he'd already checked that section."

"Mark it how?" Reg said.

"With paint down the side. If he got the whole thing marked and still hadn't found the beginning, he'd know the guy really did make it so there was no end."

"And then what would he do?" Reg said.

Trevor stared at him. "Um, complain to the chamber of commerce?" He smiled weakly.

"Huh. Brad, what have you got?"

Brad rolled his hands out to the side. "Let's be reasonable. The guy who tied the knot cheated, so there's no reason to play his game. Why should you stand there in the hot sun trying to untie some knot that can't be untied?"

"Yeah?" Reg said cautiously.

"So you walk around, see? Take careful notes, say you're going to think about it for a couple of days. Actually you go back to your camp, make a replica of the thing, and replace it at night."

"*Replace* it?" Reg said.

"Yeah. You just put the whole thing on some sledge and pull it away, and put in the one you know how to open. Next day you ride into town, untie the knot, and voilà! Everybody thinks you have the right to rule Asia."

"Huh," Reg said again. "Um, Rosa?"

"It's a cart tied to a pole, right?" He nodded. "So you should pull the pole up to loosen the knot. Then it would be easier to search for the ends."

"Interesting," Reg said. He raised his eyebrows fractionally as he looked at Eddie. "What about you?"

*Crap crap crap. What would I do if I were Alexander the Great?* "If I'm Alexander, I'm a busy guy. I don't have three days to stand around trying to untie a knot. I'd just draw my sword and cut it in half." Eddie made a chopping motion with his hand.

"That's cheating!" Rosa said.

"No," Eddie said calmly. "Brad was cheating. I was innovating."

"Was it who could *untie* the knot, or who could *open* it?" Trevor said.

"No clue," Reg said. "But that's exactly what Alexander did. He just cut the damn thing apart."

*Holy smokes. Alexander must not have done his homework, either.*

Reg led them to the hangar where they'd met for the testing. They walked past where the chairs had been, climbed a metal staircase with X-bracing, and entered a small room. It opened onto the cockpit of a spaceship—the flight simulator. They grinned at each other, and Reg scowled at them.

"Sit down and open those manuals. You have control panels to learn."

They spent two hours on that, then Reg took them in the simulator and let them look at the real equipment. Eddie had to walk in a little hunched over. Reg let them take turns touching and naming the controls, and then jerked his head toward the seat.

"Think you're ready, Eddie?"

"You know it," Eddie said at the same time Brad said, "That could be a nickname."

"Those could be last words," Eddie said.

The others backed away, and Reg started a program that projected a sky onto the windows. The whole cockpit vibrated.

Eddie settled into the chair. "I run through my checks first," he said.

"Always," Reg said. "And fasten your restraint."

"The capsule's not really going to move," Eddie said.

Reg gave him a dark look and leveled a finger at him. "This is NASA. We are not stupid people. Put on the damn seat belt."

Eddie slipped into it and snapped the buckle, then touched each lever and switch and said its name as he checked it. Reg had left one lever in the wrong position, and Eddie found and corrected it, the handle cool and hard in his fist. He didn't have much luck suppressing his grin. Reg started a countdown, and Eddie tried to keep up with what he should do.

"We didn't read that far yet," Eddie said.

"I saw you peeking in the back," Reg said. "Five. Four. Three."

He braced himself.

"Open that compartment. There, under the manifold pressure indicator."

Eddie pushed the button, and the door dropped down like a glove compartment. A snake jumped out at him, uncoiling as it flew straight at his chest. He tried to stand, but the belt kept him in place, and the big diamondback smacked into his sternum, and he punched it with a solid uppercut that connected, but nothing was there. And then Eddie understood. It was an inflatable snake—very lifelike, very light. He turned to give Reg a murderous look.

"No one," Reg said, "is holding the controls. This craft just crashed into"—he checked his laptop—"Orlando. Oh, Eddie, there are easier ways to get to Disney World."

Eddie unsnapped the belt and stood, bumping his head on the ceiling.

"Anything to say for yourself?" Reg said.

"Yeah. Screw you."

"Careful, or you'll be contributing to the swear jar in the lounge."

"NASA has a swear jar?"

"How do you think we fund this stuff? The money sure isn't coming from Congress."

Eddie stepped out of the capsule and Brad took his place. Reg ran the countdown and Brad did pretty well, but he missed checking a couple of instruments. Eddie couldn't help himself—something about Brad irritated him, and this was a perfect opportunity to harass the guy.

"You didn't check your altimeter," he said in a stage whisper.

"Shut up," Brad shouted. He turned and stuck a finger out at Eddie. "I do not need your interference."

"And blastoff," Reg said. "You know this thing's liftoff speed? It would be nice if the pilot was looking where he was going."

"It's just space," Brad said. "It's empty."

"I do not like that attitude," Reg snapped. "And your trajectory would have brought you nose-first into an Iowa cornfield. Out."

Brad unbuckled, glowering at Eddie, and got out of the seat. Rosa took his place. She started her check.

"I'm missing something," she said.

"What's that?" Reg asked.

"My copilot."

"Huh. Trevor, get your ass in the second seat."

"Yes, sir," Trevor said, grinning.

When Rosa was four seconds into liftoff, Reg pitched a glob of green goop at the side of her face. It hit her cheek and then slowly rolled down her jawline and hung suspended for a moment, trying to decide whether to follow gravity or the property of adhesion. It went for adhesion and followed the curve of her neck, rolling into her shirt.

"Oh," she said, but kept her hands on the control. "Oh. Oh."

"It was in the fridge," Reg whispered to Eddie, clearly pleased with himself.

"Oh," she said again.

"Miss Hayashi," Reg said, "you did an admirable job of keeping your hands on the control wheel. However, you paid no attention to what you were doing with it."

Rosa looked at the controls and made a correction.

"Too late," he said. "Unpleasant shearing forces have already occurred." He turned to Trevor. "Someday we'll discuss the concept of copilot." Reg waved him toward the pilot's seat. Rosa unbuckled and stood by Eddie.

"He totally knows something's coming," she whispered.

Eddie nodded.

"I mean, how can Reg torture him now?"

"Electrocute his ass?" Eddie said. Rosa laughed.

Trevor took a look under the seat as he sat down, and ran through his check with one eye on Reg. He sank into himself during the countdown, and during liftoff, when the capsule began to shake, he threw one elbow over his face.

Reg rocked back on his heels. "Is this how you shoot off to face the future? Cowering, with an arm over your face?"

"Pretty much," Trevor said, his voice muffled. "It's my usual MO."

Reg sighed loudly. "You're done."

Trevor peeked over his arm, then unbuckled the harness and got up. "You didn't do anything to me."

"Didn't have to. You did it to yourself."

Reg led them back through the building, stopping at the bathrooms so Rosa could clean up her neck. "You get to see a movie now."

"Is it a cautionary tale about swearing?" Eddie asked.

"No, it's a training film on . . . oh, hell," Reg said, pulling up as he rounded a corner. They stopped behind him, duckling-like. A man and a woman, both in dress uniforms, were walking through an open door down the hall. "Okay, behave yourselves and get in here now," he said, running his ID badge over a pad by the door. A light turned green and he pulled the handle, jerked his head, and they filed in. Heels clicked on the floor, coming down the hall toward them.

Reg looked a little green. "That's a situation room down the hall," he said. "Something's going on."

The door was shutting softly on pneumatic hinges when a set of red-painted fingertips caught it and pushed it open.

"Mr. Davis," the woman said crisply. "I need to borrow"—her eyes ranged over them—"that one." She pointed at Eddie.

"These are the trainees," he said. "They are in no way prepared for, well, anything."

"Undeniable," Trevor whispered. "Still—ouch."

"We just need somebody at the door," she said. "There was a snafu with the guard assignment."

Reg looked at her, then at Eddie, obviously reluctant. "You can watch the training film later," he said. "Just go do whatever she tells you."

Eddie followed the woman down the hall. She didn't say anything—no introduction, no handshake. He was the local bicep. She stopped outside the door.

"You stand here," she said. "If somebody has a green badge, you let them in. Like this." She inserted a metal stub straight into a hole above the doorknob, then handed him the lanyard. Eddie wrapped it around his wrist. "This is a green badge," she said, showing him both sides. "Green, they get in. Anything else, they don't. Got it?"

He nodded. He wasn't an idiot.

She held out her ID, and he stuck the key stub in the slot and opened the door for her, and then he was alone in the hall. The room was soundproof. A couple of guys came around the corner, the same way Reg and the trainees had come, passed the room where Rosa, Brad, and Trevor were watching a film, and flashed their green at Eddie. He took both badges, checked their photos against their faces, and let them in.

The door had just closed when four men came from the other direction, guys in their fifties, serious men having a hushed conversation. Something about data curves.

Three of them showed their IDs and stood there, waiting for him to open the door.

"Your green badge, sir?" Eddie asked the guy in the middle. The guy in charge.

"You're kidding, right?" he said, looking Eddie in the eye, but he didn't seem to find it funny.

"Sir, I need to see your green badge."

The men around him stirred.

"Do you know who I am?"

"No, sir."

"I'm John Taylor Templeton. I'm the head of NASA, and this," he said, gesturing vaguely, "is my house."

And he was. Eddie recognized him once he said it. He'd seen his photo on the wall near the entrance.

"Yes, sir," Eddie said, because what even the heck? Even Reg with his Ping-Pong balls and fake snakes couldn't bring in the head of NASA to torture him. This wasn't fake torture. It was real.

"Son, I have a meeting," he said, pointing an index finger at the door. "Let me in."

He outranked the woman who had told Eddie not to let in anyone without a green badge. And Eddie was on the bubble. If he screwed up in front of the head not just of IA but of NASA as a whole? Trevor or Brad would have his spot, and Eddie would be supersizing in Oolitic.

Eddie held his hand out. "Badge, please."

His face darkened. "Do you know who I am?" he said again.

"Yes, sir. You're John Taylor—"

"I was a Rhodes Scholar. I piloted three shuttle missions. I have two doctorates, and I attend meetings with the president." He stared at Eddie, his hazel eyes boring into Eddie's blue ones. They were exactly the same height. "Who the hell are *you*?"

"I'm the guy who's going to see your green badge before you go through that door," Eddie said.

John Taylor Templeton reached out and gripped his shoulder. Eddie stood very still.

"Reg told me about you, but I wanted to see for myself." He squeezed Eddie's shoulder and turned to the door. The guys around him were smiling.

"Sir? The ID?"

He laughed out loud, showing perfectly even teeth, and flashed a key. "You think I need you to get me through a door in my own building?" And then they were inside. Eddie stood alone in the hall, guarding something that didn't need guarding from people who could get in when they wanted. A moment later Reg stuck his head into the hall and motioned him back. Eddie walked down the hall, feeling stupid and not knowing why.

"This trick was *his* idea?" he said.

Reg grinned. "Yeah. I ran into him in the bathroom. Told him one of the trainees was thinking with his spine, and he wanted to meet you."

"I . . . what?"

He clicked a couple of keys on his laptop and set it on the desk for them to see.

"There was no training film, was there?"

"Nope," Trevor said.

The laptop showed the feed of Eddie in the cockpit. Reg took it frame by frame as Eddie opened the compartment Reg told him to.

"No-o-o-o-o," Trevor said in a horror-movie voice.

"And there," Reg said, pointing to a time stamp at the bottom of the screen. It was calibrated in thousandths of a second. "Look at your legs—your thighs are bunched, your head is back, and your arm is already coming up. You're already reacting."

"You launched a snake at me. So, yeah."

"Mm-mm," he said, running it back a few frames, then forward again. "There wasn't time for the impulse to get to your brain, have it make a decision, and get word back down to your limbs."

"What?" Brad said.

"People have a little bit of gray matter in their spines. You don't write poetry with it." Eddie snorted. "But you started to react before news of the snake reached your brain. You made that decision in your spine."

Trevor and Rosa tilted their heads at the same angle as they looked at him. "NHL goalies do it," Reg said, "because the game's just so fast."

"What if you can't think with your spine?" Brad said.

"Then you're not an NHL goalie," Reg said. "They have to develop that pathway so they get an immediate response when they see a threat come down the ice. You seem to have already done that." He looked at Eddie, but Eddie didn't say anything.

After a moment Reg tapped the computer again and brought up Rosa in the cockpit.

"I didn't react superfast," she said.

"Nope. But see, right there?" He paused the feed. "You looked at the chair, then mentioned a copilot." He looked at Eddie. "Took her three point seven seconds to think of working cooperatively."

Rosa put a hand over her face.

"What?" Reg said.

"That's not a strength," Rosa said.

"Yeah, it is."

"Eddie wouldn't have said it," she said.

"*Eddie* has understudies," Reg said.

"I'm right here," Eddie said.

"Yeah," Trevor said. "Us, too." He twisted a little, like a washcloth wringing itself out. "I didn't do anything special."

"No," Reg agreed. "Of course, you're the only one who didn't crash a one-point-seven-billion-dollar spacecraft."

# CHAPTER TWELVE

The next day Reg drove them to a park in town. He made them run laps while he shouted math questions at them. It wasn't hard, and it felt good to be outside. Reg had brought a box of fried pickles and sat on a shaded picnic bench eating them, so he was pretty much in heaven. Trevor found a garter snake, picked it up on a stick, and pestered Eddie with it. All in all, an enjoyable day.

Before he dismissed them, Reg gave them an assignment.

"Tomorrow we start working on teamwork. You have to learn to trust each other."

"We're not doing trust falls, right?" Brad said. Reg snorted.

"You will each have to lead a blindfolded teammate through a maze. You can neither talk to them nor touch them."

"Uh," Trevor said. "How do we lead them through the maze, then?"

"That's your problem," Reg said. "You can bring props. Be prepared to lead any of the other three."

He grinned at them. "By the way, you have to find a way to let the person know they're the one you're leading."

"What do you mean?" Eddie said, frowning.

"I'll blindfold the other three. You have to get the right one to follow you." He turned to walk back to the car, clearly pleased with himself.

When Reg pulled the IA car to a stop at the guard booth and flashed his badge, the guard peered in. "These the trainees?"

"Yeah, that's them," Reg said.

"Their parents are here."

Rosa sat up straighter.

"They're getting the tour."

Reg and the trainees caught up with the parents in the IA administration lobby. Rosa's parents were standing with two other couples and Friesta Bauer. Her father was impeccable in a suit, and her mother was impeccable in black dress pants and a red blouse. One of the other couples was in khakis and matching polo shirts.

"Let me guess," Rosa whispered to Trevor. "Those are your parents, right?" He nodded. "They dress alike? That's kind of cute." He rolled his eyes.

Brad's parents stepped forward. His dad shook his hand, and a woman in a short gold dress—way too young to be his mother—air-kissed him on both cheeks. Rosa flared her eyes at Trevor, but then her dad grinned at her and she forgot the other parents. Rosa's mom threw her arms out and took a couple of steps as though to run at her, then thought better of it and waited till Rosa walked into her arms. She gave Rosa a hug that smelled like an expensive department store, then pulled back to look at her, holding Rosa's upper arms.

"We are so proud of you," she said, smoothing a stray strand of Rosa's hair. Her dad gave her a bear hug and then did a handshake they invented when she was ten that included a lot of finger action and ended by tapping elbows. She could have killed him, except she was grinning too much.

"Doctors Hayashi, Doctors Clayborn, and Mr. and Mrs. Quatro," Friesta Bauer said, "why don't you go ahead and unload your cars? Then our IA director would like to invite you to dine with him at a local restaurant this evening."

"Sounds good," Trevor's dad said.

Rosa hadn't even thought of Eddie till she turned. He was standing halfway across the room, fists thrust in his pockets.

"Eddie," she called. "Come meet my parents." But they all walked over to him and there were introductions all around. "Your parents couldn't make it today?" her dad asked.

"No, sir," Eddie said. "My old man has a hard time getting away."

"I can understand that," Dr. Hayashi said.

They all walked back to the apartment building together, and mostly the parents talked, since they weren't allowed to discuss the testing. But Rosa's dad asked in a whisper if she'd acquitted herself well, and when she said she thought she had, he squeezed her shoulder.

When they got to the cars Brad's stepmother sat on the retaining wall. Her heels were too high to let her carry luggage. "No porters?" his dad said, looking around. Eddie headed for the building, but Brad's dad called out to him.

"Excuse me, uh, young man?" *He's already forgotten my name*, Eddie thought. "Any chance you could give us a hand here?"

Eddie stood for a second, then came back, and Brad's dad handed him a big box, and by the time Brad got to his room, Eddie had already set it down and gone back out for another load.

"Seems like a nice boy," Mrs. Dr. Hayashi said as she and Rosa carted a trunk up to the second floor.

Rosa wanted to tell them how anguished he was. Everybody looked at Eddie as though he was dangerous, but he seemed more vulnerable than anyone she knew. She wanted to explain what it felt like to see him hold a houseplant like it was his only friend. That after those goons attacked her, he sat on her floor in his boxers and told her terrible knock-knock jokes. She wanted to say that she was worried about him because he thought with his spine and because his parents weren't there. But she didn't know how.

Rosa had gotten mostly unpacked, and her mom had helped her put up pretty toile curtains when Trevor's mom poked her head around the corner.

"We're going to caravan to the restaurant," she said.

"You can finish unpacking tonight," Rosa's dad said, ushering them to the door. "And tomorrow, and the next day . . ."

"Ha-ha," she said. "Such a funny man."

The restaurant was a nice place. Eddie was the only person in jeans, but no one said anything. Director Smithson talked about their futures, then compared notes with Rosa's dad about running a big agency and listened to Brad's dad talk about real estate. Rosa's mother ordered French food and then complained about it, which was both embarrassing and predictable. Trevor and Eddie talked basketball with Trevor's dad, and Rosa's mom chatted with his mom. Brad's stepmother rearranged the food on her plate. When the check came, Director Smithson put his credit card in the leather envelope the server left.

"I've got that," Brad's father said expansively, tossing a credit card on top of Smithson's. He winked at his wife and gave her leg a squeeze.

"Thanks, but IA has this," Smithson said, handing the card back to him.

"Oh, come on!" Mr. Quatro said. "I can buy and sell all of you a dozen times over."

"Actually you can't," Rosa's mother said. "That would violate the Thirteenth Amendment."

Mr. Quatro started to laugh, then realized she was serious. He waved his fingers in the air, but he took his credit card back.

Rosa said good-bye to her parents outside the apartment building. She hadn't really been lonely until they came to visit— she started missing them when she saw them again. That seemed messed up. She watched them until their taillights were past the guard booth. She felt very adult, and very alone.

# CHAPTER THIRTEEN

At breakfast the next morning all four of them carried a bag with things they might need for the maze exercise. They walked together to the gym. A couple of men were pushing a final hay bale into place, completing a maze only one bale high. Reg stood with them, supervising. He looked up. "This is John Doepker and Bob Richtig," he called from across the gym. "Team 2. They stopped by to impart some words of wisdom." He introduced the four of them as Team 2 walked forward.

"Hey," Doepker said. "It's nice to meet you guys. We just wanted to say hello and see if you have any questions."

They glanced at one another. "Um," Rosa said, "what do you think are the most important things for us to work on at this stage in our training?"

"Teamwork," Doepker said. "And communication. Get to know one another so well that you know what the others will do in a situation that's never arisen before. What they're thinking."

"Like passing the ball to where your teammate is *going* to be," Eddie said.

Richtig jutted his finger at him. "Exactly."

Doepker rubbed his hands together. "Reg said we can help train you today." He grinned at them. "Your job is to lead someone through the maze without letting them touch a wall at any point."

"The lanes are pretty wide," Rosa observed.

"One step in the wrong direction, and how wide will it be?" Richtig said.

"Um."

"Yep. So," Doepker said, "the rules are you can make noise but you cannot talk or sing. You cannot touch the person. And you'd better be leading the right person through that maze."

"How exactly is this training?" Brad said.

Reg threw an arm out and pointed through the ceiling. "Out there, you don't know what you'll encounter. Neither do we. But you better be able to communicate clearly and effectively, and you better be able to trust each other." He gave them a serious look. "Learn what you can from the maze exercise, because after this we're working with live explosives."

They pulled their heads back and stared at one another.

"It would be swell," Reg said, "if you learned teamwork by then."

Doepker turned to Rosa. "You're going first." He blindfolded the guys, then pointed to Eddie. "Lead him through the maze."

Rosa unzipped her duffel. She pulled out a basketball, tried to spin it on her finger and it fell off, the sound echoing through the gym. Eddie grinned and stepped forward. Rosa stood in front of the guys and dribbled for a moment, then backed up into the maze. Eddie followed her. Trevor and Brad stayed where they were, and Reg removed their blindfolds so they could watch.

The maze was low and not very complex. Eddie followed perfectly until she lost her dribble and he thought she was turning. He realized the problem when the bounces tapered off, and stood still, knowing he was facing the wrong direction, and waited until the dribbling was strong and regular again before he turned back and continued on.

When they reached the end and exited, the three men applauded. "Take off your blindfold, Eddie," Doepker said. Eddie ripped it off, saw they were through the maze, and gave Rosa a high five. "Nice job," Richtig said. "Eddie, you're leading."

They walked back to the start, and when they were all blindfolded, Richtig pointed at Trevor. Eddie nodded and pulled a bottle of isopropyl alcohol out of his duffel. He opened it and waved it under their noses. Trevor and Rosa both stepped forward. Eddie looked to Reg in alarm, but Reg just shrugged. Eddie passed the bottle past them twice more, afraid he was going down in defeat but still enjoying the way Rosa wriggled her nose. Then she took a step back.

Eddie walked backward into the maze, holding the bottle out toward Trevor. Trevor followed him. It was slower than following a noise—even in the closed gym there were plenty of air currents, and a couple of times Eddie thought he was going to lose him. But they made it to the end, and Trevor pulled off his blindfold, leaped onto a hay bale, and took a bow.

"Bunch of crazy people," Reg muttered.

"Hey, Rosa, what did you think it was, anyway?" Eddie asked.

"Nail polish remover," she said, smiling. "I figured that would be for me."

Brad went next and led Rosa with a bottle of actual nail polish, then Trevor led Brad through with a handful of change that he shook repeatedly.

When they were done, Doepker looked at Rosa and Eddie. "What were you two going to use if you got Brad?"

They said, "The same thing" at the same time.

"You were all three going to lead him with a fistful of coins?" Doepker said. "Get to know him a little better. You suppose there's more to him than just that his family has money?"

Rosa, Eddie, and Trevor exchanged a guilty look.

Reg sighed. "Okay, fifteen-minute break and then . . ."

"I'd like to try one more run through the maze," Richtig said. "I'd like to see Eddie lead Rosa."

Eddie walked over to his duffel.

"No props," Richtig said.

Eddie stared at him, then at the others.

Reg shrugged. "I don't know what the man's doing."

Rosa and Eddie walked to the beginning of the maze, and Trevor blindfolded her.

"Just a second," Richtig said. "I want to rearrange the maze a little, in case you've got it memorized."

The three men pushed a few hay bales around, changing the first three turns. Eddie stood, looking at Rosa in her blindfold. He couldn't touch her, or lead her with smell, and he couldn't talk or sing to her. He sighed.

Then he sighed louder. Rosa took a step forward. He sighed again, open mouthed, puffing air out. Rosa took another step.

"No noise from your mouth at all," Richtig said.

Eddie hesitated for a moment, then stamped his foot. He moved backward, stamping again, and Rosa followed him. They made the first turn like that—right this time, instead of left—and Doepker called out, "Eddie can't make any noise with his feet."

Eddie gave them a murderous look, and then he started clapping as he backed up. Rosa followed. The adults let them get through the next turn before Richtig shouted, "No clapping."

Eddie snapped his fingers, and Rosa took a step forward.

"No finger snapping."

Eddie looked behind him. They still had three-quarters of the maze to get through. He hesitated.

"I'm going to take one step forward," Rosa said. "If that's right, put your hand where I can touch it." She jutted an index finger in the general direction of the men. "You said he couldn't talk or touch me. You didn't say I couldn't touch him."

As Rosa reached out tentatively, Eddie put his hand where she would touch it. When she felt his knuckles she gave his hand a little pat, smiled, and took a step forward. They repeated it twice, and then Rosa felt an elbow, not a hand.

"I'm going to take one step right if I feel your hand," she said. Eddie extended his hand so she could grab his fingers.

Rosa touching his hand was a good way to spend a morning, Eddie thought, but it was taking forever. So he slipped his shoes off and crouched, smacking them down with his hands.

"Hey!" Doepker called.

"You said I couldn't make any noise with my *feet*," Eddie shouted back. "My feet are sock-foot silent."

Dopeker inclined his head, and let Eddie lead Rosa out with the sound of his shoes smacking on the gym floor. When Rosa and Eddie rejoined the others at the start of the maze, Richtig and Doepker shook their hands.

"They did terrific," Doepker said. "Whatever we threw at them, they found a way around it. And Rosa realizing that she could take over leadership even while she was blindfolded? Magnificent."

Rosa beamed.

"Those two are good," Richtig said, pointing to Trevor and Brad, "but these two are exceptional." Reg nodded, and Brad glowered. Richtig and Doepker raised their hands in farewell and left the gym.

"Okay," Reg said. "Fifteen-minute break, then meet at the zipline platform behind the hangar."

"I don't want to zipline," Trevor whispered, but Reg heard him.

"You won't be," he said. "You'll just be defusing a live bomb. The rest of us are watching from the tower because it's a good observation post, and safe in case you blow yourself sky-high." He smiled. "So cheer up."

"I wish I was ziplining," Trevor whispered, and Eddie snorted and thunked him on the back.

# CHAPTER FOURTEEN

When they reassembled, Team 2 showed up again. "We've got a meeting with Smithson in a couple of minutes," Doepker said to Reg, "but we wanted to see what you're doing with that platform."

"It's a very simple exercise," Reg said, fingering the binoculars around his neck. "Two of them get on the platform and we raise it."

"It's hydraulic," Doepker said to the trainees. "And it can go *high*." He grinned at them. "I saw the flight mechanics wheeling it out earlier and figured Reg had to be behind it."

"There's a live bomb on the platform," Reg said.

"What the . . . ," Doepker said. "Crap, Reg, did you get clearance for this?"

"I did," he said. "The director required an emergency egress system in case the defusing doesn't go well. Hence the big yellow mat at the bottom."

"The big yellow mat is *single use*," Richtig said. "Like a car's air bag."

"Yeah," Reg said.

"If one of them jumps on it, it deflates."

"Yeah," Reg said again.

"There are going to be *two* of them on that platform? With a *bomb*?"

"That's right."

"What the hell, Reg? If they have to get off there, they've got to jump at the same time. Otherwise one of them is stuck," Doepker said.

"They've got two shots at teamwork," Reg said. "First, when defusing the bomb. If that doesn't go well, they can jump together. If they can't pull off either of those, they don't belong here."

They were all silent for a moment. The trainees exchanged sober glances.

"How high are you raising the platform?" Richtig finally said.

"Three stories."

"Crap, Reg," Doepker said.

"You remember when I crashed?" Reg said, leaning forward, invading Doepker's space. "You know what happened?"

"I know how much it cost. That's mostly what Smithson mumbles about."

"Yeah," Reg said. "My pilot panicked and used the emergency egress system. By himself." His nose was a centimeter away from Doepker's. "Leaving me to land the craft by myself." He turned to the trainees and barked, "It was a two-person landing procedure. It's a *miracle* that I brought it down at all."

"Did they fire him?" Brad said.

"No," Reg said, and he didn't sound angry anymore. "They buried him. Idiot used the capsule for a water rescue and we were over land." He sighed. "We have some work to do here. You guys want to stick around and play?"

"I think we better get to our meeting," Richtig said. "I'm not sure what our liability is if we're here, and I don't want to find out." He clapped Reg on the arm.

"Good luck," Doepker said to the trainees. "Listen to this guy. He's as smart as he is crazy."

"Yeah, yeah, yeah," Reg said. Team 2 walked away.

"Wow," Rosa said. "I'm so sorry . . ."

Reg waved her off and clipped a cordless mic to her collar. "Rosa and Trevor, scramble onto the platform there. Don't touch anything."

They walked over to the platform, a gray contraption with a metal ladder dropping off the side. It had five steps. Rosa reached up and grabbed ahold and climbed onto the platform, and Trevor followed her. It had a low railing, and there was a stand holding a box, a stapled document, and a blindfold. Reg pressed a button and the platform began to rise.

"Why is there a blindfold?" Trevor said. "Reg?"

"Oh yeah," Reg said, grinning. "Put that on. You're going to be defusing blindfolded."

"No," Trevor said. "That's not a thing that's going to happen."

"Rosa, make sure the blindfold's tight, then glance at that booklet." She looked down at them, her face pinched. The platform was rising slowly, but they were already too high to use the ladder to climb down. "You're going to give him instructions on what to do. Trevor, you have to do it without being able to see what she's talking about."

Rosa waved the printout. "I just tell him to do each of these steps? And we don't go boom?"

"That's right," Reg said. "You can't do any of it yourself."

"Okeydokey," Rosa said, her voice tight.

"Don't start till we get up to our observation post."

"Oh god," Trevor said.

Reg, Eddie, and Brad walked to the zipline tower and climbed its corrugated aluminum steps in silence. When they got to the top, Reg shouted, "Get that blindfold on, Trevor!" At three stories tall the platform was well below them, and fifty yards away. Rosa gave them a thumbs-up, then turned to Trevor.

"Okay, Trev. The first thing is to put your hands out." He did and she grasped them. "I'm here. Feel me?" He squeezed her hands. "I'm right here, Trev, and we're going to do this together. Then we're going to think of something really awful to do to Reg."

On the tower, Reg grinned.

"Now turn back around," Rosa said. "A little more to the right. There you go. Put both hands forward, about shoulder width apart, and lift the lid straight up."

Trevor reached forward, got ahold of the box covering the bomb, and lifted. "I want to release a variety of airborne pathogens in his office," he said.

"That's the spirit!" Rosa said. "Now turn to your left and lower the lid to the platform."

The device was the size of a shoebox, had a half-dozen color-coded wires and a digital timer with a blank display screen.

"That screen comes on if they accidentally activate it?" Brad whispered on the tower. Reg nodded and kept watching through the binoculars. "Does it really have live explosives?" Brad said.

"Yeah," Reg said. "It really does."

Rosa gave directions one step at a time, guiding Trevor in picking up the tools, clipping wires, and pulling a pin out of the device. When they were done, Trevor took his blindfold off and sat on the edge of the platform, limp, his arms draped over the railing. Rosa sat beside him.

Reg climbed down from the tower and lowered the platform, then removed the defused bomb and replaced it with another device covered with a box. "This one's different," he said to Brad and Eddie. "So if you memorized how to defuse the first one, forget it."

"Wish he didn't think of everything," Eddie muttered.

"Brad, you're in charge," Reg said. "Eddie, get the blindfold on."

Reg, Rosa, and Trevor trudged up the tower steps while Eddie and Brad clambered onto the platform. Eddie waited until it finished rising before he put the blindfold on.

"Okay," Brad said. "Take the lid off." Eddie reached forward, got ahold of the lid, and lifted it. "Well, put it down," Brad said. Eddie hissed through his teeth and set the lid down on the platform. "Pick up the screwdriver," Brad said.

"Um?" Eddie said.

"You have to remove a screw to get to one of the wires."

"I don't know where the screwdriver *is*," Eddie said.

"Well, obviously it was under the lid, or you'd have seen it. So put your hand out and feel around a little."

Eddie put his hand out gingerly, felt the edge of a tool, and slid his finger along its surface. "These are wire cutters."

"Yeah," Brad said. "So put them back. They're for later."

"You get that you could be more helpful?" Eddie said.

"You're 'exceptional.' You figure it out."

"I don't like this," Rosa whispered on the tower.

"Brad's right there, though," Trevor said. "He's going to be an ass, but he can't do worse than that."

"Okay," Brad said. "Unscrew the third screw from the left on the bottom row."

"You want to give me some overall visual of this?" Eddie said. "Just describe it in general?"

"It's more complicated than the first one," Brad said.

Eddie waited. "Oh-kay," he said. He waited another moment, then reached out and felt the device, running his right index finger along, feeling for screw heads. "This one?"

"Sure," Brad said.

"Is it or isn't it?" Eddie snapped.

"Yes," Brad said. He flipped the microphone off. "You know, I get that you were raised in a barn, but you could still be more polite."

"I was raised in a barn?"

"I can tell by your clothes," Brad said. "And you're from Indiana."

Eddie removed the screw. "You get that there isn't one giant barn over Indiana, right?"

Brad shrugged. "If there were, I wouldn't know about it. My dad does real estate in Manhattan."

"What's next?" Eddie said, pocketing the screw and ignoring the provocation.

"Get the wire cutters and cut the black wire close to its source. That's the one that arches over the top of the device."

Eddie picked up the wire cutters, felt around for the wires, and said, "This one?"

"Yeah," Brad said. Eddie traced it back and snipped it. "Now detach the red wire from the timer." Eddie reached out, felt a rectangle, and found a wire leading from it. "This one?"

"Yeah," Brad said. He flipped the mic back on.

Eddie clipped the wire.

The digital display snapped on: *15 seconds.*

"Oh god!" Brad said. "You *idiot!*"

*14 seconds*

"Eddie, take off your blindfold!" Reg shouted.

Brad took one step to the edge of the platform, lowered himself off the railing, and dropped onto the yellow bag below. It billowed up around him and he sank slowly in the middle as it deflated. Eddie tore his blindfold off, saw the display: *12 seconds,* at the same time he realized he was alone on the platform. He stepped to the edge and saw Brad sprawled below him, riding the bag down. *Single use.* If he jumped now, the fall would be uncushioned.

Rosa grabbed the zipline apparatus and jumped off the edge of the tower.

Eddie saw her coming and crouched on top of the railing, facing her. Rosa hurtled down the line toward him. As she slammed into him, Eddie grabbed for the nylon line clipped to the pulley, his fingers closing over hers and his legs wrapping around her.

The impact was hard, ribs knocking together, the irresistible force of Rosa's speed hitting the immovable object of Eddie's bulk. They began rotating, still swinging downward toward the far platform.

They spun in hard, Eddie taking the brunt of the landing with his shoulder. They went down on the landing platform in a tangle of legs and elbows.

That's when the bomb went off.

A small crack came from the center of the field, and a white cloud rose six feet over the raised platform and then showered it with fine dust.

Rosa brushed herself off and stood. Eddie sat, feet dangling over the edge, and stared at her.

"That is the most badass thing I have ever seen," he said.

"What *is* that?" Rosa demanded. "What kind of bomb *is* that?"

"Maybe powdered sugar?" Eddie said. "I can't believe you . . ."

But Rosa pounded down the stairs from the landing platform and bolted across the field. Reg and Trevor were halfway down from the taller tower when she reached the bottom and shouted up at them.

"What kind of bomb was *that*, Reg?"

"I said it was a live explosive. I didn't say it was a big one."

"What the hell?" she said, and started shaking.

"Damn it, Reginald," he said softly, trotting down the last stairs. "You okay?" he asked her.

"No, I am not okay!" She couldn't stop shaking. "I thought Eddie was going to *die*."

"Me too," Eddie said, reaching them. "Thanks for your crazy-ass heroics. It's been a while since a girl swept me off my feet."

Trevor grinned at him. Rosa put her hands on her knees and sucked in great ragged breaths. Eddie put his hand on her back.

"What happened out there?" Reg barked to Brad.

Brad walked toward them from the shadow of the building, where he'd run. His face was twisted. "He screwed up and nearly killed me. Would have killed me if that had been a real bomb."

"John Glenn's nuts!" Reg said. "You were responsible for talking him through it. Why didn't you?"

"He was too busy insulting me to describe anything precisely," Eddie said.

"That's not true!" Brad said.

Reg stared between them, his face dark. "This is my takeaway from this *team building exercise*," he finally said. "Rosa Hayashi has crazy courage. Trevor can handle his fear. And something *I don't like* is going on between you two."

He stalked toward the building. The trainees exchanged an uncertain look, and then followed.

"Rosa," Reg said, not turning around. "Did it occur to you just to send the zipline handle down to Eddie without swinging yourself? If that had been a real bomb, you both could have been killed."

"It goes faster with weight on it," Rosa said. "And the blast would sever the zipline. Eddie had to make it to the landing platform before the bomb went off. I thought we needed the extra speed."

Reg shook his head and clapped slowly.

"Knock knock," Eddie whispered to her.

"Who's there?" Rosa said.

"Angel."

"Angel who?"

"Ain't gelatinous scattered body parts because of you. That was incredible." He brushed the back of her hand with his fingertips. "Thank you."

# CHAPTER FIFTEEN

The next morning Reg took them back to the simulator and had them each run over the controls separately, without review. Then he taught them physics the old-fashioned pen-and-paper way. No projectiles were involved. They talked a lot about gravity. Brad and Eddie sat with an empty chair between them.

Finally Reg stretched and said, "I want to give you a little background on our present situation." They looked up at him, and Rosa flipped to a new page in her notebook. "No, no notes on this. There's some disagreement as to how much we should tell you until you're fully trained. I'm of the opinion that if you're going to be IA Teams 3 and 4, you need some information.

"IA exists because we know there are worlds out there with intelligent life. We believe that at least one of them has achieved travel capacities far beyond our own. Our deep space sensors have indicated that. Which means that someone out there is ringing doorbells."

"What have the sensors shown exactly?" Brad asked.

"Gravity flutters."

"Gravity flutters?" Brad said.

"Gravity doesn't seem like a thing that should flutter," Trevor said.

"Yeah," Reg said heavily. "I'll give you an outline of the math in a minute—you won't really understand it yet." He glanced out the window. "We're accelerating all our programs here, not just the training program. If they ever come here, we want to be ready."

"Ready for what, exactly?" Rosa said.

"We have no idea." Reg sighed. "But your training is broad. We have a course in recognizing life-forms—because if someday you meet an alien and it's not carbon based, you don't want to walk right past it. Or accidentally step on it."

Trevor laughed, and Reg shot him a look.

"You'll learn the ins and outs of space travel, and also take anthropology, sociology, ethics . . ."

"*Anthropology?*" Eddie said.

"Yep. We're preparing you to deal with space travel, and with potential contact with another world. Pay attention in Space Geography—the lines are shifting all the time. Did you know the Russians are claiming Mercury is theirs?" Reg scowled.

"Will we help negotiate space boundaries?" Rosa asked.

"No, those decisions are made at a higher level. But you need to recognize them. You're going to be flying diplomats with ray guns."

"Do we really have ray guns?" Rosa said. The guys pointed their fingers at one another and made sizzle noises.

"Sure," Reg said. "They're just lasers. Had 'em for years. And we're developing a line of Tasers to work on different neurological systems."

They were silent for a moment.

"*Are* we going to meet aliens?" Trevor said.

"Yeah. Maybe not now, but someday. Something's causing those gravity flutters."

"Could it be a black hole or a supernova?" Eddie said. "Something like that?"

Reg shook his head.

He showed them some of the math, and he was right, they didn't understand it. He was giving them some homework when his phone buzzed. He checked the screen, then motioned them up and led them to a building they hadn't been in before. The trainees peered into rooms as they passed—lots of equipment and a faint chemical smell—some kind of lab building.

"Is this headquarters for the resistance to the zombie apocalypse?" Trevor asked Reg. Reg snorted.

"This is Newton Hall," he said. "But we call it Nightmare Hall."

Trevor caught Rosa's eye. "Zombies," he mouthed.

Reg led them into a room with a tile floor and two hospital beds. They had wood-grain head- and footboards and thin white sheets. There was equipment on the wall behind them—suction machines, blood pressure cuffs, oxygen nozzles.

"Um," Trevor said.

"They must have heard about your ass," Eddie whispered.

Trevor flushed.

"Day after tomorrow you're going to do your duty for science," Reg said. "And Eddie, we're going to need that permission form. Did you get it back yet?"

Eddie's flush rose into his blond hair. *Like a plow going into corn*, Rosa thought. *Maybe. I'm from New Mexico—I've never actually seen that.* "Uh, yeah," he said. "I'll get it to you after class."

"Good," Reg said. "Can't let you do this without it."

Eddie nodded, but didn't look at Reg.

"Some crackerjack neurobiologists designed this for us," Reg continued, rubbing his hands together. "This is classified. We don't want bad guys getting ahold of it and using it for the wrong thing."

"Hospital beds?" Trevor said. "I hate to tell you, but the rest of us know about them."

"But you can totally see how bad guys could use these to destroy the world," Rosa said.

"They'd probably race them down the hall," Eddie said. "I know I would."

"Listen up, you knuckleheads," Reg said. "Because they're going to take your blood in a minute." Reg rubbed his hand over his scalp. "This isn't a test for you, understand? We're sending you in order to get data for the people designing this thing."

"Sending?" Rosa said.

The trainees looked at one another.

"It's a simulation," Reg said. "They'll inject you with some significant drugs, show you a video while you're going under, and your brain will continue the movie. You'll experience everything as though you were actually there. They're practicing syncing people, so ideally you see the same thing."

"Couldn't you send some secretaries or something?" Brad said. "We're valuable assets. You shouldn't experiment on us."

"Being a 'valuable asset' is a position of service, not privilege," Reg said. "But if you have to know, they want guinea pigs who have psych and intelligence testing on file so that they can evaluate the results."

"Oh," Brad said. "They need smart people."

"He's one 'et' short of being an asset," Trevor whispered.

"How can you make someone see what you want?" Brad said, ignoring him.

"Hell if I know," Reg said. "They dim the lights and give you some drugs and stick wires on your scalp. You'll give Frankenstein a run for his money."

"A helpful analysis, Reg," a woman in a white lab coat said as she walked in. A phlebotomist came in with her and set her plastic tub down on one of the narrow tables that swung over the beds. "I'm Dr. Sue O'Donnell. Nicole's going to take your blood while we talk." She motioned them to the beds and they perched on the edges. Nicole and her cheerful frog scrubs approached Rosa first.

"We've been able to induce detailed hallucinations for some time," Dr. O'Donnell said. "The trick was synchronizing them with another patient's, and making them interactive. The short version is that we change your frontotemporal interactions."

"What's the long version?" Trevor asked.

Nicole ripped open an alcohol wipe, and its sharp scent cut

the air. It was cold on the inside of Rosa's elbow. She drew Rosa's blood and moved on to Brad.

"Keeping in mind that you signed a nondisclosure agreement," Dr. O'Donnell said, giving Trevor a long look—probably thinking about his doctor parents—"we alter the connectivity among the temporal, prefrontal, and anterior cingulate regions."

"I'm with you," he said.

"We synchronize the gamma oscillations in your thalamocortical networks. We inhibit prefrontal and limbic attentional systems to allow the hallucinations to work. The mind wants to hallucinate," she said. "Just think about dreaming—you stop daytime sensory input, and the mind makes up its own. Or take Charles Bonnet Syndrome."

"When you lose sight," Trevor said, "you have visual hallucinations. Researchers think you always have them, but everyday visual input overrides them."

"Very good," Dr. O'Donnell said. "We just work with your brain's natural inclination, and give it direction."

Nicole dropped three vials of Brad's blood into her plastic tote and moved over to Eddie. He stuck his arm out and sat like a fossil, listening to Dr. O'Donnell.

"We'll have you wired up. You'll see out of your own eyes—your own brain, actually. The person monitoring you will see what's going on and will give prompts to produce the story line they want. You'll hear their voice, but you won't find that odd."

"Will one of us do the monitoring?" Brad said. "Will one of us be in charge of it?"

"No," Dr. O'Donnell said.

"Maybe," Reg said. "Good idea, Brad. I'll look into that."

Brad beamed, but the doctor gave Reg an inscrutable look.

Nicole labeled Eddie's vials and started working on Trevor. He scrunched up his face and turned away.

"You'll experience the world the way you do every day— your senses will be intact, they'll just be stimulated a different way. You walk by a lemon, you'll smell a lemon, understand?" Dr. O'Donnell said. Rosa nodded. "You won't know it's a simulation."

"So the person in the sim will just react on instinct, right? They won't know they're being manipulated?" Brad said.

"That's right," Dr. O'Donnell said.

"Can we die doing this?" Eddie asked.

"If you're stabbed, you won't bleed and you won't die, but you will see blood and you will feel pain. You'll think you can die." She looked at each of them in turn. "The physical effects won't be real. The psychological ones will be. What you experience, you will really experience."

Nicole walked out, carrying her plastic tote with twelve vials of their blood. She hadn't given Rosa a sticker or a princess bandage. Her pediatrician at home still gave her candy. They laughed about it, but she always left the place with a grape sucker in her mouth. For some reason, the tan bandage on her arm made her feel like an adult more than the apartment had.

"Tomorrow night, no food or drink after midnight." She raised her clipboard and uncapped her pen.

"What's the simulation going to be?" Brad asked.

She smiled at them and her eyes crinkled. "We're just trying to see if we can get you synced up, so the situation itself doesn't really matter." She shrugged. "Don't worry about it. You're just guinea pigs."

"Who could worry about that?" Brad asked.

"Once we get this perfected, it could be an incredibly effective training tool." She smiled again, nodded to Reg, and left the room.

"Do you know, Reg?" Rosa asked. "Do you know where we're going?"

"I do. But I ain't telling you."

"I hope it's historical," Eddie said. "The Middle Ages! I want to joust." He faked a lance thrust.

Trevor blew his lips in derision. "I'd want to go to Renaissance Florence and hang out in Michelangelo's studio."

"They're not sending you to 'hang out' anywhere," Reg said.

"What about you, Rosa?" Eddie asked.

Rosa flushed. "I want to go to prerevolutionary France, when the dresses were gorgeous. I want to go to a ball." She couldn't believe she said that out loud. *Rosa Hayashi—space pioneer, and fashionista.*

"You're not going back in history," Reg said.

"What about you, Brad?" Trevor said. Brad shook his head. He wasn't giving these people any more information about him than he had to, because he had an idea.

"I'll come to your ball," Eddie said to Rosa, "but I'm wearing my armor."

"Yeah, Michelangelo and I will come to your partay," Trevor said.

Reg sighed deeply and led them out of the room. "Yeah," he said. "That's exactly how it's gonna happen."

# CHAPTER SIXTEEN

The next morning Eddie took the signed permission form off his dresser and walked it over to the main office.

The secretary looked at the form and frowned slightly, and for a moment his stomach turned to cement, but then she looked up. "You're Eddie Toivonen?"

"Yeah?"

"There's a package for you in back. Hold on."

She went to a back room, and a moment later came out with a big box.

"Do I need to sign?" he asked, and then flushed, because that was not something to bring up.

"Nope," she said. "You're good."

The return address said it was from Bruce Jarboe, his best friend at home. It wasn't heavy but it was bulky, and when he staggered back to the apartment with it he almost wiped out Reg, Rosa, Brad, and Trevor leaving breakfast.

"You're late," Reg snapped.

"I took my consent form in, which I couldn't do till eight a.m., and they gave me this." Eddie shuffled sideways so he could see him.

"I do not have time for this," Reg said. He sighed. "Okay, everybody follow Eddie and his big fat care package." He motioned at him.

"I'll just meet you guys . . ."

"I don't want any of you loose today," Reg said. "Not a day to bother the grown-ups."

Eddie hesitated a moment, trying to decide how insulted he wanted to be, but Trevor came up and grabbed one end of the box. Between the two of them they got it to the building and into Eddie's apartment. So they were all standing there, in his place.

"You gonna open it?" Reg said.

"I thought we didn't have time." Eddie did *not* want to open it with them there. He had no idea what was in it.

"Your mama might have sent cookies, which you could share," Reg said.

Rosa looked down. She'd figured out that his mama wasn't sending any cookies. Eddie sliced the box open with his pocket-knife and pulled out his old blue sheets, some clothes, a few framed photos that he laid, facedown, on the dresser, and a brand new Nerf basketball hoop for over the door. He'd stored some stuff at Bruce's—he knew what to send. There was a note, too:

*Eddie, WTH? They said you made it? You're an IA trainee? If I'd known you were that smart, I'd have*

*cheated off you in calculus instead of sitting behind*
*Emma Alexander so I could smell her hair. Here's some*
*of your crap. The rest is still in the basement. It's okay to*
*leave it for a while. Good luck boldly going where no man*
*has gone before, or whatever you do now.*

*Hey, there was an article in the paper about you. No*
*fooling. You're as famous as the Joe Palooka statue—*
*Oolitic's two claims to fame. You have less bird shit on*
*your head. Or you did last time I saw you, anyway.*

*Bruce*

*PS: Dude, I gotta be honest—I would rather smell*
*Emma Alexander than pass calculus if I had to choose.*

*PPS: Don't get any bird shit on your head. You're*
*representing all of us now.*

Below the note was a bag of cookies Bruce's mom had made.
Eddie tossed a sweatshirt back in the box to cover them before anyone saw. Somebody made him cookies—and he was not sharing.

Reg led them to the tarmac beside the hangar. It was a bright
morning, and the sun glinted off a small silver airplane.

"We're flying?" Eddie said hopefully.

"Yeah," Reg said. Eddie gave the others a high five. "A friend
is letting us use it. I want the first craft you actually lift off the
ground to cost less than the net worth of Idaho."

Reg walked them around the outside of the plane, identifying
the different parts, then did the same for the inside. There were
pilot and copilot seats, and four seats in the back.

"You've got controls?" Rosa said.

"Yeah, it's a teaching plane."

He talked them through the preflight check, then had them each run through it. When they were done, he held up a finger for them to wait and exited the plane. They stayed seated for a couple of minutes, then Brad poked his head out. Reg was leaning with his palms against the plane, eyes squeezed shut.

"Reg?" Brad said.

"Get back inside," Reg snapped. He came in a moment later, made no eye contact, and took off without a word. Once he was in the air, he seemed to relax. He flew around the compound, and then landed where they'd taken off. "You feel that?" he said, grinning at them. "No, you didn't, because it's not possible to land more smoothly than that."

They each got a turn taking off and landing, and then Reg ushered them out of the plane.

"We survived," Trevor said. "I was afraid the Big Bang was going to happen right here on this runway."

"It did," Reg said. "The Big Bang occurred everywhere. Did you ever think about that? Even though the universe was a pinpoint when it occurred, it took place everywhere within that space at the same time."

"The universe is bigger now," Rosa said, "but wherever you are, that's where the universe started."

"You're saying the Big Bang took place in Trevor's colon?" Eddie said.

Reg grinned. "I am."

"Hey!" Trevor said.

"What gets me," Eddie said, "is that everything is held in place by its distance from everything else. Something gets too close and it disturbs that."

"Wow," Rosa said. "That's actually very self-revelatory."

"I'm talking about astronomy," Eddie said. He hoped. She just looked at him.

"Guess it's a good time to break for lunch," Reg said. "Just work on your math problems this afternoon—I've got a meeting."

Reg led them back to the cafeteria, but he ate with some other adults in huddled conversation. Eddie got tomato soup and grilled cheese and four iced molasses cookies. They didn't talk much. He'd eaten three of the cookies when a man in a crisp blue IA shirt approached the table.

"Eddie Toivonen?" he said, but it wasn't a question. "Come with me, please." Eddie gave him a wary look and took his time standing, so the guy said, "You have a visitor."

Eddie got up and followed him. It was another IA trick. Because no way did he have a visitor.

# CHAPTER SEVENTEEN

The man took Eddie to the director's office, knocked, and pushed the door open to reveal a utilitarian desk and file cabinets. Nothing mahogany, no leather-bound volumes. No bronze ducks. There was a framed photo of a spectacular space explosion on one wall. The director was sitting behind his desk, tapping his fingers. Eddie's escort motioned him in, and shut the door behind him as he left.

"Eddie." It was his old man's voice.

Eddie stiffened, but then managed the turn casually. It wasn't possible for the old man to be there—and it sure as hell wasn't fair.

"Eddie," Director Smithson said, "have a seat."

The old man was standing. Eddie wasn't sitting while he was standing. Rule Number One.

"What are you doing here?"

The old man smiled. He had one less tooth than the last time Eddie saw him, but he was still big as a bear. The guy's chest was huge, his T-shirt pulled tight over hard muscle. He had a couple of days' worth of stubble on his chin, as if his inside was so full of sharpness that it poked right out of him.

"I heard you were here. I'm concerned about your safety."

Eddie snorted softly.

"Um, your father tells me he didn't sign your release."

*Please don't get it out.*

Director Smithson pulled the paper from a folder on his desk. "Our understanding was that your grandmother has legal custody of you."

"She does."

"I didn't sign that," the old man said.

"We weren't aware there was any kind of issue," Director Smithson said, his hands tilting open in apology. The head of the Interworlds Agency, apologizing to the old man. *Unbelievable.* The universe is infinite, so everything happens somewhere—but not this.

"What are you going to do with him, anyway? I mean, you testing drugs on him or anything?"

"No," Smithson said. "Of course not." He blinked at him, then looked between them. He'd picked up on the dynamic.

There was a question Eddie was dying to ask, but he couldn't say it here—too humiliating. The old man knew it, too. So Eddie said, "Have a safe trip," and turned his back on him. Dangerous, but Eddie had good hearing and he was watching Smithson's eyes. If the old man moved at him, he'd see it there.

The old man adjusted to the situation, though, you had to give him that. He figured out how to humiliate Eddie. He answered the unasked question.

"Some guy on death row confessed in order to stall his execution. They had to give me a new trial, and part of the evidence in my case had gotten lost." Eddie turned back and his old man grinned. The missing tooth was on the right side of his mouth. He'd gotten popped by a southpaw. "I'm now an innocent man."

"No, you're not. You're a guilty man who got out on a technicality."

The old man stared at him for a moment, his gaze full of broken dishes and shouting in the night. He was supposed to seem smaller, the way your elementary school does when you drive by years later. He still looked big. But Eddie had seven years' growth that was new to him. The old man stuck his hand out to Smithson.

"Lemme see that form."

Smithson half stood to hand it to him, his chair scraping unnaturally loud. The old man took the paper and Smithson hung suspended for a moment, his butt in the air, then slowly sank back into his seat, as though even gravity knew to move slowly around the old man.

He looked the form over. It was more than the standard release—it specified that Eddie might encounter serious injury or death on this or any other Earth, or in transit between. Eddie wasn't worried about him seeing that, and he wasn't all that worried about the signature, either. He could do it pretty well. What worried him was the date.

The old man's eyes went over the page, slowly. He was going for careful father, but he didn't have a lot of experience with that, and was projecting illiterate con. "If he gets hurt doing any of this," he said, waving the paper vaguely, "it's gonna cost me. Hospitals aren't cheap."

He'd missed the date. Eddie should have been relieved, but a fireball of fury grew in his gut. He shouldn't have missed it. Asshole.

"Oh," Smithson said, relieved because he didn't understand anything. "He's covered by NASA. We do take safety precautions, but if he got hurt, we'd take care of it."

The old man reached an arm back and scratched his neck, his elbow pointing at the ceiling. "Still. I could encounter expenses," he said.

The room was quiet for a minute. Interworlds Agency Director Stanford Smithson, PhD, sat in his neatly pressed shirt, processing that statement. The old man was more alien to his world than if he'd been a tentacled Martian.

"You want . . . money?"

"I'm starting over, see? And I had assumed me and my son would be going into business together."

*Yeah. There's a lot of money in bar fights.*

"Seems like if you withhold my son's labor from me, I should be compensated for that loss." He shrugged.

"Eddie," Smithson said. "When do you turn eighteen?"

"February." It occurred to him that he should have said "next week." The old man might not have remembered.

"Huh." Smithson looked up at the old man. "Mr. Toivonen, are you aware that your son has won entry into an extremely prestigious training program that will lead to multiple job offers within the astrophysics and space industry? Eddie's future is set."

"That's good," he said. "You did good. I'm proud of that." He held Eddie's eye. He meant it—Eddie had made him proud. Eddie didn't begin to know how to process that. "But if he did so good, if he's such an asset," he said to Smithson, "then I should be compensated."

"There's really no way to do that," Smithson said. "But you can rest assured that he's being taken care of. It's one thing off your mind."

"See, that doesn't really work," the old man said. "If I don't have a little nest egg, I'm gonna have to pull him out so that we can work together."

"You would do that?" Smithson said. "You'd withdraw him?"

The old man shrugged, rippling his yard-hard muscles. "No choice, really."

Smithson stood. "Mr. Toivonen, I'm going to have to ask you to leave. Don't come back until you have legal custody."

The old man's eyebrows lowered and he worked his jaw side to side. Smithson didn't flinch. Another guy might have moved to stand beside the director, to show some solidarity. Eddie took a step toward the door. Smithson saw it—and Eddie figured that now the director thought he was a coward. But the old man saw the step, too. He knew what Eddie was doing—separating, so he couldn't take them both down in one motion. So if he had to, Eddie could come at him from behind.

The blood rushed in Eddie's ears, and a vein ticked in Smithson's neck, and then the old man smiled and said, "Getting custody's not gonna be that hard." And he turned and left the office, leaving the door open behind him.

Smithson stood for a moment, then took a deep breath and turned, smiling wanly.

"I'm so sorry," Eddie whispered. "God, I'm so sorry."

The director said something, but Eddie was out of there, walking as long as he could, and then he was running.

# CHAPTER EIGHTEEN

Eddie wasn't at dinner. Rosa, Trevor, and Brad ate together, which seemed strange—it had never been just the three of them. They were eating butterscotch pudding and talking about their favorite books when Reg came up and sat at their table. He leaned forward on one elbow.

"You seen Eddie?"

They looked at one another.

"Not since lunch," Rosa said.

"What's going on?" Trevor said.

Reg tapped the tabletop for a moment, thinking. "Look, his dad was here, okay? He left the compound, but Eddie doesn't seem to be here now."

"Maybe they ate out," Trevor said.

"Or went shopping," Rosa said.

"Yeah," Reg said, "that's not what happened. We want to keep them apart, but we don't know where Eddie is. If you see Mr. Toivonen, let me know right away, okay?"

"What does he look like?" Brad asked.

"Like Eddie on steroids, only thirty years older and a hundred years meaner."

"Ouch," Brad said.

Reg tapped the table again and stood. "We're concerned about Eddie," he said. "I want you to take this seriously."

"Of course," Rosa said.

"Have you checked the rec center?" Trevor said.

Reg looked at his watch. "He can't be there. It's closed."

"Hmm," Trevor said. "We're gonna need the key." Reg pulled his head back and squinted at him. "If we find him, he may need some Hoosier therapy."

Reg thought about it for a moment. "Yeah, there's a key in the office. One of you can pick it up."

"I'll get it," Brad said. "I'll leave it on top of the mailboxes."

They nodded. Reg left and they dumped their trays, then Brad took off for the office.

"You thinking what I'm thinking?" Rosa said.

"Yeah," Trevor said, sighing. "And my butt already hurts."

Rosa hesitated. "Should we take Brad?"

Trevor shook his head. "The fewer people who know we've been off campus the better."

They made sure they'd lost Reg and Brad, then walked to the place where they'd crawled under the compound's electric fence the night they went to the pharmacy. Rosa went

first, and Trevor gave her sad cow eyes as he dropped to his
belly.

"Keep your butt down," she reminded him.

He grunted and pushed forward with his toes, inch by inch.
Finally she got fed up and grabbed his wrists and pulled him
through. He stood, brushing himself off.

"Last time we did this it was dark," he said.

"Yeah," she said. "Let's get moving."

If Eddie was off campus, he had probably walked into town.
It was the only place they knew to go, which meant it was all he
knew, too.

They'd walked a couple of miles—long enough for the light
to soften—when they saw him ambling down the road toward
them. He was wearing jeans and a plain white T-shirt and he had
a fist wrapped around the neck of a bottle in a paper bag. He was
singing.

"This is not good," Trevor said.

"At least we found him. We didn't have to check every alley
in town."

Trevor grunted.

"*Don't matter how far I travel, I can't get awaaay,*" Eddie
sang with a bluegrass twang, then he saw them and raised his bag
in greeting. "*He's the one who done the crime, and I'm the one
who paaays.*" When he got close they stopped, but he kept walking, so they turned and flanked him.

"This," he said, waving the bottle in the air, "is classic. A brown
paper bag!"

He put it to his lips and took a gurgly swig. Rosa looked around him to Trevor.

"Um, can I have a drink?" Trevor asked.

Eddie passed him the bag, and Trevor took the opportunity to pull the bottle out. His eyes widened, and he held it up to show Rosa. Vodka. Not full. He took a swig, coughed, and spat it on the road. Eddie tried to take the bottle back.

"*So help me drain the bottle, help me hoist a glass,*" he sang.

"Maybe you've had enough," Trevor said.

Eddie wrenched the bottle away from him.

"*The earth will spin around the sun, but this will never pass.*"

"Hey, Eddie?" Rosa said, not sure she was doing the right thing. "We heard you saw your dad today."

"Yes," he said, turning to her. "He has come to take me home."

"Home?" she said. "You can't stay?" She felt sick.

"No," he said, his breath washing over her. "All I have here is a chance at meaningful work and a respectable life. There I can evade the police and sleep in the back of a truck with chickens." He took another drink and wiped his mouth on the back of his hand. "My old man killed a guy in a carjacking—Lamar Sensenbrenner."

"Who was that?" Trevor said.

Eddie shrugged. "Just some guy who was unlucky enough to run into my old man, and get run over by his own car." He pointed a finger at Rosa. "Have you ever slept in a truck with chickens?"

"No," she said.

"*Don't ask me why I'm drinking, don't ask me why I'm*

*drunk—the old man showed back up today and now my future's sunk."*

"You live with your grandma, though, right?" Rosa said. "The cool one?"

"Yes!" Eddie said, and took a long drink. He raised the bottle high. "To Grandma, may she rest in peace!"

"What?" Rosa breathed. "Oh, Eddie, no."

"She died a month ago," he said. "She signed the first waiver, but this second one we had to do? I forged it."

They didn't say anything.

"And the old man looked at it, and he didn't even think about the date. He didn't even notice that she was buried when I signed it, because he wasn't thinking about her."

"Or about you," Rosa said, then bit her bottom lip, because maybe that wasn't something to say out loud.

"No," Eddie agreed amiably, "definitely not about me."

Then he started crying. He pulled the T-shirt up over his head and walked that way. Trevor tried to take the bottle, but Eddie yanked it back, and between sobs he took a long swig under the shirt. A dribble of vodka ran down his stomach and into the waistband of his jeans.

"I'm so sorry," Rosa said.

They were almost to the IA compound when he said, "I really miss her." His voice was muffled and boozy and miserable.

"Could your mom—" Trevor said.

"No." Eddie cut him off. "She's not in the picture."

"We should go around," Rosa said. "We can't just walk through the guard booth."

"Why not?" Eddie said. "You know they've got cameras, right? They know either way." He pulled his shirt down, then wiped his face on the tail, exposing his muscly stomach again. Rosa thought that under the circumstances, it was really, really wrong of her to notice. Eddie headed straight for the guard booth. Trevor put a hand on his bicep.

Eddie stopped and held very still for a moment. "You realize," he said, slurring his words, "how embarrassing it will be to get beat up by a guy as drunk as me?"

Trevor took his hand off Eddie's arm. Eddie sauntered up to the guard booth and stood, swaying, peering at the guard with his blurry red eyes.

"I am Eddie Toivonen, reporting for duty," he said. "Sir!"

Rosa and Trevor sidled up behind him.

"Um, Reg Davis wants us to bring him back in," Rosa said, making an effort at a smile.

"Yeah," the guard said, looking them over. "We were notified about this. You need any help?"

"No, sir," Rosa said. "Thank you."

He waved them through and they walked down the sidewalk.

Once he'd succeeded in going into camp through the main entrance, Eddie didn't seem to care where he went. Rosa steered him toward the rec center, and Trevor ran off to the apartments to get the key Brad had left. By the time Eddie and Rosa got there, Trevor had the place unlocked. There were emergency lights at the ends of the halls, but the place was dim and absolutely silent save for their footfalls. Trevor heaved open the gym door and they walked in. The emergency lights were on there, too, glowing dimly in cages on the walls. It was a full court, and there was a metal cart with two rows of basketballs by the wall. Trevor rolled it out to the half-court line.

"This," Eddie said, "is heaven."

Trevor held his hand out, and Eddie passed him the bottle and staggered to half court. Trevor stashed the bottle in the hall so Eddie wouldn't see it. Eddie chose a ball, gave it a trial bounce, then carried it under his arm as he walked toward the basket. He stopped ten feet away and stared at the rim.

"Traditionally," he said, "the basket holds still. I believe that's one of the rules."

He swayed, took a step back, turned around to see if the other basket might be closer, then pivoted and sank the shot.

"That went in, right?"

"Yeah," Rosa said. "You done good."

Eddie wailed for whiskey in a spot-on Janis Joplin imitation.

"That is one drunk Hoosier," Trevor said.

Eddie shot from the left, but stumbled backward and missed. "I don't know what good drinkin' can do, Janis," he said. "Let's find out." Rosa got his rebound and bounced it to him. Trevor moved under the basket, and Eddie walked to the free throw line.

"You know what sucks about this?" Eddie said.

"What?" Rosa said.

"I did this. Getting in here—that was *me*. And he gets to take it away because I'm not eighteen yet?" He shot. The ball made a pretty arc and dropped with a swish, never touching the rim. Trevor whistled, and Rosa bounced the ball back to him. "I'm more responsible than he'll ever be."

"Maybe he won't come back," Rosa said. "I mean, he left, right?"

Eddie spun the ball between his hands. "Won't matter. Once people get a whiff of him, they look at me different. This one time I was supposed to meet the track coach in the school office. Nobody else was there, and when the secretary came back in and saw me, she went to her desk and checked her purse. Right in front of me."

"That stinks," Rosa said. "But you earned your spot, Eddie. Nobody is going to take it away from you."

"Yeah?" he said, tilting his chin up. "That's what Trevor and Brad are here for. Because of my anomalous, overaggressive test results." He shot, got the swish, and Trevor snagged the ball. "I was on the bubble before. Congratulations, Trevor. You're in, and you didn't even have to screw me over to get the job. The old man did it for you."

Trevor stood holding the ball.

"Where is my only friend in this world? What did you do with it?" Eddie stumbled in a circle.

"Do I want a spot here?" Trevor said. "Of course I do. But I'm not trying to get rid of you." Eddie snorted. "That bottle's not your friend, and I am. The more time you spend with it, the less there is of both of you. That's not a friend."

"You," Eddie said, pointing at Trevor, "have a future teaching Sunday school."

Trevor flushed.

"He's right," Rosa said. "We *are* your friends."

Eddie staggered away from the free throw line, heading toward

the door. "What do you know about it? Your daddy runs the
Los Alamos National Goddamn Lab. Until recently, mine was a
valued worker in the laundry room at Pendleton Correctional."
He stumbled across the floor, then turned in circles, looking for
the vodka Trevor had stashed outside. Eddie started to cry again.
He crouched by the wall and pulled his shirt back over his head. His
stomach shook with his sobs. "I've lost everything," he said. He sank
against the cinder block and sat there, crying under his shirt.

Rosa and Trevor went over and sat beside him.

The wall was hard against Rosa's spine, and her sneakers
squeaked when she shifted positions. Eddie cried for a long time.
Trevor knocked the ball sideways with his straight leg, rolling it
past Eddie. Rosa tapped it back to him with her ankle. It reminded
her of tempting her cat to play by dragging a string past her.
Finally Eddie stopped crying, pulled his shirt down, and wiped his
nose on his sleeve. That sleeve was getting seriously snotted.

"This is so embarrassing." He didn't look at them.

"No it's not," Rosa said. That got him to peek sideways at her.
"I'm sorry, but you have real problems. You can't live with your
grandma, and you don't want to live with your dad. So if you get
dropped from IA, what happens to you?"

"Oh wow, Eddie," Trevor said. "I didn't even think of that."

"And you're worried *he'll* take your place?" Rosa said. Eddie
almost smiled.

"You were under way more pressure than the rest of us,"
Trevor said. "At the tryouts? Holy crap. You *had* to make it."

"That," Rosa said to Eddie, "is why you are only runner-up at
embarrassment." He shifted to look at her. "You've got reasons.

Nobody begrudges you one bottle and some surprisingly good drunken shooting. I, on the other hand, had to wake up two guys to help me get accessories for my lady parts."

Trevor flinched and looked away.

"You think you're embarrassed?" Rosa pointed past Eddie to Trevor. "He thinks my vagina wears a hat."

"Oh my god," Eddie said, rolling away from her. "This day keeps getting worse."

"I can't believe she said the word," Trevor said. He stood and extended a hand down to Eddie. Rosa stood, too, and together they hauled him to his feet. "I'm proud to know both of you. You've both got weaknesses," Trevor said earnestly, "but you've got such great strengths, too."

"Wait," Eddie said, raising his index finger.

"We both have weaknesses?" Rosa said, arching her eyebrows. "What's mine?"

"Um, needing tampons?" Trevor said.

"And there," Eddie said, dropping the finger like an ax. "You know I'm not gonna be sober enough to bury you until tomorrow, right?"

Rosa gave Trevor a kill-you-later stare, and they shuffled Eddie out of the rec center. Trevor slipped back in to throw away the bottle under the guise of locking up. They hauled Eddie to the apartment building, and he insisted on climbing up on the retaining wall but couldn't coordinate his feet well enough to make the jump. Trevor clambered up and threw his hand down. Eddie shook his head.

"I am the lone wolf, howling at the moon."

"If you took my hand you could howl five feet closer," Trevor said.

Eddie threw himself at the wall a half-dozen times before he pulled himself up, knees bruised, but counting it a victory. He threw his head back and howled. Rosa and Trevor exchanged a look and then hustled him into his apartment. Trevor warmed a washcloth and tossed it over Eddie's head, and Eddie wiped his face. Rosa walked over to the photos his friend had sent, lying facedown on his dresser.

"Do we want these up?" she asked.

He hesitated a second. "Yeah," he said.

She tilted the frames up and stood back to look. One was a photo of Eddie at about three years old, sitting on the back of a pony. The second one was of him and his grandma. She had shoulder-length gray hair and was standing on a barn roof holding one end of a homemade rocket launcher. One hand rested on Eddie's shoulder, and they were both grinning. "I miss your grandma," Rosa said. "And I never met her."

Eddie nodded.

The last photo was of Eddie and an even taller guy with dark hair. They were wearing orange vests and holding sticks to pick up garbage with one hand, and flashing peace signs with the other. Both were smiling. "Um . . . ," Rosa said.

"Community service," Eddie said blearily, following her gaze. "Bruce's mom is a nurse at a GI clinic. He stole a bunch of stationery and we sent out notes all over town telling people it was time to get a colonoscopy."

They stared at him.

"Dude, that's epic."

Eddie nodded. "Thirty-seven people got butt scopes in response. Two of them had early colon cancer."

"You saved two lives," Trevor said.

Eddie fell onto his bed. "Probably. And we picked up a lot of trash along a highway."

Rosa laughed and propped a pillow up behind him.

"No," he said. "Eddie go night-night."

"No," Rosa said. "Eddie get hydrated, and fast. You can't eat or drink anything after midnight, remember? Tomorrow is the simulation."

# CHAPTER NINETEEN

Rosa knocked on Eddie's door the next morning, checking to make sure he was up. He opened it.

"You're pretty, but you're too damn loud."

"Clean clothes. And a shave?" she said. "I'm impressed."

Brad and Trevor came out of their apartments. Brad looked rested and was wearing a tailored shirt. Trevor had dark circles under his eyes, but he gave Eddie a fist bump. They walked together to the building where the simulation would take place.

When they got to the room where they'd been before, Dr. O'Donnell was there but Reg wasn't.

"We're going to go ahead and get you prepped," she said.

"Is Reg coming?" Rosa asked.

Dr. O'Donnell frowned. "He was delayed." She hesitated. "There was a break-in at the office."

They exchanged an alarmed look.

"Someone went through your personnel files."

"How can they tell?" Brad said.

"Every document has an embedded thread. The photocopy machine keeps a record of the chip numbers—what was copied and when. Last evening someone copied parts of your files, including the twelve-page psychological profiles you filled out before you came here."

They were silent for a moment.

"Couldn't it just have been someone involved with this?" Trevor said. "Sort of reviewing our charts?"

"No," Dr. O'Donnell said. "They would have recorded it properly. We're very good at recording things properly." She gave a wry smile.

"That's a little creepy," Rosa said.

"No kidding," Brad said.

"Um, you said you're trying to sync two people, right?" Trevor said. "But there's four of us."

"Two trips!" Dr. O'Donnell said, her blue eyes shining. "We're sending Brad and Trevor first."

"Give Michelangelo my best," Eddie said.

The nurse—Nicole—came in and started IVs for Brad and Trevor.

Reg came in a few minutes later, looking as disheveled as a bald man can.

"We still on here?" Dr. O'Donnell said.

"Yeah," Reg said. "They want to get the data from the simulation." He added, "They're going to dispatch Young and Moloney—send them to the source of the anomaly."

"I didn't give the trainees anything yet," the doctor said, "in case you needed them, too."

"No," Reg said. "We wouldn't send them no matter how bad it got."

"How bad what got?" Eddie asked. "What anomaly, exactly?"

"It's nothing," Reg said, and they learned something new about him: he was a terrible liar. "Just a little gravitational disturbance."

Trevor stared, bug eyed, at Rosa and Eddie. He reached over, grabbed a pen out of Nicole's plastic phlebotomy cart, and dropped it. It fell down, just like it was supposed to.

Reg rolled his eyes. "This," he said, "is why we don't send trainees."

Friesta Bauer knocked on the door and opened it at the same time.

"You start yet?"

"No," Dr. O'Donnell said.

Ms. Bauer glanced at her watch. "Go ahead." She turned to the trainees. "I'm your monitor—I'm going to be seeing everything you're seeing, but I'll see it through my own eyes. It'll be like I'm an observer in the crowd."

"We give you a modified paralytic so you won't thrash around much," Dr. O'Donnell said. "But you'll still be able to talk."

"I don't want any paralytic," Eddie said.

"You'll be able to move in the simulation," Dr. O'Donnell said. "It's similar to what they give you for surgery to keep you still on the table. But unlike surgery, when you wake up you'll remember everything. It will make a memory, even though it never happened."

"This is deeply weird," Rosa muttered.

"This is fascinating," Trevor said, walking over to examine

the syringes that Dr. O'Donnell had laid out. She beamed at him. "Reg, would you lower the lights, please?" He did, and Eddie was grateful for the darkness. The doctor motioned Brad and Trevor onto the beds.

"Don't you have to be in bed?" Rosa asked Ms. Bauer.

"No," she said. "I don't get the drugs. I'll know what I'm seeing is a simulation."

Nicole picked up a syringe, held it upright, and tapped it sharply, then inserted the needle into a side branch of Brad's tubing. "This may feel a little cold," she said. Then she did Trevor's. Trevor wiggled his toes—must not have been the paralytic. A couple of techs came in and put five round electrodes on his chest, then skinny leads on his scalp. Then they wired Ms. Bauer to them, and Dr. O'Donnell injected more drugs.

They switched on a screen, and a video montage started—fields in midsummer, and then a tornado, dark and twisting, and the sky an eerie green. A woman screamed for a little boy as he abandoned his toys and ran into the house. A bike lay in the yard beside a stuffed monkey. On the porch a pile of yellow Legos spilled out of a sand bucket—pictures to give them images to draw from.

Rosa gave Trevor what she hoped was an encouraging smile, then exchanged an uneasy glance with Eddie. They were next, and she was not comfortable with public hallucination.

Dr. O'Donnell placed Ping-Pong balls cut in half over Brad's and Trevor's eyes. She picked up two final syringes and injected two cc of clear liquid into their tubing. A couple of heartbeats later their breathing became slow and rhythmic. Rosa didn't know where the two of them were, but they weren't in a room in Nightmare Hall.

Their muscles twitched like dreaming dogs. They were both struggling with something no one else could see—except Friesta Bauer. She sat with her eyes closed, frowning, watching what was happening inside their heads for a couple of minutes. Trevor mumbled, "I want to go home."

"Stop it," Ms. Bauer said, opening her eyes. There was an authority to her voice that made even Eddie want to obey. Dr. O'Donnell gave another injection and removed the Ping-Pong balls from their eyes. She caught Rosa's and Eddie's gaze and held a finger to her lips.

Brad and Trevor blinked and looked around the room, then at each other, and gradually came back to the room in Nightmare Hall.

"You kept taking them," Trevor said. It was an accusation.

"They were *mine*," Brad said. "It was a private beach and you shouldn't have been there."

"They didn't sync consistently," Friesta Bauer said flatly. "They saw each other, but neither gave up his version of what was happening."

"Any better than the last attempt?" Dr. O'Donnell said.

"Definitely, in terms of picture clarity and lack of bleed

through. Sensory was perfect, but their minds wouldn't cooperate."

"What did you see, Trevor?" Dr. O'Donnell asked.

"There was a pile of yellow bricks, and I tried to make a road with them so I could get out of there. There was a witch on a bicycle and a tornado, and a flying monkey beat my head with its wings."

"Are you freaking kidding?" Brad said, laughing. "You were in *The Wizard of Oz?*"

Trevor flushed.

"That's why you were wearing those shoes!" Brad turned to them. "He had on Chuck Taylors, but they were covered in red sequins!" He barked a laugh and Trevor's flush deepened. "Your flying monkey was just a stuffed animal I threw at you so you'd stop stealing from me."

"It felt like it was flying around my head," Trevor mumbled. "It was actually kind of disturbing." Rosa looked at Eddie. This was real—Trevor had been trying to build a road to get himself out of there, and a monkey had been flapping around his head, harassing him. For Trevor, it had been a real experience.

"What did you see, Brad?" Dr. O'Donnell said.

"I was on a *private* beach building a sand castle. I found a pile of gold bricks and I tried to stack them, but he came along and kept carrying them away. I guess to build his stupid road." Brad crossed his arms and sat stonily on the bed. "He threw a bucket of sand at me."

"It was a bucket of water!" Trevor said. "I was trying to make you melt."

Eddie pushed his fist against his mouth and stared at the floor.

Ms. Bauer sighed. "The picture was great, but they couldn't agree on what they were seeing."

Dr. O'Donnell nodded.

"Probably you don't need to send us, then," Rosa said. "Since you got the data you need."

"They need to run a scenario with a different pair," Reg said. "This is an important experiment. And I like Brad's idea of having one of you wired up as the voice."

Dr. O'Donnell turned her back and began to prepare syringes.

"But we already know the scenario," Eddie said. He grinned at Rosa. "The sequined shoes are all yours."

Trevor scowled.

"This will be a different situation," Reg said. "In every way."

There was something in his tone that seemed off to Rosa, an undercurrent like a riptide. Something more dangerous than whatever the simulation would do to them.

Eddie caught it, too, and he knew what it was. There'd been a break-in at the office and they thought he'd done it. People always thought he'd done it. And they were going to give him drugs and put him in a stressful situation and try to trick him into confessing. That's what Brad was for—a second witness. Eddie would be drugged, paralyzed, and without representation. And he couldn't refuse to do the sim. That would be an admission of guilt, and guys like him didn't get a second chance.

And then Dr. O'Donnell turned around, syringes raised.

"Time to go," she said.

# CHAPTER TWENTY

"Any changes in your health history in the past day?" Dr. O'Donnell said, once Rosa and Eddie had hospital gowns on and IVs started.

"I'm a little dehydrated," Eddie said.

She gave him an inscrutable look, then said to Nicole, "Let's bolus him at a half liter of normal saline over thirty minutes. We'll just piggyback." Nicole nodded and retrieved a saline bag, hung it on an IV pole, and attached the tubing to the needle in his arm.

Dr. O'Donnell and Nicole worked together to put electrodes on them. Rosa took longer because of her hair. Trevor pulled the bed rails into position with a loud *clickclickclickclick*.

"Dang, Trev," Eddie said. "That is seriously too loud for my head."

Then Reg nodded at Brad, and Brad beamed, and they hooked him up as well as Friesta Bauer.

Dr. O'Donnell glanced at Reg, then took a breath and said, "Both Brad and Friesta will be able to see what's going on in the simulation. I'll get you started but Brad's the monitor, so once we're under way, if someone talks it will be him. You'll hear his voice, but you won't find that odd."

"Why would he be talking?" Eddie said.

"To help the simulation," Reg said. "Or just if he thinks he can clarify anything, since he's been through this once."

Brad nodded from his chair.

Eddie opened his mouth, but Dr. O'Donnell gave them an injection, and Reg switched a screen on, starting another video montage. The light hurt Eddie's eyes, but that wasn't why his head was swimming. He was confused, but didn't know what he was confused about. On the screen rain came down, drops, then sheets, then torrents. Eddie saw a river, maybe thirty yards wide, rain driving craters into its surface. It was deep, and he could hear its urgent rush.

"He's gonna have a tough day," Dr. O'Donnell whispered. "A hangover and then this?"

On-screen the video flipped from image to image: a yellow church bus with "Trinity AMC" painted on the side, a two-lane highway, the faces of smiling people in choir robes. Other traffic— trucks, a police cruiser—again the swollen river. Dr. O'Donnell put the Ping-Pong balls over their eyes. *Reg threw Ping-Pong balls at us once.* Eddie remembered that. "What is it with you people and Ping-Pong balls?" he said.

Then he heard the thrum of a motorcycle over the roar of the river, and saw the back of the yellow church bus, glimpsed heads bobbing inside, and caught a snatch of singing. And then he was on the motorcycle. Eddie could feel the seat between his legs, the stirrups under his feet, and the warm press of a girl behind him, her arms wrapped around his waist. The pavement was slick so he slowed down.

He was Eddie Toivonen. He was riding a motorcycle. He saw a bus full of people slide off the road, across the muddy shoulder, and into a raging river.

Eddie pulled over and Rosa jumped off the bike. They pulled their helmets off, and instantly rain was running down their faces and staining her dark hair darker. Ahead of them a police car pulled over, wallowed for a moment on the shoulder, and an officer jumped out.

Great muddy gouges from the bus's tires cut the bank. Beyond it, the bus settled in the river a dozen yards downstream, snagged on something under the water. It shuddered, then came to a rest, pointing upstream. The water was already up to the bottom of the lettering on the bus, which meant the floor inside was already wet. People were shouting, faces pressed to the windows, fogging them.

Eddie kicked off his shoes while he shrugged out of his leather jacket.

"Eddie, I can't swim," Rosa said. "Oh god, I can't swim."

*You can't help,* Brad's voice said. *You weren't prepared, Rosa, and now you're failing.*

"I can swim." Eddie trotted up a few yards, toward the police officer. The water would carry him downstream fast—he needed to start higher if he was going to intercept the bus.

The cop stepped forward. "Stay on the bank. I radioed for help already," he said in Brad's voice.

"The bus will get swept away," Eddie said.

The police officer shook his head. "It's way too dangerous to go in the river. Besides, they might make it to shore on their own." He popped his trunk and took out an orange-and-white-striped barricade.

"They got shaken up and they're scared," Rosa said.

*You shouldn't talk, Rosa*, the voice said, and it was the cop's voice, but the cop wasn't talking. *You have nothing to add.*

"Screw you, stupid voice," Rosa said. "Can you get out?" she bellowed, her hands cupped to her mouth.

"Door's stuck," the driver shouted.

"Break a window!" Eddie shouted. "Kick out a window!"

"Or just lower it," Rosa said.

A woman near the back dropped the top half of her window and shoved her head and shoulders through, but the opening was too small to crawl out, and the bottom didn't open.

"There's an emergency exit!" Rosa shouted at Eddie, then turned and yelled at the driver. "There's an emergency exit!"

"It'll let the water in!" the woman shouted, the rain driving down onto her short dreadlocks, making them writhe.

The driver had his window open, too. "Call for help!"

"I did!" the cop shouted. He'd set up the barricade and was dragging a second into place, blocking access to the bank. "Now we wait."

"We don't *wait*," Eddie said. "When that bus sweeps away it'll tip and sink."

"But I'm in charge," the officer said. "And I'm giving you a direct order. Stay on the bank."

"Their best chance is to get out *now*."

The woman with the locs and another woman kicked out the bottom of her window, but they couldn't bend the frame out of the way. More people rushed to the window, pulling at the metal with desperate hands. The bus listed toward the bank. Inside, people screamed and backed away from the window. Even with the weight redistributed, the bus stayed tilted.

"Break the front windshield and bring them up the center aisle," Rosa shouted.

Eddie studied the current. When he picked his way forward, the officer stepped in front of him and jutted a finger in his face. "Stay here!"

"Why are you being a jerk?" Eddie said. "I'm trying to save those people."

"I am in charge here!" he shouted. He was wearing a hat with a little brim, and water sheeted off it like he was behind his own private waterfall. Then he grabbed Eddie's arm.

"Get your hand off me."

The man squeezed Eddie's arm harder and tried to haul him away from the water. Rosa ran at him.

"Stay back!" he shouted. "You'll fall down the bank and get hurt, just like you almost fell down the steps at the dorm. You don't want that, do you?"

She stopped. Eddie twisted free of the cop, kicked over the barricade, and dropped, feetfirst, into the river.

The water pulled at him, trying to drag him under. He struck out hard for a point ahead of the bus. He caught spray in the face from the churning water, and rain pelted his face.

The bus was huge and yellow above him in the water. The current pitched him hard, and his hands slid down the side, scrabbling for a hold, then caught the frame of the driver's window. He pulled himself onto the hood and punched both heels at the windshield. It cracked and the shock traveled up his legs to his spine. Inside, the driver picked up a fire extinguisher and drove it into the web he'd made, breaking the glass, then clearing it with the extinguisher. The driver laid his jacket over the edge.

The water in the bus was knee deep. The choir—eleven people— sat stiff in their seats so the bus wouldn't tilt farther. A couple of them were a little bloodied up, but they weren't panicking. All in all, one tough church choir.

"Go!" the driver shouted. "Anybody who can. Go, go, go!"

A man crawled out onto the hood, trying to steady himself on its slick surface, but he slid off the side. Everyone's heads snapped to the windows as he swept past the bus, then struck out for shore. He'd wind up pretty far downstream, but Eddie thought he'd make it. The woman with dreadlocks, another younger woman, and the driver crawled out the front and started swimming, too.

Which left Eddie with eight people. And the woman on the back bench, sitting in the middle, was really large. Stricken, he met her eyes. There wouldn't be time to get everyone, and she would be last. She wouldn't make it and she knew it. She gave him a calm smile that made him desperate to save her.

"You," he barked at an older woman. She wrapped her arms

around his neck and when they eased into the water her triceps floated out to the side. She kicked for all she was worth, though, and they landed, coughing and sputtering, a hundred yards downstream. Rosa was already there. She waded in and took the woman from him, helping her up the bank. Eddie stopped long enough to strip his sodden jeans and shirt off and went back in.

The third time back the cop was waiting by the bank, by Rosa and a mat of reeds she'd constructed to keep people out of the mud.

"Get out of there!" he called. "You're facing charges! You're just like your old man!"

Eddie didn't waste any air on him. The bus was sinking. The woman he was carting had taken a lungful of water, and he didn't think she could make it up the bank herself, so he carried her to where Rosa could grab her. The police officer came at him, but Rosa stuck her foot out and sent the guy sprawling headlong in the mud.

"Oops," she said. "It's slippery along here." Eddie shot her a grin before he dove back in.

Eddie made three more trips, and the cop stayed away from him, biding his time. There was no point intervening if Eddie was going to drown. The bus wasn't that far away, but the current was deadly and it was still raining a steady drumbeat. There were two more people—a rangy woman in her seventies, and the big lady. And Eddie was exhausted. He caught his breath on the bank for a moment, palms cupping his knees.

"Eddie," Rosa said. "You should stop."

He dove back in, fought the river, and this time hit farther back on the bus. It was harder to control his muscles, but when he pulled himself up to the windshield, the rangy woman was waiting. He didn't look at the large lady on the back bench.

Eddie and his charge struggled against the current, and when his foot finally hit a rock, he pitched forward and they both slammed into the bank. But Rosa was there, helping, pulling the woman out, and then she had his wrist and hauled him out and he let her. Eddie lay on his belly, exhausted, and coughed out water. He felt like a stripped tire, or a toothless gear.

His head was turned toward the river. The water would override the hood any moment and flood the bus. It would slam into the lady in the back and dislodge the bus, which would break free. And before she drowned she would be spinning loose in the world, all alone in a two-degrees-above-zero universe.

He hauled himself to his feet and trudged up the bank, past the silent, mud-caked cop. It would take him longer this time to work his way to the middle of the river. He was spent.

He dove in.

The water tugged at him, and the wind shifted so the rain was full in his face. He fought the gray sky and the gray river for the yellow arc of bus, thinking of the big woman. She wasn't afraid, and that made him desperate to save her.

By the time he reached the hood it was covered, and water was pouring over the edge of the dashboard, a thin waterfall but a fast one. The woman on the back bench was sitting in water to her waist, humming.

She stood up and plodded to the front of the bus, her skirt sticking to her legs. Eddie sat in the driver's seat and rested while she walked forward.

"A white boy in his underpants." She shook her head, then smiled at him, and it was a great smile. "Who's carrying whom?"

"I don't know," he said. She grabbed the dash and hauled herself up, and he put his shoulder low, bent his legs, and heaved her out onto the hood. Eddie hoisted himself up, but then she came flying back and they fell into the aisle as the river overtopped the hood and rushed in. Eddie grabbed a pole and she grabbed a seat as the water pressed past them and slammed the far wall and the bus rocked and tilted and pulled loose from whatever had snagged it below.

They began to spin.

"We've got to get out of here!" he shouted. She was already working her way forward, eyeing the gap where the windshield had been. And then the water was to the ceiling and there was no more air. Eddie pushed her as she swam, and she was through the opening and he followed her, out and up. He broke the surface, pulled in a lungful of air, then grabbed her arm and set out for the bank. Behind them the bus turned in slow circles as it careened downstream.

The wind ran across the current so the waves chopped into their faces. The woman helped all she could—she kicked, but it rocked them and they lost as much in sideways movement as they gained going forward. Eddie's eyes stung and he couldn't see. He wasn't even sure they were heading for the bank. What direction had the bus been facing when they swam out of it? He thought they might be swimming straight upstream, and would keep going till they drowned—or reached the headwaters.

They were going to drown.

He heard coughing over the wind, and then—fragments of a song. It was the choir, on the shore. Eddie and the woman turned together toward the music, and pushed harder.

And then he saw Rosa, standing in the water, leaning out for him. The driver was holding her waist, and the rangy woman was holding his. The choir was lined up in the river, reaching for them. But they were too far away. Eddie dug deeper, but there was nothing left. Three feet closer and Rosa could have snagged them.

Rosa tugged at her shirt.

"Hey!" the cop said in Brad's voice, "Stop it! That would be *embarrassing*."

She pulled her shirt off and wrapped it around her wrist and cast it out to Eddie, and he lunged and caught the edge. He worked hand over hand until he reached her, and then the driver had him and the lady holding on to him, and the choir reeled them in. They were still singing.

They laid them on the reed mat, Eddie and the big lady, and they looked at each other and smiled with their eyes, because everything else was too tired.

Rosa kissed his cheek.

"Your shirt ripped," the police officer said, "and you don't have another one."

Rosa walked to the back of the motorcycle and began rummaging in the storage compartment.

"Are you *kidding*?" she said. "I definitely do. And it's cute." She pulled out a blue top, eyed it, and it changed to red. "There." She slipped it on.

# CHAPTER TWENTY-ONE

"Bring them up," Ms. Bauer said.

The gray of the sky above them turned blue, and the blue was a wall, in a room with two hospital beds, in the IA compound.

Dr. O'Donnell was standing at their bedsides.

"It was so real," Rosa whispered. "The river, and the people." She felt her hair. Water had sheeted off it a moment before, but now it was dry.

Dr. O'Donnell nodded sympathetically. "The brain's a marvelous instrument."

"Did you see the things I saw?" Rosa asked Eddie. Thinking about her shirt.

"You created it together," Dr. O'Donnell said. "We've never been fully successful with that before. Your brains interacted to produce a picture together. It's a fascinating process." She smiled. "We intended it to be a car-crash scenario, but you turned it into a river rescue."

"We did that?" Rosa asked.

She nodded, and her blue eyes sparkled. "Guess Eddie was solving his hydration problem."

Reg snorted.

There was something Eddie knew, but he didn't know what it was. "Rosa," he said, but he couldn't remember what he wanted to tell her. Rosa stretched a hand out across the space between them, and the tape around her IV site pulled. He took her hand and gave a little squeeze, then let it go.

"He's going again," Friesta Bauer said. "Solo."

"There's no need," Dr. O'Donnell said. "He can't sync by himself."

"There's something else we want to check," Ms. Bauer said.

"I don't want to send him straight back," Dr. O'Donnell said.

"Yeah," Reg said. "Do it."

Dr. O'Donnell gave him a long stare, then crossed the room and began drawing up another set of syringes. Reg crouched by Eddie's head.

"Because the psychological effects of the simulation are real, you can learn from it. You understand? What happens isn't real, but the choices you make—you're really making them. So even though the simulation will seem brand-new to you, it'll be like you already know how to work it."

"Like a video game you've played a hundred times, and you know what order you have to do things in?"

"Exactly." Reg ran his hand over his scalp, then moved aside as the doctor approached and gave Eddie the first injection. Friesta Bauer lowered the lights and started the video montage—the driving rain, the yellow AME church bus, the churning river. Reg dropped the severed Ping-Pong balls over Eddie's eyes, and Dr. O'Donnell approached with the final syringe.

Eddie reached out and grabbed Reg's wrist. "Four!" he said as the doctor injected two cc of clear liquid into a branch of his tubing. "Rosa . . ." He tried to take the Ping-Pong balls off his eyes, but his arm fell away from Reg's and he couldn't lift it and he couldn't tell Rosa what he knew. And then the bus skidded off the road and Eddie pulled his motorcycle over. He was drenched.

A police officer dragged a barricade between Eddie and the bank as he ran for the river. The guy threw his hand up. "Stop right there!"

Eddie hurdled the barricade without slowing and jumped feet-first into the river. He fought to get to the bus, but no matter how hard he flailed he didn't get closer, and then he realized he wasn't wet anymore. He was swimming through the sky, and then he was in a hospital bed, wired up, with people looking down at him.

He wasn't saving a choir. He was paralyzed, and Brad could see inside his head.

"He is a dangerous guy," Brad said. "Wow, does he have a problem with authority."

Rosa stood up. "Four," she said, pointing a finger at Brad. "There were *four.*"

Reg looked between them. "Get those leads off him," he snapped. Dr. O'Donnell began to pop the wires off the electrodes on Eddie's scalp.

"Reg, those guys who attacked me. There weren't three of them." She turned to stare at Brad. "There were four."

"You're crazy," he said.

Trevor looked between them, then moved to stand by Rosa. He didn't know what was going on, but he knew who he was with.

"It never made sense to me," she said. "Those guys weren't close enough to the top to benefit from knocking me out of the competition. But *Brad* was."

Reg slowly turned his head toward Brad. There was an ancient menace in the movement, something that spoke of slashing talons, of predator and prey.

"He could afford to pay them," Trevor said. "To attack you, and to shut up afterward."

"Yeah," Rosa said. "You son of a bitch."

"That's not true!" Brad said, taking a step away from Reg. "She's . . . *overwrought*."

"I. Am. *Overwrought?*" Rosa said.

"There's no evidence," Brad said. "Eddie was hallucinating because he's vulnerable to drugs, just like his father. Hallucinations aren't proof."

"You said I might fall down the stairs again," Rosa said.

"And there," Eddie said weakly from the bed. He raised his forefinger and let it drop.

"IA never released what those guys were going to do to me," Rosa said.

"I never said anything about stairs!" Brad said.

"I heard it," Friesta Bauer said. She was still disconnecting the wires from her own scalp. "Reg, you were right. He's obviously the one who read their personnel files."

"Yeah," Reg said heavily. "Did he push their buttons in the sim?"

Ms. Bauer snorted. "Oh yeah. Not a master of subtlety, this one."

"Still trying to get someone kicked out?" Reg said. "Always working it, trying to move up? Is that what happened with the bomb?"

Brad blanched. "That wasn't a real bomb," he said.

Reg took one fast stride forward and they bumped noses. "You didn't know that!" he roared. Brad scrambled behind a chair. He looked scared.

"Get the hell off this compound," Reg said.

"Consider that a formal dismissal," Friesta Bauer said with a frosty smile. It didn't reach her eyes.

"You're all going to die in space, anyway," Brad said. He paused in the doorway. Reg took a step toward him, and Brad scurried away without a final word.

"The smart people aren't always good," Reg said heavily, "so the good people have to be smart." He shook his head.

"Hey," a guy said, stepping into the room and looking at Friesta Bauer. "We need you in the Flight Control Room. We've got a situation."

She turned, the smile fading from her face. Dr. O'Donnell crossed her hands over her chest. Reg flexed his fingers at his side, like an Old West gunslinger.

"The gravity leak?" Ms. Bauer said.

"Yeah. It's a lot worse."

This wasn't a simulation.

# CHAPTER TWENTY-TWO

Reg hustled them out of there. He offered Eddie a wheelchair but he refused it. The paralytic had worn off, and he felt terrible, but he could walk.

"Dude, what was with the song?" Trevor said.

"What?"

"In the simulation. You were singing, man."

"That wasn't me. That was the choir." *There was no choir.* "Rosa?"

She shook her head. "I don't know that song."

"I was *singing*?"

"Yep."

"Maybe that's why Brad was out to get me."

"I thought it was to move up, and because you foiled his plot against Rosa," Trevor said. "But the singing is a better explanation."

"Not to change the subject," Rosa said, "but what's going on? The 'situation'?"

Reg pulled them aside by a planter in front of the building. There was more sidewalk traffic than they'd seen before, people getting places without slowing their pace when they passed one another.

"My thought is that if you're going to be on Team 3, you need to know some things." He glanced over his shoulder, like maybe not everyone agreed.

"IA sensors picked up gravity microvariations weeks ago, but they've gotten steadily greater."

"I don't get what this means," Eddie said.

"We have incredibly sensitive sensors pointed out there into the dark," he said, "measuring gravity as far into the universe as we can. Because this is how you detect another world."

Reg started to walk again. "We know there are an infinite number of stars and planets and Earths out there. Within an infinite universe, every possibility will occur."

"So you're saying you found another planet or something?" Trevor said. "Because they do that all the time. I mean, think how much they discovered after they installed the Tyson telescope on Pluto."

Reg shook his head and ushered them into a building that had been off limits before—the command building. It was at the edge of the compound, overlooking the helicopter pad and the launch tower for vehicles that would leave Earth's orbit.

"Those don't cause gravitational disturbances," he said. "Think." He tapped his forehead. "You only get a disturbance like this when something changes, something moves—when something is out there that didn't used to be."

"You mean . . ." Eddie wasn't even sure how to phrase it. "You mean something is *coming*?" The hairs on his neck rose.

Reg gave him a sober look. "We don't know what it means. But something is off in a way it has never been before." He yanked on the door handle and they walked into the building. It was a hive of activity. He pulled them over against the wall. "I'm going to try to sneak you into the Flight Control Room. It's where the data comes in and is analyzed in rough form, and the satellite feeds come in to the screens there. It functions like a combination of the White House war room and an air traffic control tower."

"That's where they launch the probes?" Trevor said.

"Yeah. Any craft we send up. That's where the countdown takes place. It'll be the best learning experience of your life if you can lie low and keep your mouths shut." He looked at Eddie, which Eddie didn't think was entirely fair. Then something occurred to him.

"Is that why the head of NASA is here?"

"Yeah," Reg said.

"I didn't think he was just here to torture me with green badges."

Reg gave a little snort then led them, trotting, up a staircase. They flattened against the wall at the landing when a woman raced past them. Reg stopped them in the hall and said, "These are serious people doing serious work. Keep your wisecrackery to yourself."

They nodded, and he pushed open the door under the Flight Control Room sign and they slipped inside. The room was humming, vibrating. John Taylor Templeton was leaning over a computer bank, one arm propped against the wall. The room was the size of two basketball courts. To the right were windows over-looking the launch pad, about a mile away, where one deep space vehicle was attached vertically to a launch tower. There had been two—Young and Moloney had already shot off, then. The trainees looked through the window, hoping to see their contrail, but there was nothing.

To the left was a bank of large screens showing views of space fed from space-based telescopes. They pressed against the wall, watching the place vibrate. It looked like chaos at first, but after a couple of minutes Eddie began to see that it was actually several interconnected systems operating within the same space. Rosa was staring at the deep space screens.

"It doesn't make sense," the IA director said. "We've been tracking this gravitational anomaly for weeks. We sent Young and Moloney off a couple hours ago, and now the anomaly's coordi-nates have shifted."

"Yeah, that's crackers," John Taylor Templeton agreed. "Did we send our team to the wrong location?"

People were ducking heads and averting eyes.

"Get Richtig and Doepker ready to go," Smithson said. "They're still prepping?"

"Yes, sir," someone said.

The IA director was silent for a moment, then swore under his breath. Eddie didn't catch all of it, but was impressed by the creativity of what he did hear.

"They should just give him a plaque and retire the swear jar," he whispered to Rosa. Reg shot him a look.

"Did we send Team 1 on a wild goose chase?" Smithson said, then roared, "Well? I want an answer."

"Sir, all the data were consistent on the location of the anomaly," a man said.

"And now it's coming from nineteen degrees to the left. Nineteen degrees! We can weigh a *proton*, and we were off by nineteen degrees?" He punched a fist into his open hand.

"Are we sure it's not coming from both places?" John Taylor Templeton said.

"It seems to be coming only from the new location now, sir," a woman at the computer bank said.

The NASA director's mouth tightened. "We could send a probe," he said.

"They're unmanned," Smithson said. "If it runs into something, it can't deal with—by the time we dispatched a team, it could be too late."

Eddie and Rosa exchanged a glance. *Too late for what?*

They stood against the wall, watching and listening for an hour. Eddie felt conspicuous. Rosa was small, and Trevor had an angularity unusual for a biological life-form. He was well camouflaged for a room like this. But Eddie was all bunchy muscle and attitude. The only thing about him that stood at attention was his hair. People were too busy checking instruments and running calculations and swearing to notice them, but when someone did shoot them a look, it was Eddie they saw. He kept his mouth shut and watched the hive vibrate.

The woman who'd almost flattened them in the stairwell was

back in the room. She was on the phone, tapping at a keyboard while she talked, and then she stood up and looked for Smithson.

"Sir? The Russians say their data are the same as ours. The source of the readings has shifted."

Rosa was trying to catch Reg's eye. "Couldn't it just have moved?" she whispered. Eddie had been wondering that, too.

Reg shook his head. "Distance we're talking about? With a terrific energy source and a few hundred years, sure. This is what I meant by gravity flutters. We get a reading, and then it just shuts off. But it's never been this close before."

"How close?" Rosa whispered.

"Close enough that we think we can make contact. That's why they sent Team 1."

They all stared at the huge screens showing deep space. It stretched in lonely darkness forever. Smithson worked the room, walking down the rows of computer banks, talking briefly to each person in turn. Once he turned and shouted, "What are the Chinese saying?" A woman rose and yelled back, "They appreciate our leadership in this time of crisis."

"Oh, screw them," Smithson said. He finished his rounds, then stood under the screens at the front, the cosmos hanging over his head. "Okay, we're sending Team 2. Somebody tell Richtig and Doepker to get their suits on."

Reg jerked his head into the hall and the trainees followed him, but they were reluctant ducklings. None of them wanted to leave the Flight Control Room.

Reg kept his voice low, even though the door shut behind

them. "It's gonna take a while to get Team 2 ready to go. They've known this was a possibility so they've been prepping, but they're still fueling the craft. That takes a while."

Eddie nodded. They were dispatching their last team, and whatever needed doing from now on would fall to Rosa, Eddie, and Trevor. They weren't well trained—they weren't really trained at all—but he was ready. Whatever IA needed them to do, Eddie was itching to do it.

"You guys go get some lunch," Reg said.

*Ouch.* Eddie'd been hoping for a tougher assignment.

"They're just gonna stare at screens and go mad for a while. You can watch the launch later."

Smithson stepped into the hall just then, stared intently at the trainees and then at Reg. "I just heard that you lost one of your trainees."

"Yeah," Reg said.

"I authorized a live explosives exercise . . ."

Reg laughed. "He didn't blow up."

Smithson blew air out loudly. "You get that working with you takes a couple years off a guy, right?"

Reg grinned, then turned sober. "He broke into the office and he tried to injure—possibly kill—two other trainees in order to secure a spot."

"We're sure he's off the compound?"

"Yeah," Reg said. "The guard booth texted me a few minutes ago."

Smithson nodded. "You're going to have to cut one of them

now," he said. "If we don't have two teams, we need one. Not one and a half."

"I'm keeping one as an understudy."

"Reg," Smithson said. "NASA doesn't have understudies."

Reg shrugged. "Consider it a redundant system, then."

"Everything is turning to crap in there," Smithson said, jutting a finger at the Flight Control Room. "I don't want to think about this. Cut somebody."

"I'll make that decision later," Reg said. "When things have quieted . . ."

Rosa and Trevor exchanged an uneasy look, but Eddie looked at the floor. He'd seen this before.

"Which one is the understudy?" Smithson asked.

Trevor squirmed.

Reg hesitated, then nodded at Trevor.

"He's the understudy for . . . ?" Smithson said.

"Eddie," Reg said. "He had some unusual test results."

"Eddie, thanks for your time," Smithson said, "but you're gone."

"The hell?" Reg said.

"I do not need any more goddamn unusual test results! I am up to my ass in anomalies," Smithson shouted.

"He's a remarkable—" Reg said.

"Is there any chance they're not all remarkable?" Smithson snapped.

Reg squeezed his eyes shut. "We could make even teams by *adding* another—"

Smithson shook his head and stalked back into the Flight Control Room.

Reg stared through the wall, then softly said, "Damn it." Finally he looked up. "Eddie, you were terrific. I'm sorry."

Eddie stood very still as Reg disappeared back through the Flight Control Room door, leaving them in the hall. He'd lost his place. Brad tried to blow him up and got cut for it, leaving the teams uneven—and *he* was getting cut as a result. There was no Eddie on any Earth with worse luck than his.

"Come on," Rosa said quietly. "Let's order a pizza." A guy walking past them into Flight Control glanced over. "You can't," he said. "The compound's on lockdown." He disappeared through the door.

They headed toward the cafeteria without speaking. How long would a lockdown last? Eddie didn't want to stay there while Trevor took his place, while Trevor went off in the morning with Rosa. But where would he go? Oolitic, he guessed. Could any of his friends drive this far to get him? Trevor and Rosa would be making trial space flights, and he'd still be hitching east down I-74.

They went through the food line.

"Can I take the tray outside?" Eddie mumbled.

"Get the dishes back before two o'clock," the cashier said.

He nodded and took an extra plate of cookies. He didn't ask Rosa and Trevor to come with him, but they trailed him out of the cafeteria.

"Where to?" Rosa said.

Eddie shrugged. "Someplace in the sun." It felt like a last meal.

He wanted the sun burning his forearms. He wanted to breathe free air.

They found a grassy hillside and sprawled across it. Eddie should have been thinking about what he was going to do now that they'd kicked him out, but he couldn't stop thinking about the Flight Control Room. He knew he'd be thinking about it for the rest of his life. He didn't want to leave. He just didn't. He took a bite of his grilled cheese.

"Congratulations, Trev. Tomorrow they'll measure your flinty little head for a space helmet."

"I'm sorry."

Eddie snorted.

"You know, it's not my fault you have to die on every hill," Trevor said. "You're the one who decided to jump over that barrier."

Eddie looked up at him, his face twisted. "You think the simulation's what did it?" He shook his head. "It's because they met my old man." Eddie bent his spoon until it snapped and tossed the pieces into the grass. "They look at me and you and decide I'm the one who has to go. Why do you think that is?" He snapped his fork. "They think I could be the old man. Or like Brad."

"Smithson was just stressed," Rosa said. "He—"

"And maybe I could be," Eddie said. "I mean, how do you know what you might do?" He speared the broken fork into the ground.

"Dude," Trevor said. "You are *not* like Brad."

"When Ms. Bauer tried to get us to fight," Eddie said, looking up at Rosa, "I thought about it. About hitting you."

"They were trying to make you think about it," Rosa said. "I thought about hitting you, too."

He smiled faintly.

"During the simulation, the voice—Brad—tried to provoke us into doing something stupid so we'd look bad or maybe get kicked out. He read our psych profiles," Rosa said. A shudder ran up her back.

"He was in the office to get a key to the rec center," Trevor said. "I wondered why he was being helpful. It gave him an excuse to go in there."

"The reason it bothers us is that the voice wasn't really him," Rosa said. "Brad was talking, but the voice is the one inside our heads, right? I worry that I'm not like my dad, and you worry that you are like yours."

Eddie nodded but didn't look at her.

"How do we know who we are under the weight of all the expectations?" she said, twisting the broken spoon in the grass. "Good and bad."

A crow flew in and landed on the slope beside them, the sun gleaming off its black back. It tilted its head, examining them. Trevor tossed it a french fry, and it took a trial peck at the food.

"You can trust yourself, Eddie," Trevor said.

"How do you know?"

"Because you wanted to hit me a minute ago and you didn't."

Eddie gave him a half smile. "I want to hit you a lot."

"Further proof!" Trevor said. "And you're a friend to church choirs everywhere."

The crow snatched up the fry and flew away with it trailing from its beak.

"You need to give yourself a break," Rosa said. "You're having a rough day."

"You almost drowned today and got blown up a couple days ago," Trevor said.

"The day before that wasn't so great, either," Eddie said. He picked at a piece of grass, splitting it with his thumbnail. He had no idea what he was going to do next.

They returned their dishes and then sat outside to watch the launch. Reg texted that they couldn't go back in the Flight Control Room, so it seemed as good a place as any.

"Knock knock," Rosa said.

Eddie looked at her. She was trying to make him feel better— he could see it on her face, all lit up in the Iowa sun. "Who's there?"

"Oswald."

"Oswald who?"

"Oswald my gum and now I don't feel so good." She smiled expectantly at him.

He groaned. "How long did you work on that?"

"Two days. A piece of gum was harmed in the creation of this joke."

Team 2 exited their transport and walked across the tarmac to the launch tower. Rosa, Eddie, and Trevor ran through the equipment check they'd be doing, but they must have missed some things because they finished before Team 2 did. Then the tower pulled away from the spacecraft, and moments later a bloom of flame appeared underneath it. The needle vibrated.

"I get why the engines wobble," Trevor said, "but watching it still freaks me out."

"It's because the initial explosions aren't evenly distributed," Eddie said. "Once the engines get to full power the explosions will even out and the engine bell will stop rocking." Eddie knew Trevor understood it. He needed Trevor to know that this was stuff he knew.

Rosa grinned and ratcheted back an imaginary control, and then the ship shot into the sky. A wave of heat blew over them as far away as they were, and the wind buffeted their faces and whipped Rosa's long, dark hair across Eddie's face. His eyes stung, but it wasn't because of her hair. They filled and made the craft looked wavery as it shot up, and a drop of water rolled down his cheek.

It was Newton's fault—equal and opposite reaction. For everything that went up, something had to come down. Eddie just didn't know why the thing that went down was always him.

*Screw Newton.*

# CHAPTER TWENTY-THREE

The next morning Rosa got three texts from her dad, to go with the seven he sent the previous night—tips on comportment (read: don't embarrass me) and advice to start a journal because it would help someday when she wrote her memoirs. Rosa loved her dad— he was the best—but she got some satisfaction from muting her phone and dropping it in her bag.

She went downstairs and found Trevor waiting in the hall. They both looked at Eddie's door, uncertain whether they should stop for him or not. They left without knocking. When they got to breakfast Eddie was there. They slid their trays in next to him, and he jerked his head and grunted at their appearance but didn't lessen the rate at which he was eating.

"You think it's okay if I go in and ask if the lockdown is over?" he asked when they were done eating and stood to leave.

He didn't know how to handle it, either.

"Yeah," Trevor said, maybe too quickly. "Walk with us."

Eddie shook his head. "I'll catch up with you," and he stood there till they walked off. When they were outside, Rosa looked back through the window and saw him wrapping biscuits in a napkin and sliding them in his pocket. Not knowing where his next meal would come from, afraid of being hungry. She wished she hadn't seen that.

Nobody was on the sidewalks as they walked to the administration building.

"This is a little spooky," Trevor said, and Rosa nodded.

Ruth in the front office looked up from sharpening a pencil when they walked in. The pencils were all short, and exactly the same length. She'd been sharpening pencils for a while. "Any word?"

"Um?" Rosa said.

"The gravity," she said. "You don't know anything?" They shook their heads and looked at each other, confirming their ignorance. "It got worse overnight."

"Do you know where Reg Davis is?" Rosa said.

"He's not one to check in. But everybody who can squeeze in is down at the Flight Control Room."

"Thank you," Rosa said. They turned to go as Eddie walked up.

"Is the lockdown still on, then?" he said.

"Oh, definitely," Ruth said.

"Oh." He turned but didn't look them in the eye. "Guess I'll go back to the apartment."

*The* apartment. He already wasn't calling it his. Rosa and Trevor exchanged a glance.

They walked out of the office, and Ruth returned to sharpening pencils that already had lethal points.

"She seemed a little on edge," Rosa said.

"Hey, stay with us," Trevor said as Eddie started to walk away. "There's something I don't understand."

Eddie stopped and looked at him warily.

"This gravitational anomaly isn't large, right?" Trevor said. "Or we'd be aware."

"Yeah," Rosa said. "I think it's just the fact that it's there at all."

Trevor made shut-up eyes at her, and she remembered that they were trying to draw Eddie out. Rosa sat on a ledge by the sidewalk, and the guys hopped up, one on either side.

"Gravity is the only force that exists across dimensions," Eddie said. "The strong force and weak force stay in the dimension that generates them, right?" They nodded.

"Suck it, strong force," Trevor said.

"But gravity can cross dimensions. It's the only force that peeks around the edge."

Rosa nodded. "The point is that a gravity leak isn't coming from anything we can see or hear. It's coming from, or through, another dimension."

"*Gravity exists across the dimensions*," Trevor said excitedly. "So if something is right there, parked right next to us, the only way we'd know it is a . . ."

"Gravitational anomaly," they all said together.

"It got bigger overnight," Eddie said. "A bigger anomaly means that whatever is out there, it just came closer."

A shiver ran down Rosa's spine. "That's why they're down at Flight Control," she said. "Something is out there, and it's coming this way."

They ran to the last building, the big one that oversaw the launch pad. A guard outside recognized them but stopped them anyway. "Reg Davis," Rosa said, although they didn't want Reg— they wanted to see what was going on. He hesitated, then pointed to a staircase. They followed it up and came to a glass-fronted room that overlooked Flight Control from the back, like an observation gallery in an operating room. They squeezed in. Rosa couldn't see the screens below at all—her eye level was filled with blue sleeves. She bet Eddie could see them, though. She tugged on the back of his red T-shirt.

"What's on the screens?"

He bent toward her, his face flushed with excitement. "Just like yesterday. It's views of space. I don't see any little green men."

"There's Reg," Trevor whispered. "Do you think he'll kick us out if he catches us in here?"

"I don't think so," Rosa said. "Yesterday he wanted to let us see everything."

There were speakers embedded in the walls of the overflow room, so they could hear Smithson and Templeton barking orders in Flight Control, overriding the whispered conversations and general rustle of shifting feet.

Eddie leaned down and whispered right in Rosa's ear, "Come on." He took her hand so they didn't get separated, and it was warm and dry and wrapped perfectly around hers. Rosa reached back and pinched Trevor's sleeve and pulled him with her in

Eddie's wake. When they got to the glass wall, Eddie pulled Rosa in front of him so she could see.

The big screens were before them at eye level, and to the right they could see out the window to the empty launch area a mile away. Young and Moloney, Richtig and Doepker had gone. Someday Rosa and Trevor would be Team 3—Hayashi and Clayborn. They would be authorized to negotiate for Earth. It was an immense responsibility, and Rosa's dad would probably still be sending her texts to keep her from screwing up. And, she thought, she might need them.

"Anybody got a mass on whatever's out there?" Templeton barked.

"Approximately 5.9723e24 kilograms, sir," someone shouted from one of the workstations.

There was a momentary hush, both below and around them. Because 5.9723e24 kg is Earth's mass.

A couple of people stood at their stations, leaning forward, tapping keys, scrolling furiously. "The sensors are going nuts," the man next to them breathed. "Jesus."

"Talk to me!" Smithson shouted.

"My god," Templeton said. "Are they bringing their *planet*?"

"There's a small presence at seventeen point two degrees northeast, five thousand meters out," someone shouted. "And closing." They all turned to stare at the launch pad. There was nothing there.

And then, with an audible hiss, there was. A spacecraft hurtled down the runway. It slowed before it was halfway down the tarmac, and then turned, pointing back up the runway toward the northeast. That was the direction from which it had arrived, but it sure wasn't where it had come from.

The place erupted. NASA was going to need a second swear jar.

And then again silence, because the hatch opened. Everyone stared at the giant screens in the Flight Control Room as an arm waved from the spacecraft, and then a man's head emerged. He swung down from the cockpit and flexed his knees a couple of times as though testing the ground, then unstrapped his helmet and tossed it back in the craft. He moved to the side, and a woman came out, put her palm down on the ground, looked up at the sun, and shook her head. Two more men got out behind her— Richtig and Doepker. They all tossed their helmets and gloves in the craft and walked toward the building, swiveling around like tourists.

"I thought Team 2 launched," Trevor said. "We *saw* them launch."

"Director!" someone shouted.

"I see them," Smithson's voice said through the speaker. "But I don't believe it. How did they do that?"

The guy next to Rosa grinned. "Teams 1 and 2 took off at separate times in separate crafts, and are returning weeks earlier than expected—in a craft we've never seen before."

"That's not ours!" a woman said, shouting across him. "Somebody somewhere built that, and it wasn't us. Proof there's intelligent life out there."

"We already knew that," Trevor said.

"Yeah," she said, "in theory. But we only had mathematical proof."

"Until right now," the guy said.

"Mark this moment," Smithson said. "The history of human-kind just changed forever."

"Get a med crew down there," Templeton barked. "Make sure they're okay."

Rosa, Eddie, and Trevor watched the screen as Teams 1 and 2 shook off the med team's assistance, but let the medics drive them up to the building and hustle them into the Flight Control Room. The technicians stood at their stations and applauded as the dazed team members strode slowly forward, staring around them as though they'd been gone for a century.

"I don't understand how you did it," Smithson said, shaking their hands and gripping their shoulders, one by one, "but by god I'm glad to see you again."

The room hushed to hear what they had to say.

"This is amazing," a team member said. "And you can't imagine how much we appreciate that welcome. I was a little afraid you'd shoot at me when I poked my head out of the spacecraft."

Everyone laughed.

"That's Young," the guy next to Rosa whispered. "He's senior." She nodded. She'd seen their photos on the wall in the lobby, but it wasn't like she would instantly recognize him. Not like his colleagues did.

"I'm speechless," Young said. "It's a thrill to see you all, but completely disorienting."

There was a little stir at that. It made sense to Rosa—something had clearly gone haywire with their mission. Young looked across the banks of computers.

"Our Flight Control Room looked like this about thirty years ago," he said.

The place went silent.

Young glanced at Moloney. "We're going to have to scrap the mission," he said, and she nodded. "But we should get acquainted before we go," he said with a smile. "One thing I already know is that you people are an awful lot like us."

"Young?" Smithson said.

Young stuck out his hand to shake again. "Are you called Smithson?"

Smithson stared at him for a beat, then said, "I am."

"We bring you greetings from Earth." Young grinned. "I always wanted to say that."

The crowd began to buzz.

"Um, *we're* on Earth," Trevor murmured.

"You're not the Young we sent out, are you?" John Taylor Templeton said.

"No," Young said, his voice disappointed. "You have one of me? It's a shame I missed myself. That would have been something."

A few of the assembled scientists scrambled onto chairs to see better. Nearly everybody put their phones on hover so they could take video of the scene at the front of the room, or selfies with the visitors in the background.

"I'm glad we're up here," Rosa whispered. "Downstairs they probably can't see past all the phones."

Young rubbed his forehead. "Is there one of everybody here? I mean, is your personnel exactly the same as ours?"

A woman at the left station in the front row called "Kendra

Alexander." "Steve Yoon," the man next to her said. The two IA teams at the front of the room shook their heads at one another as one by one, everyone in the room called out his or her name. When they were done, Young massaged his forehead again and Moloney rubbed her neck.

"It's a pleasure to meet you all," Young said. "But man, is it weird."

Everyone laughed again.

"Hey, Steve!" Moloney called. "You owe me twenty dollars."

"Cool!" Steve Yoon said. "Here, I owe you fifty."

Everyone laughed again.

"I'd sure like an explanation," John Taylor Templeton said. "You went to a lot of trouble to reach us."

"Yeah," Young said. "Well, the trip isn't so bad. Developing the technology was the tough part." He glanced at his team members. "It was a biological research mission, but we're going to have to scrub it. We needed an Earth with life, but not human life. Certainly not identical life."

"We can locate other Earths," Moloney said, "but we can't get precise readings of the development of their life-forms. We just have to land and take a peek."

"Your world have an epidemic?" Smithson said.

"No," Young said, "we're good. It was a research mission." He glanced around the room again. "I'd love a tour of this place, though."

Smithson and Templeton began talking with the four visitors, showing them around the Flight Control Room. A big professional camera swooped in, and the brass posed together by the NASA and IA logos on the wall, then it snapped some photos of the room at large.

"We have some things to learn from you," Templeton said, and Young nodded.

"I hope they let us stay for a good visit," he said. "I'd love to see the town. Do you have a Joe's Café?"

"Best ravioli in a hundred miles," Templeton said. "And Joe plays his tenor sax when it's not too busy."

Young shook his head. "Just unbelievable. It's like landing on Earth."

"This *is* Earth," Smithson said.

"Well, you know. Like our Earth," Moloney said.

"Hey," Templeton said. "We got conflicting readings from a couple of locations. We sent a team to each of the points of origin. Are either of them going to land on you?"

The alien teams exchanged a glance.

"What was going on with that, anyway?" Smithson said.

Rosa looked back at Eddie and Trevor, because she'd wondered that herself.

"We fly through the extra dimensions," Moloney said. "Our passage temporarily opens a window into the part of the universe we left. You would get gravitational readings, but they'd only last briefly."

"It would appear like a flicker to your sensors," Doepker said.

"The gravitational flutters," Templeton said.

"Once we realized that happens, we started using it as a safeguard," Young said. "We knew this planet was advanced—we just didn't know how advanced. So we sent two craft out to punch through the extra dimensions and set up gravitational anomalies. If you were advanced enough you'd investigate, and it would draw your best people away from your planet." He shrugged.

Smithson looked taken aback. "You faked the location of the anomaly?"

"Yeah," Young said. "Sorry about that. But you thought it was prudent."

"I . . . Ah," Smithson said. "Well, it's nice to know I'm director over there, too. Do send me my greetings."

"Will do," Doepker said, smiling. "You're deputy director, actually. Lamar Sensenbrenner is director."

Eddie gasped. Rosa tugged on his sleeve, but he stared over her head into the room below.

"Do you have a Lamar Sensenbrenner?" Doepker said, scanning the crowd.

Smithson frowned. "I've never heard of him." Smithson and Friesta Bauer shook their heads.

"Huh," Doepker said.

"Do you think he's why you're ahead of us?" John Taylor Templeton said.

"No way," Young said. "Our ascendance would have started before him." He scratched the back of his hand. "I assume you've done all the things you can to get an educated citizenry? Fully funding schools and libraries, making sure talented students get to great colleges? The no-brainer stuff?"

"Yeah," Templeton said heavily. "We've for sure got some no-brainers."

"Eddie," Rosa said, turning to face him. They were squished in close, so she was staring up at him from under his chin. "Isn't that the guy . . ." She trailed off, unsure of how to finish.

"That my old man killed?" he whispered, his lips brushing her ear. "Yeah."

She stared at him.

"I think it's time we contacted Director Sensenbrenner," Young said to Moloney.

"Oh my god," Rosa whispered. "He would have been the director of IA?"

"Yeah," Moloney said downstairs, her voice coming through the speakers in the wall. "Do you have a quantum interface for communication?"

"Uh, no," John Taylor Templeton said.

Young looked disappointed. "We'll have to route the call through the craft, then," he said, pulling what looked like a phone from his jacket. "We've got to contact our director."

"I hope he says to eat at Joe's before we go," Richtig said, and everyone laughed.

Young told his phone to expand and it did, pulling into tablet size.

"Whoa," Trevor said.

Young touched the screen, typing something—entering some data.

"It doesn't move," Rosa whispered. "It's hanging in the air but he can push against it."

She could feel Eddie nod, but none of them looked away from the scene below.

Young typed, then waited, then typed again. "I'm letting him know it's an advanced civilization," he said. "We have a case full of bacteria on the craft that we wanted to release somewhere." He paused as he typed again. "And watch how it played out. It causes a mutation in plants that causes extremely rapid growth. You plant—*bing*—you harvest. If we released it at home, it would increase our food supply immeasurably. No more famine."

"That's fantastic," Smithson said.

"Only problem is that if you eat one of the plants, you get cancer," Moloney said. "Almost every time."

Smithson grimaced.

"We want to release it somewhere and watch the animals. See if the population develops an immunity—if the creatures that survive pass on a resistance to their offspring."

"And if enough animals survive to keep a species going," Doepker said. "That's the part we can't do in a lab."

Young stared at the screen of his tablet.

"Eddie," Rosa whispered. He leaned over her to hear better. "He looks like someone hit him in the solar plexus. You kind of do, too."

And he did. Sensenbrenner's name had been a gut punch.

Young tilted the tablet so that Moloney, Richtig, and Doepker could read it.

"Can I treat you to ravioli tonight?" Smithson said.

"I'm afraid not," Young said, and his voice was strained.

"I wonder why they didn't just talk," Eddie said. "Sensenbrenner could communicate directly with our people. You'd think he'd want to."

"Yeah," Rosa said. "You'd think he would."

# CHAPTER TWENTY-FOUR

Young turned and pointed up at the observation room, crowded with people in blue shirts—and Eddie, in a red T-shirt.

"Hey, can you guys come down?" He turned to Smithson. "I want to meet your best people. We've got a problem we're going to have to work on together."

"Sure," Smithson said. "Do you need a rocket mechanic, or what?"

"Why don't you introduce me to everybody to start with?"

Smithson shrugged. People were already surging out of the glass-fronted observation room, heading down the staircase to the hallway outside the Flight Control Room, thrilled to get a chance to meet the Earth aliens.

"I think I'm going to go now," Eddie said. He gripped Trevor's hand and upper arm and gave him a shoulder bump that passed for a hug. He gave Rosa a real hug. Somebody was motioning them into the room, but they pulled out into the hall. Eddie felt like a salmon fighting his way upstream.

"Because of their IA head?" Trevor said. "Who is he again?"

"The guy my old man killed."

Trevor gaped at him, his eyes attaining a degree of liftoff from their sockets. "Are you messing with me?"

"Yes," Eddie said. "I make up the most humiliating things possible, unlike other people who lie to make themselves look better."

"Yeah, but . . . wow," Trevor said.

"It's not because of him. It's . . . I don't think you should go in there," Eddie whispered. "Come with me instead." He tilted his head down the hall.

Rosa hesitated, but Trevor said, "You can come in, too."

"I don't like it," Eddie said. He could see the indecision play over Rosa's features.

"You're jealous 'cause we get to meet the Earth aliens," Trevor said.

The last of the people from the overflow room pushed past them into the Flight Control Room.

"If there's any trouble, we'll leave," Rosa said. "I promise. But I can't just skip out. It would look bad."

Eddie squeezed his eyes shut.

"This is like the moon landing!" Rosa whispered. "It's *bigger*. I want to be here for this."

Eddie tried to keep his voice steady. "There's a lot going on. If I have to go, this is a good time to do it."

Rosa hesitated, then threw her arms around his neck.

"Oh, Eddie. I'm going to miss you." She pointed a finger up at him. "Come back and visit. And write and let us know how you're doing."

"Or else," Trevor said.

"Yeah," she said. "Or else."

"Okay," he said, and gave them a smile that stalled at half throttle. They all knew how good he was at following instructions. He'd never write, and they knew it.

"Get in there," the guy at the door growled. "They're not waiting on some trainees." He stepped toward them.

Rosa gave Eddie a sad smile and turned, and she and Trevor walked into the Flight Control Room. Eddie touched a finger to his forehead in salute to the guy at the door and walked away down the hall.

"Hey!" the guy called. "Get your ass back here."

Eddie kept walking, but gave him a different finger over his shoulder.

He listened for the door closing or feet coming after him, but didn't hear either, so he turned around. Flight Control was packed, so the guy had left the door open, probably to get a little airflow. Not Eddie's problem.

He needed to get his stuff. His friend from home hadn't sent a lot, but it was too much to carry. Eddie still had the box. Maybe he could mail back his bedding and just carry a bundle of spare clothes.

Eddie could hear Young's voice, faint from the control room. "You don't do extradimensional travel yet, so it'll be weeks before your teams are back?"

Smithson murmured something in response. It would be

weeks—and they were going to miss their targets because there was no target there.

Something was off. Trevor didn't get it, him with his doctor parents and germ-free home life. Rosa knew something was wrong—she was too smart not to—but she had her father's legacy to think of. Leave that room, now, because of a hunch? She couldn't do it.

Eddie's old man had given him something neither of them had—the ability to sense the air parting behind him when a fist swings, so he could duck without ever seeing it. The ability to think with his spine, because sometimes what he threw was one of Eddie's books. But sometimes it was a baseball bat. Or a hatchet.

And then Eddie knew. He had to get out of there, now.

Instead, Eddie turned back and trotted down the corridor and into the Flight Control Room.

"There was a kid in a red shirt, too," Young said. "I saw him upstairs."

"That was me," Eddie said, pushing forward. "I wasn't supposed to be there." Around him people were staring. All the smart people, the steady-job people, the people who never pitched a beer bottle at the meter reader once in their life. The people with the blue shirts. "I screwed up and got kicked out," he said. He was craning his neck—the place was packed. Where were Rosa and Trevor? Then he had them. "They did, too," he said, pointing. A few yards away Rosa's jaw dropped open. "Sorry," he called to Young. "We flushed out and were supposed to be gone by now."

"I did *not* screw up," Rosa said, trembling with fury.

"You stunk the place up," Reg shouted from across the room. "Get out of here. Man, this is embarrassing."

Rosa stared between them.

"Wait," Trevor said. "Am I in or out?"

"You're out," Eddie said. "Come on, we're in the grown-ups' way."

"Sorry," Reg muttered, shoving his way through the crowd. "I'll get them out of here."

"Wait," Moloney said. "Reg Davis?" Reg nodded to her, but kept shoving through the crowd.

"He's in charge of our trainees," Smithson said. "Till he feels ready to fly again."

"Oh," Moloney said. She looked at Young.

"I think we're going to need you to stay, anyway," Young said.

"Sure thing," Reg said, pushing through faster. "I'll get these scrubs out of here and hustle right back." He reached them, grabbed Rosa and Trevor each by the upper arm and motioned Eddie on with a jerk of his chin.

As they got to the hall he turned sharply left and pulled them into the stairway leading to the overflow room.

"This better be good," Reg hissed. "I just put what's left of my career on the line following your lead. So why did you need these two out of there?"

"Um," Eddie said. "Something didn't feel right."

Reg squeezed his eyes shut.

Rosa's mouth was tight, and when she spoke her voice was carefully controlled. "Do you think you might just be upset about that Sensenbrenner guy?"

"Their IA head?" Reg said. "You know the guy?"

"My dad stole his car and killed him," Eddie said.

"Holy crap," Reg said slowly.

"I still don't get it," Trevor said. "What's going on?"

"Okay, maybe you don't want to tell the aliens that," Reg said. "But what does that have to do—"

"I don't know," Eddie snapped. "I thought they should have put their director on speakerphone."

Rosa stared at him. "That's no reason to embarrass us in front of everybody. God, Eddie, that was humiliating."

"Welcome to my world." He didn't say it nicely.

"Wait," Trevor said to Reg. "*Why* did you drag us out?"

Reg hissed a sigh. "Eddie looked like he knew what he was doing. I was hoping he had an angle on that gizmo Young was using. That he could read it."

Eddie shook his head.

"I know what this is," Trevor said, standing on the steps above him. "You got bumped out, so you're trying to screw me." He jutted a finger toward the Flight Control Room, beyond the stairwell wall. "You just told absolutely everybody important at IA that I'm a screwup. In the back of their minds, they'll always think that." He put the bottom of his sneaker on Eddie's chest and shoved, but it didn't budge him. Eddie stayed very still and looked at him. He had an urgent desire to show Trevor what a bad fight move that was.

"Stand down, Trevor," Reg said. "Did you watch their hands?" They all looked at him. "When the other three read the tablet they exchanged a glance, but then all three of them put their hand in their pocket. Three out of three."

"You pulled us out because they needed a cough drop?" Trevor said.

"A weapon," Reg said. "I'm sure they were checking their weapons."

Rosa frowned.

"I'm just going to shut this door for privacy," Moloney's voice said, feet away from them.

"What about Reg Davis?" Young's voice said in stereo from the Flight Control Room door and the speakers in the observation room.

"We'll get him when he comes back."

The door clicked shut. Rosa put a finger to her lips. Trevor and Eddie stared at each other, listening as Young's voice floated faintly down from the speakers above.

"I'm going to stand up here so I can see everybody better," he said. There was a scrambling noise. He must be standing on a workstation countertop. "Look, I don't like our instructions, but we have to carry them out." There was a pause, and Trevor sat back down.

"Director Sensenbrenner wants us to go ahead with the experiment."

"Wait," John Taylor Templeton said. "What?"

"He wants us to release the bacteria here."

"What the *hell*?" Templeton said. "No, you're not doing that."

"I'm so sorry," Young said. He sounded stricken. "I want you to know I don't agree with this."

A buzz of background noise rose up, making it harder to hear Young's voice. "Director Sensenbrenner feels that this is an ideal opportunity to see how human life would react to this kind of mutation in the food supply, if it ever happened on Earth."

Another pause. They could hear Smithson's voice, but couldn't make out the words.

The speaker buzzed with noise, then went silent.

"This won't hurt," Young said. "It just freezes voluntary muscle control for a few minutes." Then quieter, to his colleagues, he said, "Just put it on half spray. There's too many of them to dose everybody at full strength."

The room erupted in noise and shouting, but no one came out the door.

"Oh god," Trevor said. "We should call the police . . ."

"We should open the door," Rosa said, "so the people in the back can run out."

"We can't stop this," Eddie said.

Rosa gaped up at him. "Eddie?"

"You've got nothing?" Trevor said. "Come on, now's the time for an idea."

"I've got lots of ideas," Eddie hissed, "but none of them would actually work." He ran down the stairs into the hallway. "We don't have the capacity to stop them. All we can do is raise the stakes so this isn't their biggest problem."

They followed him down into the hall. "I'm in," Rosa said. "What are we doing?"

"We're taking it to them. They can't release the bacteria if they don't have it." Eddie started running. Over his shoulder he called, "I'm going to steal some very expensive wheels."

# CHAPTER TWENTY-FIVE

They ran quietly toward the far door, slipped out, and then raced down the stairwell at the end of the building. The three of them headed toward the spacecraft out on the runway, but Reg called them back.

"We've got a camera on it, remember? They'll see us from inside."

"I want them to see it," Eddie said. "That's the point. I want them to see me boosting their ride."

Reg shook his head. "It's a mile and a half away—half a mile past the launch tower. We won't get there before one of them notices and does something about it." They exchanged an uneasy glance. "They freeze us, it's all over."

"How are we supposed to get there if we can't be on camera?" Trevor said.

"Where's the car they brought them up here in?" Eddie said. "They'll see it, but we'll have a head start."

"That was a med vehicle. They return those immediately, so they're always ready."

"Even *now*?" Trevor said.

"This is NASA," Reg said. "We put our tools away."

Eddie shifted his weight, wanting to move. He had the look of a guy who might bolt into the open just to do it.

"We need to keep them from seeing us till the last second," Trevor said slowly. "So we have as much time as possible to figure out the controls."

"Bingo," Reg said.

"I know how to get a head start," Rosa said. "We use the emergency egress system."

"That's at the launch pad," Trevor said. "It's for getting off the tower."

"But we can get to the launch tower without the camera in Flight Control picking us up," Rosa said. "And then the emergency egress will shoot us from the tower to near where they're parked." She grinned. "It would be fast."

"Heck, yes, it would be," Eddie said, giving her shoulder a gentle bump.

"Oh crap," Reg said. "I've trained on that." He ran his palm over his scalp. "Yeah, that's the best plan. Then we run the last bit to the craft."

"Wait," Trevor said. "I don't understand. What are we doing?"

Reg led them around to the parking lot and pulled a set of keys from his pocket. "We're driving to the tower. They won't see us as soon, and if they chase us we'll go up the tower. They'll think they have us treed."

Eddie grinned. "Then we go *zoom* off the top."

"*Zoom?*" Trevor said.

They ran at a crouch behind Reg. An outside speaker crackled.

". . . taking him too long." It was Richtig's voice, coming from a black speaker attached to the building.

"He's one guy," Doepker said. "Not that big a deal if we don't get him."

"Oh, we'll get him," Young said. They didn't realize they were being heard outside. Someone must have thrown the audio switch, hoping to alert someone, to get some help.

Reg paused at the side of a blue four-door. "Ain't that sweet! They think I'm a threat." He started the car, then stepped across the console and motioned to Rosa to drive. "I'm gonna use that at my next performance review."

The guys climbed in the back and pulled their doors shut as quietly as they could, and Rosa eased back out of the spot, then accelerated toward the launch tower. She sneaked a glance sideways as Reg fished a receipt out of the glove box and wrote on it: *J—Love always, R*. He flipped it facedown on the dash, for his wife to find.

Rosa wished she hadn't seen it.

She roared across the lip of the launch pad and rocked to a stop at the base of the tower, cut the engine, and kicked her door open. They hit the elevator at the same time, running, and the doors didn't open immediately. Unbelievable.

"Crap," Eddie said. "It's got to be at the bottom. This tower is three hundred and seventy-three feet tall."

The elevator doors opened. They stepped in and Reg flashed his ID in front of the panel and they began the climb.

"So," Trevor said. "We're going up the elevator to take the emergency egress system down."

"Yep," Eddie said.

"And then we run for it," Rosa said.

"And we think this will be faster than just driving to their craft?"

Rosa hissed. There really was a reason he'd come in third. "This way we escape detection longer."

"I think it'll be fast enough for you," Reg said.

"I don't remember hearing about the emergency egress system," Trevor said. "What is it, exactly?"

The doors slid open, and Reg ran around the corner and jumped into the front seat of a little open cart. The wind on the tower made it noisy and whipped Rosa's hair across her face.

"It's a roller coaster!" Reg shouted.

Rosa jumped in beside him, and the guys vaulted in the back. "You in?" Reg shouted, looking over his shoulder. Eddie nodded. Trevor said, "Oh god."

Reg grinned and released the brake. They jolted forward and accelerated down the track for eight yards, then the track fell off at near ninety degrees, so they were pointed straight toward the earth. They plummeted off the edge of the tower, gray metal tubing flashing by them on the sides, the ground rushing up.

Rosa's hair flew above her. She gripped the restraint bar with one hand, the strap of her crossbody bag with the other, and screamed. Beside her Reg yelled and raised his arms over his head.

If you'd asked her that morning which of them was craziest, she'd have said Eddie. It hadn't occurred to her that it might be Reg.

Colors streaked as they shot down toward the parked craft, then bumpers burned off speed as they approached the end of the line. The car was slowing itself to sixty miles per hour, then fifty, then forty.

"Get ready to run," Reg shouted.

The roller coaster clattered to a stop and they clambered out and streamed across the half mile of open ground toward the spacecraft. Rosa didn't look over her shoulder as she ran. Her track coach had drilled it into their heads that turning meant slowing, and slowing meant losing. Still, she was itching to check the windows of the Flight Control Room. She couldn't see anything that far, anyway—but they had cameras out here, and if anyone was watching, they'd see them.

There were a hundred people in Flight Control being systematically frozen so that the alien teams could get out here and release their freaky alien bacteria in Iowa farm country. It would be the end of Earth's food supply. The end of this world.

Eddie was the first to disappear into the alien craft, with Reg on his heels. Trevor shot Rosa a nervous look as they pulled themselves in. The shell of the craft gave slightly, soft and firm and ultrasmooth under Rosa's hand.

"Did you feel that?" Reg said. "The outside feels like a boiled egg."

"Looked like it, too," Rosa said, staring at the inside of the craft, studded with switches and controls.

Reg grabbed a helmet off the commander's chair and lowered

himself, bouncing on the seat. "Comfy. Hope this guy doesn't have lice." He strapped on the helmet.

"Reg, this is way more complicated than what we trained on," Rosa said.

"There are switches on the ceiling," Trevor said. "All across it."

"No time for sightseeing," Reg said. "Get your helmets on and strap in." He patted the seat next to him. "Rosa." She was being invited to be copilot on an unplanned space journey with equipment they didn't understand. She pulled her hair into a low ponytail, then slipped the helmet on.

"This would be a great time to check in on Social Earth," Trevor said. "Trevor is at: alien spacecraft!"

Eddie gave him an appreciative snort. Reg began a preflight systems check, clicking items off rapid-fire. He knew what he was doing. He'd done this before.

"We don't have time for that!" Trevor said.

"Forward Reaction Control System Module," Reg said, checking a switch. "I'm looking at what we know, and what we don't."

"All that stuff in the middle of the panel—about sixty switches worth? We don't know that stuff," Eddie said.

"Very helpful, Eddie, thank you," Reg said. "Okay, looks like they're burning monomethylhydrazine fuel and nitrogen tetroxide oxidizer."

"They'll burn when they touch," Rosa said, "even in an environment without oxygen."

"Yeah," Reg said. "They're in separate tanks so they don't go boom."

"Pressured by helium?" Rosa asked.

"Looks like it," Reg said. "Probably spring-loaded solenoid valves. Maybe they've got something better."

Reg kept running down his checklist, all the while scanning the panels of switches before them and overhead. There were control panels aft where Eddie and Trevor were sitting, too.

"Your controls look like backups to ours?" Rosa whispered to them, trying not to interrupt Reg's preflight systems check.

"Looks like we've got life support back here," Trevor said.

"I like life support," Eddie said.

"I think we've got chemical carbon dioxide canisters to remove the $CO_2$ by reacting it with lithium hydroxide," Trevor said.

"Do we know if they were ready to make a return trip?" Rosa said. "I mean, do we have extra $CO_2$ canisters on board? Do we have *fuel*?"

"I think so," Reg said, finishing his check. "It's all pretty familiar, except for the part I don't understand at all, not even the terms."

"You know," Eddie said, "we're more likely to get the bacteria out of their hands if we can actually start their buggy."

"Do we need space suits?" Trevor asked. "There aren't any spare suits here."

"We'll be okay," Reg said. "As long as everything runs perfectly. And if it doesn't, they wouldn't have saved us."

Rosa glanced back at the guys and caught their sober return looks. They all knew this. Hearing it from Reg was different.

Reg examined the switches on the main panel—the ones they didn't understand. He took a deep breath and flipped one. Nothing happened.

"Maybe we should have gotten help, instead of trying to steal a spaceship," Trevor said. He shot Eddie a look.

"Listen, Mr. Cautious, I never invited you along. I said *I* was going," Eddie said. "You could have gotten security if you'd wanted to. But if they can hold off a hundred people, do you think a couple of guards are going to make a difference?"

Reg flipped another switch. Nothing.

"Maybe you have to start it traditionally?" Rosa said. "Get it going, then switch to extradimensional?"

"That's what I think, too," Reg said. "I wish I knew what I was doing." He started the engine, and the craft began to vibrate.

"You gonna switch into drive?" Eddie called.

"Got to get the engines to ninety percent before we take off," Reg said. His forehead was beaded with sweat.

"I don't know if we have time," Trevor said. "They have to have picked us up by now."

"Oh, they'll see us all right," Reg said. He pulled on the throttle, but it didn't move.

"Do you have authorization to fly this vehicle?" the spacecraft asked in a woman's pleasant tone. They stared at each other for a moment.

"Roger that," Reg said.

"Verify authorization," the craft said.

"Damn it, Reginald!" He looked around wildly. Rosa pointed—there at the bottom of the rudder control was a little rectangular panel. She held up her thumb and raised her eyebrows. Reg nodded and pressed his thumb against the screen.

"Welcome, Commander Davis," the spacecraft said.

They exchanged a sober look. It's one thing to hijack an alien spacecraft. It's another thing when the aliens are you.

He pulled back on the throttle and the boiled-egg craft shot down the runway, the force pushing them hard against their seats.

"When do we turn on the extradimensional capacity?" Rosa asked.

"Dunno," Reg said. "But realistically, that's when we'll die."

Rosa swiveled in her seat. Eddie's and Trevor's faces had identical expressions. She bet hers mirrored theirs. They hurtled down the runway and rose into the air, then banked hard left. Reg grinned over at Rosa.

"Um . . ."

"We want them to see us, right, Eddie?" Reg called back.

"Yep," Eddie shouted over the engines.

Reg swooped past the command building, cutting his speed and swinging right past the fourth-floor windows of Flight Control. Rosa craned to see past him. They shot by too fast to get a good visual, but she thought she saw Young staring out the window.

"Ha!" Eddie shouted. "We boosted your ride, asshats!"

"I want to moon them!" Trevor shouted. "Can I unstrap, Reg?"

"Not advisable," Reg said, pulling back on the throttle. They rose and curved backward, making a loop-de-loop in front of the Flight Control window.

He pulled them out of the loop and swept toward the ground, pulling up at the last minute to shoot straight up past the window like a rocket.

"Um, considering there's apparently some lethal bacteria on board," Trevor said, "maybe we should get out of here."

Rosa had a different concern. "Reg? You doing okay with flying again?"

"Yeah," he said, shooting away from the command building and arcing right, in the direction from which the ship had originally come. "I crashed one of these. Well, a much simpler craft, of course."

"That's comforting," Eddie said.

"Three, two, one," Reg whispered in a private countdown. He simultaneously flipped two switches in the extradimensional travel panel, then another overhead. Nothing happened. He gave a quick glance at Rosa, took a breath, and flipped another switch. Nothing.

"This is an incorrect sequence," the craft's voice said pleasantly. "Is your flight crew disabled?"

"Um, yes," Reg said.

"Would you like to fly on autopilot?" the voice said.

"Yes!" Reg said. "Oh god, yes."

"Confirming: Do you wish to enter extradimensional flight mode?" the voice said.

"Yes," Reg said. "Engage extradimensional flight on autopilot."

"What is your destination?" the voice said.

They all exchanged a glance. "Home," Reg said. "Take us home."

"Confirming," the voice said. "Destination: Earth. Do you wish me to have a medical team standing by at Flight Control?"

Reg's eyes widened. "No. Let's cut off communications, too. We'll surprise them."

"This is an incorrect procedure," the voice said. "Communications should be maintained at all times."

"Not this time," Reg said. "We're flying in without notification."

"Don't blame this on me," the voice said, and Reg grinned. The ship shuddered slightly and began to spin, and then everything outside was black. The interior lights stayed on, dim against the outer gloom.

"Are we still spinning?" Rosa asked. "It doesn't feel like it."

"I don't think so," Trevor said. "My stomach feels a lot better than when Reg had the throttle."

"I think we're in extradimensional travel," Reg said, his voice hushed. "God, I hope we live to tell about this."

"I thought there would be streaking lights and glimpses into the past," Eddie said. "Something like that."

Rosa's hair rose around her and her purse floated free. "Wow. I need a special space purse."

"I can't believe you brought that thing," Trevor said.

"I do not travel light."

They all stared out into the blackness, with no idea what it was or how long it would last. Then Reg said, "What's the first thing we do when we're traveling in space?"

"Selfies!" Trevor said.

Rosa snorted, but Reg said, "Rightamundo!" and reached back to give Trevor a high five. Reg pulled his phone from his pocket and motioned them together. "Let's get all the pirates in the picture," he said. They leaned in and smiled, and when they were all in focus, the phone snapped the shot.

When they were done, Eddie wandered off to look for snacks. The inside of the craft wasn't roomy, but he found a cupboard with packets of food fastened to the sides. He frowned, rummaging through the cupboard.

"No root beer? What the hell, NASA? We have to travel through dimensions we don't understand to face a future of untold danger, and there's no stinking root beer? This is not okay."

"The carbonation and the soda don't separate in microgravity," Reg said. "No root beer in space."

Eddie threw his hand over his heart and staggered.

"Well, they *could* develop a microgravity dispenser," Reg said.

"Why has this not been a priority?" Eddie demanded.

Rosa rolled her eyes.

"Yeah," Reg said. "You'd think they'd have gotten around to it by now. I gotta say, though, I love their technology. They didn't just make the craft better, they made it easier to use. Brilliant."

Eddie snorted. He was still ticked about the root beer. He pulled a biscuit from his pocket and let it float. "Lightest biscuit in history," he said. "I could be one of those TV chefs." He snapped it out of the air like a crocodile.

"I found the bacteria," Trevor called. They all swiveled to look at him. "The case is locked, but that's got to be what's inside. The whole thing's about the size of a lunch box."

They were quiet for a minute after that.

Finally Trevor said, "Is this freaking anybody else out? This— nothingness?" He put his hand against the window.

"It feels like everything to me," Rosa said. "Like every possibility is out there."

Then they settled in for the pitch-black glide into the parallel Earth.

# CHAPTER TWENTY-SIX

They didn't know where they were, or when they were. They sat looking out the windows into nothing, glad they weren't alone.

"I thought going into extra dimensions might hurt," Trevor said. "Like getting folded. I was worried about my testicles."

Eddie snorted, and Trevor blushed. Eddie didn't want to harass the guy, but . . . okay, he kind of did. "What did you think would happen to your balls? Death from loneliness?"

"Who knows what this could do to guys our age!" Trevor said. "Why do you think there *are* extra dimensions, anyway?"

"Because three dimensions aren't enough to hold my genius," Eddie said.

"Three dimensions aren't enough to hold Rosa's luggage," Trevor said. Eddie laughed.

"I hate to interrupt this," Reg said, "but does anyone have a plan for landing?"

"You're the guy with experience," Eddie said. "If autopilot goes off, can't you just land it regularly?"

"Yeah, I can land it," he said, emphasizing his words. "And then what?"

"Their teams won't be on our tail," Eddie said. "We don't have anything that could get them home, right?"

"Nothing," Reg said.

"We're so far behind, it'll take them five years to design the ship, and fifty to persuade Congress to fund it!" Trevor said. "We suck!" He gave Eddie a high five.

"But when we land this craft and they discover the bacteria has returned and their teams haven't, they're likely to have some questions," Reg said.

"Aw, hell," Eddie said.

"Swear fine just went up to fifty cents," Reg said. "Fundraising to get ourselves one of these babies."

"What do we do first?" Trevor said.

"Run?" Eddie said.

"I have no idea when we'll leave extradimensional travel," Reg said, "but from the supplies Eddie found, they clearly weren't set up for a long trip."

"No frickin root beer," Eddie grumbled.

"So we need to make a plan, and we need to make it now."

"You just land," Eddie said. "And then we need to get away from their Flight Control Room as quickly as possible. Put some distance between us."

"No," Rosa said, shaking her head. "We're going to need help.

We know their Earth is extremely similar to ours, but it can't be exactly the same."

"Lamar Sensenbrenner is alive there," Eddie said, "so it's at least a little different."

"We need to find allies," Rosa said.

Eddie snorted. "Who's going to help us?"

She turned square to him and looked him in the eye. "*We're* down there somewhere. We have to find ourselves if we're going to survive."

They let that sink in for a minute.

"Where would we be?" Trevor said. "I mean, we might not be trainees there." He turned to Eddie. "What would you be doing, Eddie? Try to think like yourself."

"I'd be punching you."

"Okay," Trevor said. "We can find me in the hospital. That's a start."

Reg grunted as the craft shuddered slightly and they blinked at the light all around them, at the arc of blue and then their own weight settling on them again. Just like that, they were out of the extra dimensions. Rosa's hair floated down around her.

Straight ahead was a beautiful blue marble. Earth—but not theirs.

"It looks like an eye," Trevor said. "It's watching us come in."

Reg was taking command back from autopilot and was absorbed in his switches.

"It's like looking in your own eye," Eddie said. He didn't turn to them when he spoke. None of them could tear themselves from the blue sphere, beautiful and alien and home. "Death is a cyclops."

"Or maybe," Rosa said, "we're the other eye."

# CHAPTER TWENTY-SEVEN

"Leaving extradimensional travel," the craft announced, as though it wasn't obvious. The cabin heated as they rocketed through the atmosphere, melted air pouring over their boiled-egg skin. They strapped in, and Reg chewed on his lower lip while he flipped switches. Rosa glanced sideways at him but didn't want to break his concentration.

They hurtled toward alien Earth, and there was the sun and the moon, and North America spread below them. The ride was smoother than Rosa expected. Maybe the advanced Earth had perfected shocks.

"Do you wish to reestablish communications?" the craft asked.

"No," Reg said. "No, I sure don't."

They were lower now, able to pick out rivers and forests.

"Damn it, Reginald!" Reg muttered, shaking a toggle.

"Okay?" Rosa asked.

"Yeah."

"Hey, Reg?" Trevor said. "When you crashed one of these, it wasn't on landing, was it?"

"Sure was," Reg said. "But I keep telling you, it wasn't one of these. It was a simpler model. And I didn't have a chatterbox in the cabin."

None of them said a word until they could see the IA facility spread out below them, and Reg aligned the vehicle with the runway.

"If they can't already see us, they're about to," he said, and pulled back on the throttle and hit two switches overhead.

"Push the black button," he said to Rosa, nodding toward a control in the middle. Rosa pushed it. "You just flew an alien spacecraft," he said, which was an exaggeration, for sure, but still made her flush. She hoped they'd let her tell her dad about that.

Then they were hurtling like a plane down the runway, straight toward the IA Flight Control Room, just like the alien teams had done when they visited Earth. Of course, the aliens knew how to stop the craft.

"Engage brake!" Reg shouted as he shoved a lever down.

The craft braked hard and spun as it slowed, shedding the excess momentum in torque. It moved like a top down the runway, shot off the end, and dug a shallow trench in the ground between the launch area and the building. It came to rest fifty yards from the brick wall.

"Well," Reg said, "that worked pretty well."

Rosa unsnapped her belt and stood, wobbly from the carnival ride down the runway.

Eddie high-stepped away as Trevor's vomit splashed over the

seat and dripped, heavy, onto the floor. Eddie threw open the door and fled the vomit. Reg and Rosa jumped down after him. Trevor grabbed the case of bacteria and hopped out last.

"They'll think it's their own teams returning," Reg said. "We should have a minute before they scramble after us."

Eddie took off running toward the building.

"You crazy?" Trevor shouted, but he followed.

"We've got to go on the assumption that we're trainees here," Eddie called over his shoulder. "It's our best bet."

"Where would we be, Reg?" Rosa said.

They passed a woman carrying some folders. She smiled at them and moved out of the way. She didn't understand yet—but Rosa bet the people in the Flight Control Room were starting to process it.

Reg caught Eddie and pointed around the corner. "Kirkwood Hall," he said. "If those guys hadn't shown up today, I'd have had you working on symmetry problems. Room 319."

That's where they'd been before, where they'd talked about the Gordian knot.

"I always thought aliens would be little green men," Trevor said. "But we're not."

Rosa looked at him as they dashed through the door. *We are aliens to this world.* "You were green a minute ago," she said.

"Ha," Trevor said. "Good point. But I have nary a tentacle."

"Speak for yourself," Eddie said. "My tentacle is just fine."

"Seriously?" Rosa said. "Now?"

"It's always time to defend Edward the Great."

"Oh my god," she said.

Reg pulled them aside in the third-floor stairwell so they could catch their breath. "Hope this is a good idea."

They were quiet for a moment, hearts slamming in their chests, wondering if someone was already pounding down the steps from the Flight Control Room.

"How much do you trust yourself?" Rosa said. "That's what it comes down to, doesn't it?"

"Yeah," Reg said. They looked at each other, silent, then he said, "Let's go find ourselves."

They walked down the hall, quickly and quietly, Reg in the lead. Rosa wasn't sure if she was more scared that they wouldn't be in Room 319 or that they would be. Reg grasped the doorknob, inhaled, then pushed the door all the way open, and they stepped inside.

In the room, another Reg looked over from the marker board, his hand suspended in midair, half a problem written on the board. His eyes widened for a fraction of a second, then he adjusted. Eddie2 had already scraped his chair back and was standing, his elbows tilted out at his sides. Trevor2 had taken a step backward. Rosa registered all of it, but she was staring at a small girl with her hair pulled back in a neat ponytail. The girl looked up at them, then calmly smoothed her skirt and stood.

"What the hell?" Reg2 said, slowly capping his marker with a click.

Eddie stepped forward and tilted his head at his counterpart. "Nice ass," he said.

"Yeah, you, too," their Eddie said. "I mean, I knew it was good. I just didn't realize it was that good."

"Welcome," Rosa2 said. "What an unexpected pleasure." She laid down her pencil and walked over to them, stopping a couple of feet away.

"Don't touch it!" Trevor2 said.

"*It?*" both Rosas said, each of them raising an eyebrow. Eddie smirked. Rosa2 extended a hand and Rosa looked her in the eye and shook. She had no idea what to say, but figured that meant Rosa2 didn't, either, so she'd understand. Finally she said, "It's very nice to meet you." Rosa2 smiled.

"I'm wearing makeup," Trevor said. "Why am I wearing makeup?"

It was true. Trevor2 had on smudgy black eyeliner, and it looked kind of good on him.

"We're going to need some kind of explanation," Reg2 said.

"Roger that," Reg said. "But I suspect Flight Control is after us by now, and I'd like to move to a secure location."

"Why is Flight Control after you?" Reg2 said, lifting his chin.

"They tried to release a killer bacteria on our world. We're returning it to yours." Trevor raised the case, and Reg2's eyes widened.

"You armed?" They shook their heads. He hesitated. "Yeah, come on."

He led them back into the hallway and down the stairs to the back door. They trotted along with him. They knew the building.

"You're from another world?" Rosa2 asked.

"Yeah. It looks just like this," Rosa said.

She nodded, taking that in.

"I should probably be turning you in," Reg2 said. "Don't know why I'm not."

"Yeah you do," Reg said. "We have the bacteria. Besides, you know if I'd do this, you would, too."

"I know no such thing," Reg2 said sharply. "I don't even know if you're human."

Eddie pulled out his pocketknife, flicked out a small blade, held Reg2's eye, and stabbed the tip into his own forearm. Blood gushed out and he held his arm away from his body.

"That could get infected," Trevor said at the same time Trevor2 said, "That is so unsanitary!"

"You're leaving a trail," Rosa said, nodding to the floor.

"Crap." Eddie felt in his pocket, then pulled his shirt off and wrapped it around his forearm.

"It'll clot soon," Rosa2 said to Rosa. "It wasn't deep." Rosa nodded.

"I'm willing to believe you're human," Reg2 said. "Also stupid."

Eddie grinned. "That sounds like Reg." Both Regs scowled at him.

They exited Kirkwood Hall and hesitated. "We should get off campus," Reg said. "They'll look for us here."

"I've got a car . . . ," Reg2 said.

"Yeah, but we park by the command building," Reg said. "We don't want to go that direction."

"This is *not* comfortable."

"I'm parked near the gate," Eddie2 said.

Eddie's head snapped up and he stared at the guy. He opened

his mouth, but Reg2 said, "Tell me about the bacteria before I take you off this base."

They followed Eddie2 toward the parking lot inside the main gate, on the opposite end of the compound from the launch pad. He had a set of keys in his hand, and they jingled as they jogged.

"Your Teams 1 and 2 showed up on our planet, after sending out deceptive signals to draw our teams away," said Reg. "They had orders to release a bacteria that causes a mutation in the food supply. It would kill almost everyone."

"I heard about that bacteria," Reg2 said, "but it's supposed to be antifamine research. Who gave the order to release it on a populated world?"

"Lamar Sensenbrenner," Rosa said. "Your director."

Reg2 was silent. His mouth twisted, as though Sensenbrenner's name tasted sour.

Eddie2 buzzed open a red pickup and climbed behind the wheel. The Regs slid in beside him, and the rest of them clambered into the bed. Eddie2 started the ignition, backed out, and stopped. A moment later Reg got into the back.

"Too many Reginald Davises for the guard booth," he said by way of explanation.

The Trevors unrolled a tarp and they all lay under it as Eddie2 pulled through the guard booth and out onto the road. Had he ever walked down it swinging a bottle in a brown paper bag? Had Rosa2 tried to figure out what to do about it? They stayed down until the window on the cab slid open and Reg2's voice said, "You can come up now." The truck stopped long enough for Reg to climb back up front so he could confer with himself.

Rosa was starting to fix her ponytail when the other Rosa smiled a little shyly and said, "Here, let me." Rosa handed her the elastic. "Do you want a French braid?" asked Rosa2.

"Sure," Rosa said, then, "You're better than a mirror." Rosa2 smoothed Rosa's hair, gentle hands moving over her scalp. Rosa's own hands.

"This is deeply strange," Rosa said.

"Are we the same person?"

"Yeah. I think so."

"Do you have a scar on your right knee?"

"No," Rosa said, twisting to look at her. "But I have one on my left knee." Rosa2 snapped the elastic into place and leaned back against the side of the truck bed.

Across from them, Trevor kept sneaking sideways glances at Makeup Trevor. Rosa caught Rosa2's eye and jerked her head, and Rosa2 suppressed a smile. She seemed . . . nice. Like someone who could be a friend. This was the craziest thing ever, Rosa thought—she wanted to make friends with herself.

Eddie pulled his T-shirt off his arm and inspected the small wound where he'd stabbed himself.

"Is your Eddie crazy?" Rosa asked.

"Oh yeah," she said.

He scooted up to the cab window and rapped on it to get the other Eddie's attention, then slid the bloody shirt back over his head.

"That's disgusting," the Trevors said together, then looked at each other with surprise.

"So how'd you get wheels?" Eddie called through the window.

"I got the truck when I was coming out here, for the tryouts. Seemed like I needed one."

"Okay," Reg2 called back. "We've decided to hide out for a little bit while we make a plan, and I decide if I really believe all this."

"Believe it," Trevor said.

"We're going to hole up in Oolitic," Reg said.

Eddie2 grinned into the rearview mirror. "You guys haven't lived till you've tasted my grandma's biscuits."

"Oh," Rosa whispered. "I think we just found another difference between our worlds."

Eddie looked like he'd been slapped. "Wait," he said. "What?"

# CHAPTER TWENTY-EIGHT

"*Grandma?*" Eddie said. "Grandma's *alive?*"

Eddie2 stared at him in the mirror. "Yeah. What, yours isn't?"

Eddie slumped down against the front of the truck bed.

"Wait!" Eddie2 shouted from the cab. "What happened?"

"She died, asshole."

Eddie sat by himself, hands dangling off his knees. To his right were two Rosas, to his left two Trevors. In the cab behind him were two pickle-eating Regs, and one son of a bitch who should be him, but who had a truck and a grandma. Even with himself he was alone.

They drove for hours, mostly off road, through fields with corn that was already knee high, even though it was no place close to the Fourth of July yet. The Trevors took apart the phones of the people who lived on this Earth so they couldn't be traced. "They insert any chips in your ankles or anything?" Trevor asked. Trevor2 shook his head. His hair was long on one side, buzzed on the other—if you averaged it out, he was just like Trevor. Except for the eyeliner. Trevor kept shooting sideways glances at him.

They were driving east. The sun gave them a long, long look as it set, rays angling lower until they snagged on the back of the bed door. It was a relief, Eddie thought, when the sun went down. It saved explaining to yourself why you couldn't look it in the eye.

They stopped twice at gas stations and paid in cash. The second time the Regs bought them prewrapped sandwiches and a flat of water bottles, and a jar of pickles for themselves. Eddie2 picked up a case of root beer, too. He ripped the end off the box, grabbed two cans, and tossed one to Eddie before he headed back to the cab.

"Let's switch drivers," Reg2 said.

"I'm good," Eddie2 said.

Reg2 held his hand out for the keys. "No need to do it all yourself."

"I got it," he said, stepping past him.

"Eddie," Reg2 said.

"Save your breath," Eddie said. "He's not gonna let you drive his truck."

Eddie2 grinned at him. "Listen to this guy," he said, pointing with a can. "He's as smart as he is good looking." Then he swung back into the driver's seat.

Reg2 sighed and walked around to the passenger side, and they got back under way. The wind that streamed over the cab and buffeted them was cool. The Rosas pulled the tarp up over their legs. Soon they were all under the stiff canvas, shoulders sticking out. They could hear the Regs murmuring to each other in the cab, their conversation punctuated by the snap of pickles.

Eddie2 took back roads, staying off the highways. The truck was a solid vehicle, well made, and well maintained—a sturdy ride as it bounced along the roads toward home. The moon was near full—a basketball that needed inflation. The Trevors dozed sitting up, and the Rosas lay curled, holding each other like sisters. Eddie sat upright, staring at the moon. The night smelled of wild roses and turned earth and home.

He didn't know he'd fallen asleep until they slowed down for the curve by the Meyerholtzes' farm. He stood up, legs spread for balance, his left hand holding on through the open driver's window. All around him were the fields of home, corn and soybeans glistening in the night, their roots sunk into the soil of this alien world. It occurred to him for the first time that people imagine aliens as little green men because they want it that way.

They turned up the lane and the house was dark, but its familiar outline made his heart contract. The yard light by the barn was on. A raccoon scurried across the road in front of them, and Eddie2 slowed. Fifty yards farther a badger's sharp nose poked out of the wild roses in the ditch, then retreated.

"You okay?" Rosa had scooted up and was sitting by his ankles.

"I just saw an alien badger," he said. "That should be a movie. Baaadgers in spaaaaace!"

Rosa just looked at him.

"Grandma is dead and alive," he said. *Screw Schrödinger.*

Eddie2 brought the truck to a gentle stop close to the barn, where oaks already in full leaf would shield it from aerial view.

They climbed out, yawning and stretching. Unless he was a lying bastard, Eddie was about to see his grandma.

It felt formal, like they should go around to the front porch, but Eddie2 led them to the kitchen door. His key scraped unnaturally loud in the dark, and the door swung inward before he could turn the knob. He looked back at Eddie, silent, then stepped into the kitchen.

"Eddie?" his grandma's voice said.

They filed in. The linoleum by the back door had been replaced—it was gray instead of the old green with white streaks. Grandma's barn coat hung in the coat closet, and on the shelf above it sat her sun hat, floral gardening gloves, and helmet. Eddie ran his finger over the pencil marks by the door—his heights, with the dates marked in her neat engineer's printing.

Grandma stood in the kitchen, her gray hair flowing onto the shoulders of her pink cotton bathrobe. She ignored the two middle-aged black men, the mismatched Trevors, and the identical girls in her kitchen. She looked back and forth at the Eddies, but when she spoke it was to the boy she'd never seen before.

"Eddie."

She had recognized his Eddiness. He felt somehow vindicated.

"This is going to require some explanation," she said. "Right now." She moved to the counter and leaned casually against it. He knew what was behind her—the knife block. She wasn't overreacting, but she was thinking. She was ready. God, he missed her.

"Eleanor," Reg2 said, "IA developed a bacteria that alters the growth habits of plants. It causes cancer, but we think it may have some potential."

Grandma snorted.

"They're hoping it mutates in a few generations and we can find a strain that causes rapid growth in plants—but not in humans."

This time Reg snorted.

"But because of pollination and bees and just the wind," Reg2 said, "it can't be contained. If it's anywhere, it's everywhere."

"I heard the botanists were up to something," she said, "but I never got the details."

"That's it," Reg2 said. "We've been looking for a world with mammals, but not humans, to test it. Let it evolve. Bring it back home and use it safely."

Grandma was listening to him, but she was looking at Eddie.

"You're from another world, aren't you?"

"Yeah." His voice was husky, but he couldn't help it. "They were going to release the bacteria there."

Grandma sucked in her breath. "On a world with humans? Identical humans? With *you?*" She shook her head. "And that's it, isn't it? In my kitchen." She pointed.

Trevor tightened his grip on the case and nodded. Grandma put her palms together and tapped her fingertips, a gesture Eddie had almost forgotten. "Set it by the door, would you? While I think this through." Trevor put the case down. "Are you hungry?" Grandma said.

"Yes," Eddie said, with her grandson and the Regs.

Grandma lit a candle and set it on the table. Then she started cracking eggs, and the kitchen smelled of egg and sulfur from the match. Eddie ran his thumb over a corner of the table and watched her for a moment, then walked to the second cabinet to the right of the sink and pulled out the blue bowl and handed it to her. She took it from him with a little nod.

"Thank you. What's your world like?"

"You're dead there."

She stared at him for a moment. "Crap. Something spectacular, I hope?" She got a package of sausage links out of the refrigerator.

"Stroke," he said. "A couple months ago."

She looked at the sausage in her hand, then put the cast iron skillet on the stove and flipped the gas on. "I'm sorry to hear that. Are you doing okay?"

"Yeah."

She flipped the links into the pan. "I don't believe that for a minute." And then she hugged him. She was soft and warm and just the right shape, but one scent in the mix was off, some different brand of lotion that told him *she's not yours.*

She pulled back and held his biceps while she looked in his eyes, and then kissed his forehead. He sat down and didn't look at anybody, because crap, she was *Grandma,* and he didn't want to lose it.

Reg2 explained about Reg and his trainees bursting into Reg2's classroom. Then Reg told the same story, including the lack of root beer on the egg craft. That made her smile.

"Excuse me," Rosa said when he was done. "We haven't introduced ourselves properly. I'm . . ."

"Rosa Hayashi," Grandma said. "Yes, I know."

They looked at each other.

"How did you know . . ."

"I got the e-mail," Grandma said. "About the new trainees."

"Oh. I didn't realize they sent an e-mail," Rosa said.

"On our world, we called our parents," Trevor said.

"I got it from my work account," Grandma said.

None of them understood that.

"Grandma's retired now, but they still send her the general e-mails," Eddie2 said. "The ones that go to everybody."

"Um," Rosa said. "May I ask what you do?"

Grandma turned, holding a pancake flipper in one hand. "Why, I was the CPE-XD."

They looked at Reg.

"The Chief Program Engineer for Extra Dimensions," Grandma said. "I ran the mission from an integration perspective—communication, troubleshooting, things like that."

"She was in charge of the whole damn egg," Reg2 said. "The entire mission."

"I guess your grandma didn't do that," her Eddie said. "I mean, since you guys can't fly extradimensionally."

"Ooh," Grandma said, rolling the sausage links over. "What did I do there? Was I a Landing and Recovery Director? They didn't let me be a pilot, did they? My eyes weren't good enough here."

Eddie didn't know what to say. "Um, you were an engineering assistant at a firm in Bedford."

"*Bedford*? Why didn't I work for NASA? I can't imagine I didn't want to."

"Because—you're—female," he said. "I don't know how you got promoted here, but you didn't get promoted there."

"Well, damn it," Grandma said. "And now I'm dead?"

"Yeah."

She grunted, and they were quiet while she put the food on the table. Eddie2 laid out plates, and shot Eddie a look when he got up to help. But Eddie needed him to know that he knew where everything was. Grandma's kitchen? This was stuff he knew. Her grandson might be Eddie, but damn it, he was, too.

"Reg, do you believe this?" she asked once they were seated. "It requires believing that Sensenbrenner would commit mass murder."

Reg2 picked at his eggs. "Yeah, I do. Guess it's hard to believe that a guy this sharp would lie to me," he said, looking at Reg. "Also, they have the bacteria."

"Yeah," Grandma said. "We need to get rid of that."

"That's why we came to Oolitic," Reg2 said. "We have to keep it out of Sensenbrenner's hands. We can't let it go back to their world—or get released here."

"We can hole up here, ditch that case, and plan—but not forever," Reg said.

Grandma nodded.

They ate quietly, the candle sending a soft orange glow across their faces. The Trevors reached for the salt at the same moment, and then pulled their hands back to let the other go first. The four Doctors Clayborn had raised them well. Rosa glanced at herself, got Rosa2's agreement, and said, "Maybe we should take an inventory of our skills. If we know what we *can* do, it may suggest what we *should* do."

"I can fly," Reg said. "And I know the personnel and facilities."

"Roger that," their Reg said, spooning himself some more eggs.

"I'm pretty good with mechanical things," Eddie2 said, and Eddie nodded.

"I know first aid," Trevor said, "and I make the ladies swoon."

"So Trevor has the best imagination," Eddie said. Eddie2 gave him an appreciative grin. Finally someone who got his humor.

"You're hurt," Grandma said, catching a look at Eddie's arm.

"Just a flesh wound," he said.

She stood up, taking her plate to the counter as she went, and got a Band-Aid from the lazy Susan with the spices. The Band-Aid was covered with little rocket ships—that made him smile. She pulled the tabs off and smoothed it, being careful not to press on the cut. Then she kissed it.

He stood up fast, his chair scraping behind him. "I'm gonna shoot some hoops," he said, not looking at anybody.

"It's three a.m.," Trevor2 said.

"Perfect."

# CHAPTER TWENTY-NINE

Eddie let the screen door slam, and a moment later they heard dribbling and the ring of a ball clanging off the iron hoop nailed to the barn.

"Sounds like his game's off," Eddie2 said.

Rosa cleared the table—both of her. It was like being a twin, and she liked it. That meant the other Rosa liked it, too, and that made her happy. If the whole world were filled with Rosas, she wouldn't have to wonder what people thought of her.

Eddie's alien grandma watched him for a minute out the kitchen window, then she put the leftover sausage links away. She hadn't eaten any.

"I'm gonna go play with him," Eddie2 said. "This is a great opportunity to see how good I am."

"Bad idea," his grandma said, then "Don't!" as he went out the back door. "Aw, crud." She smiled wanly at Rosa. "Eddie doesn't always get along with himself." She rinsed a plate. "How about you?"

Rosa blinked, startled. How did you answer a question like that?

"Um, I think I'm okay." She glanced at Rosa2, who stood up straighter. "It is odd meeting yourself."

"Is your father the head of the Los Alamos National Lab in the world you came from?"

"Yeah. Here?"

Grandma nodded and ran water in the sink. "That's a lot to live up to," she said, not looking at Rosa.

"Yeah," Rosa said. "Everybody knows my dad. I mean, I like it—but I'm going to have to do something pretty spectacular just to stay even."

She sneaked a glance at Rosa2, and she gave Rosa a little nod.

"I suspect that would upset your dad," Grandma said, squirting some dishwashing liquid into the water in the sink. "Since he's dealt with that his whole life, too."

Rosa gave a soft snort. "No, he hasn't. His parents ran a grocery store."

Grandma pointed a finger at her. "His parents were in an internment camp as children. That's where they met, when they were three years old."

"Wait. Did you know she knew Dad?" Rosa asked Rosa2.

Rosa2 shrugged. "Everybody knows him."

"What do you think that did to your dad, knowing his parents were behind barbed wire when they were tiny?"

Rosa and Rosa2 looked at each other.

"I never thought about it that way," Rosa2 said.

"*He* always felt he had something to live up to?" Rosa said. "Oh, wow."

"I hope I'm not out of line talking to you about it," Grandma said. "But we chatted once after a couple of drinks at a conference. And since I didn't know him on your world . . ."

Outside, the Trevors howled. They and the Regs had gone out to watch the game. Grandma sighed and hung her dishcloth over the sink divider. "This worries me," she said. "Eddie playing himself is like Jacob wrestling the angel, except without the angel."

They followed her out the back door, the girls holding hands as they walked. A fixture by the barn cast a circle of light but did nothing to obscure the spangle of stars overhead. It was a muggy night and smelled of soil and grass and endless possibilities. The guys had taken white wooden rockers from the front porch and set them in the dirt at the edge of the circle. Both Eddies were shirtless now, and Rosa couldn't tell which was which until she saw the flash of the Band-Aid on an arm. They walked up and stood behind the guys, and Rosa rested her arms on the back of Reg's chair.

"They're good," he said quietly.

The night was cool, but both guys were beaded with sweat, their skin flushed with exertion, their eyes bright. Quick hands darted for the ball; equally swift hands swept it away. They pushed off with elbows and banged chests and shoulders on rebounds.

Rosa swatted a mosquito from her face. A bat swooped past the edge of the concrete where they played. Eddie2 went up for a jumper, and Eddie got an arm in his face. The ball hit the rim and bounced off, hitting in the dust beyond the cement. Eddie ran for it, then stepped onto the concrete and immediately went up for the shot. He sank it. Reg and Rosa gave each other a high five.

"Hey, Band-Aid Eddie," Rosa called. "What's the score?"

He didn't respond, but darted a hand out to knock the ball away from Eddie2, who twisted and protected it, and caught Eddie's cheekbone with his shoulder. Eddie pushed him hard and made him stagger, but Eddie2 feinted with the stagger and then cut, got around him, and made an easy layup.

He flipped the ball to Eddie, just out of his reach so he had to lunge for it. Eddie grabbed it one-handed, then cut left and made a fade-away jumper. When Eddie2 started to take the ball out, Band-Aid Eddie stole it, but slammed him with his torso in the process, making Eddie2 grunt.

"That's mine," Eddie2 said, holding his hand out.

"You've already got a truck and a grandma," Eddie said, dribbling in place, looking at his own face between him and the basket. He shot a pretty arc, got the swish, and left his hands in the air, fingers dangling, for longer than was probably necessary.

"That doesn't count. And we're not even keeping score."

"Yeah, but we both know I'm up by six points."

"We said we weren't keeping score."

"I know you are in your head, chump. I'm you, remember?"

They stood facing each other, bodies slick with sweat, faces flushed, their waistbands wet. This was what Eddie could have looked like when he'd stepped into the ring with Rosa at the IA tryouts—like an animal. She shivered.

"What?" Eddie2 said. "You want to go?"

"Yeah. I want to go."

Then they lunged at each other, torsos twisted like tree trunks
in a tornado, landed on the concrete and rolled off it into the dirt
beyond the circle of light. A cloud of dust rose and settled onto
their backs. The night filled with the sound of grunts and hard
fists slamming solid muscle.

Grandma stalked over to them and shouted. "Edward Parker
Toivonen!" They ignored her. She leaned in and shouted, "Break
it up! Right now!" They hesitated for a second, and she grabbed
Band-Aid Eddie under the arms and hauled him back, sending
them both sprawling. She crawled out from under him and stood,
a hand on her back. "Damn it, Eddie, I'm too old for this." She
sighed. "Get up and shake hands."

They shuffled to their feet and gave a perfunctory handshake
without meeting each other's eyes.

"What is the issue here?" she said, and when neither answered,
"Talk. Now."

Eddie twisted his bloody mouth into a wry smile. "You can't
make me talk. You're not my real grandma."

Grandma barked a laugh. "Oh, lord. But you sure are Eddie."
She gave him a keen look. "It must be hard to see me again, after
you've buried me."

He mumbled, "My dad is a real dick. I needed you to stay alive."

"He's a dick here, too," Eddie2 said, walking over to retrieve
his shirt. "He got caught stealing a car when I was nine and went
to jail for a couple years. I don't see him much now, and I don't
want to."

"On our world, he went to jail later than that," Rosa whispered to Rosa2. "I guess he didn't get caught there. And then he did something worse." *He killed Lamar Sensenbrenner.* Her dark eyes regarded Rosa2 soberly.

"How was my funeral?" Grandma asked. "Did a lot of people come?"

Eddie shrugged. "Yeah."

"Excellent. Did you make a nice speech about me?"

He looked up at her, startled. "No. I was just trying to get through it without, you know . . ."

Grandma let that sink in. "Well, I think we should have a memorial for me."

"Like in *Tom Sawyer*," Rosa whispered.

Grandma heard and beamed. "Precisely. By all means, make a fuss. I'm worth it."

Rosa laughed. Grandma walked to the back door and brought out the case with the mutant bacteria. "Get me a shovel, would you?" Eddie2 headed into the barn. "I'm going to get rid of this, and then . . ."

"Eleanor, you can't just bury it in Oolitic, Indiana," Reg2 said.

"Why not?" Grandma said.

"Because," he broke off. "It's not *safe*."

"It's probably not a permanent solution," Grandma agreed. "But if they ever figure out who landed that craft, and that you came to Oolitic, it will drive them nuts looking for it here."

"If they look for freshly turned earth," Eddie said, "they'll find plenty." He gestured around them. "Indiana in the summertime."

"Precisely," Grandma said.

"You won't put it where a plow could break it open, will you?"
Reg asked.

"I am not an idiot," Grandma snapped. "We're going to get a
little sleep, and then we'll have a memorial brunch and see me out
properly." She shook her head. "If you want something done
right, you have to do it yourself." And with that she pitched the
ball into the barn and picked up the shovel and the small black
case of bacteria.

# CHAPTER THIRTY

Eddie woke up on the living room sofa, and for a long sweet moment he thought he'd fallen asleep on Sunday afternoon playing a video game or watching the Reds on TV. He stretched and his ribs hurt, and then he saw two Trevors sleeping on the floor, which for a second was horrifying, and not just because it was Trevor.

By the time Eddie kicked one of the Rosas out of the bathroom—he didn't know which one, but she scooted by in a towel—Trevor was coming down the hall.

"Hey," Trevor called. "Can I talk to you for a minute?"

"I gotta shower."

"Yeah. Um." Trevor looked around. "I have a multiple worlds' etiquette question."

"Etiquette? Oh, then I'm your guy," Eddie said.

"I want to make sure my butt's not getting infected."

Eddie shut his eyes and turned his head.

"What? It could be. The fence didn't necessarily cauterize it."

"It wasn't even a burn, Trev."

"I thought I could ask *him* to look at it. You know, since it's me. That would be okay, right?"

"Um . . ."

"Except I'm not sure I want him looking. I think he might be gay."

Eddie stared at him. "Um, Trev?" He just had no idea where to go with that, so he palmed Trevor's skull like a ball, turned him around, and then walked into the bathroom. There were some things Eddie didn't deal with before a shower.

By the time he got down to the kitchen, Grandma was cooking again and it smelled like buttered heaven.

"My grandma didn't have that shirt," he said.

She looked down at her navy polka dots. "There's bound to be some differences," she said. "I probably have a little more money here than I did there." He nodded, and thought about the new linoleum by the back door.

Her Eddie came in and his face looked a little lumpy and bruised, but mostly they'd gone for body punches. Eddie stood and extended a fist.

"My ribs feel like hell. Nice job."

Eddie2 grinned and bumped his knuckles. "Likewise."

"I can't believe you beat each other up," Trevor2 said.

Both Eddies shrugged. "I do it all the time," Eddie said, "one way or another."

"Eleanor," Reg said. "I'd really like to hear about extradimensional travel."

"Sorry," Grandma said. "Telling you would probably violate

some basic principle of independent development of multiple Earths."

"Says who?" said Reg.

"Captain Kirk?" Grandma said. Eddie snorted.

"We could use the help," Reg said. "Our NASA buys used parts off eBay because some of our equipment is so outdated, we can't find new ones."

She stared at him, and he held his fingers up like a Boy Scout. "Wow," Grandma said. She set a tray of blintzes on the table, hot and crackly with butter, their creamy filling oozing out. She looked at it and said, "My god, no wonder I had a stroke."

Eddie grinned at her, but across from him, her Eddie stared at his hands, and Eddie finally knew what Eddie2 had to fight about. Eddie was this guy's future—solo Eddie. Expanding-universe Eddie. Two-degrees-above-absolute-zero Eddie. Eddie2 couldn't punch the future, but he could sure hit him.

"About that spacecraft," Reg said.

"My memorial," Grandma said. "My rules."

They tucked into the food. Trevor scooped some blueberries onto his blintz. "Blueberries are great for the brain," he said.

"Don't stop yet," Eddie said, grabbing the spoon and shoveling more berries onto Trevor's plate.

"Ha-ha," Trevor said.

"So," Grandma said. "Tell stories about how great I am."

The Eddies exchanged a glance.

"Um, when I was six you mechanized my skateboard so I could get away from the bully down the block," her Eddie said. Grandma beamed.

"When I was a sophomore I got in trouble at school," Eddie said. Eddie2 looked curious. Apparently it hadn't happened to him. Not all their experiences were identical. "Some guys on the basketball team picked up the principal's car and moved it into the middle of the street so he'd get towed."

"Did you get suspended?" Rosa said, a tiny worry line creasing her forehead.

Eddie blew air out sharply. "It's Indiana. No, they did not suspend the basketball team." Her Eddie grinned. "And the thing is—*I wasn't even one of them.* But because of my dad, the principal assumed I was in on everything."

Grandma gave him a searching look.

"Afterward my grandma had to meet with him, and he was so condescending."

"Mr. Delacorte?" Grandma said. "Never did like him. He was rude to me?"

"Oh yeah. He all but patted you on the head."

Grandma stabbed her blintz.

"He kept referring to you as being older and having trouble keeping up with a kid. He made it sound like he was being understanding, but he was being a jerk."

"Tell me I got him," Grandma said.

"There was a game that Friday. Only one you ever missed. While we were on court in full view of the whole town, somebody disassembled Mr. Delacorte's car and reassembled it in the corridor outside his office."

Rosa gasped.

"And the doors were too narrow for him to drive it back out, right?" their Trevor said.

"Oh, yeah," Eddie said, grinning.

"But the security cameras . . . ," Rosa said.

"Rural Indiana."

"Oh."

"Ha!" Grandma said. "I checked the floor first for structural integrity, right? So I didn't damage the school?"

"I'm sure you did," Eddie said. "You're not irresponsible."

She smiled with satisfaction.

They told stories and ate melt-in-your-mouth blintzes and drank orange juice. Reg2 had tramped into the fields that morning and picked wildflowers. They were in a Mason jar on the table, adding to the sweet mix of scents. *It's so right*, Eddie thought, sitting there stuffing his face and telling stories. *And it will have to end*. It always did, because the universe bears everything away, faster than the speed of light.

"It's hard to believe all this is real," Rosa2 said, looking at her counterpart. "That *I* am."

"You are completely real, aren't you?" her Eddie asked.

Eddie shrugged. "Is anybody?"

Eddie2 pressed on. "We didn't have exactly the same experiences."

"That makes sense," Reg said, "as many variables as we're talking about. As many potential interactions."

"Maybe it's a psychosocial version of conservation of parity," Grandma said.

"Conservation of parity?" Trevor2 said.

"If the universe were perfectly symmetrical, you wouldn't be able to tell if you were watching things in a mirror or watching the events themselves. There'd be no way to know."

"You'd know you weren't near a mirror because Rosa takes so long in the bathroom," Trevor said. "Not much chance you're the one looking in it."

Both Rosas rolled their eyes at him.

"Things are a little lopsided," Grandma said. "Maybe it's so we can make distinctions." She shrugged. "It's the little imperfections that let you know you're real, and not a reflection."

And then it just came out. "I disobeyed a cop in a simulation," Eddie said. Her Eddie snapped his head up. "I don't think it was resisting arrest, but I'm not sure."

Eddie locked eyes with her grandson. His were serious and blue, and Eddie could have been looking in a mirror. Maybe he was.

"Reg," Grandma barked, "is there a reason you subjected my grandson to this?"

Reg shifted in his seat and wiped his mouth. "Um, someone broke into the personnel office and photocopied their psych profiles. I used Eddie to flush out the kid I thought had done it."

"I was in the simulation, too," Rosa said. "Eddie was just trying to save some people."

Grandma shot Reg a look and then stood to refill the juice pitcher. When she sat back down, she said, "Are you familiar with trolleyology?"

They looked around the table, confirming their mutual ignorance.

"It's a concept in ethics," Grandma said. "There are different scenarios, but essentially you see a runaway trolley about to
smash some people on the track. You could switch it to another
line, but there's one person on that track. If you let the trolley
proceed, five people die. If you send it another direction, only one
person will die—but you'll have deliberately killed him, because
he was in no danger at all from the trolley. His death is totally on
you." Grandma lifted another blintz onto her plate. "Do you pull
the switch lever?"

"You'd save five people," Trevor said.

"And kill one," Trevor2 said. "Imagine explaining it to his kids."

"There's a variation to the trolley scenarios," Grandma said.
"Say you're on a bridge above some railroad tracks, and a train
is coming. Its brakes are out . . ."

"Of course," Rosa said.

"And there are people on the tracks. They can't get off . . ."

"Why not?" Reg said.

"A guy with a handlebar mustache tied them to it," Grandma
said, exasperated. "Okay?"

Reg inclined his head.

"The only way to stop the train and save them is to throw
something heavy enough onto the tracks in front of the train."

"That would stop the train so suddenly that it would kill
everybody inside," Reg said.

"It's not a science problem," Grandma said. "It's an ethics
problem."

"Ah," Rosa said. "So the issue is, do you jump?"

"No. You're not big enough. But there's a stranger next to you

on the bridge who's much larger. He'd be big enough to stop it."
Grandma took a sip of her juice and wiped her mouth. "So—do
you push him?"

"I don't know," Eddie said, spearing the last blintz. "But I need
to bulk up in case I'm ever the other guy on the bridge."

"Eat a blintz, save a life," Trevor2 said. "Very public spirited
of you."

"There's no answer," Rosa said. "You can't let the people die
if you can stop it, and you can't shove somebody else in front of
a train."

"That's the answer," Grandma said. "Sometimes there is no
answer. You just do the best you can."

"I hope I never have to make a decision like that in real life,"
Eddie said with his mouth full. "I mean, so far this week I beat
myself up and almost drowned."

Grandma smiled a little sadly, and they stood to clear the
dishes.

# CHAPTER THIRTY-ONE

By the time the dogs down the road barked, the dishes were clean and dripping by the sink. Grandma exchanged a glance with Reg and walked out to the barn. Reg2 and the six trainees trailed her.

Reg climbed the hayloft ladder behind her. She raised the periscope and took a long look.

"It's Team 2," she barked. "They're alone, and they're coming fast." She twisted to look down at them. "I thought you said they were stranded on your Earth."

"We took their craft," Reg said, "and they said they couldn't communicate with your IA without it."

"Probably they missed a check-in, and IA went after them," Reg2 said.

"Damn it," Reg said, clambering back down the ladder. "Damn it, damn it, damn it."

"Okay," Reg2 said. "Eleanor, me, and myself made a plan last night for any unforeseen emergency. This is it." He hustled them out to Eddie2's truck. "Eddie, we're heading east. We're going to drive fast and leave tracks." Eddie2 grinned and swung into the driver's seat. Eyeliner Trevor hauled himself into the bed, but Rosa2 looked, stricken, at Rosa. They always knew they couldn't stay together, but neither thought they'd have to separate so soon.

"You're taking my car," Grandma said, pressing the keys into Rosa's hand.

"*She's* driving?" Eddie said.

"Reg says your reactions are fastest, but she's less likely to take a chance. Fair assessment?"

Rosa took the keys and walked toward the black Mercedes parked by the house.

"Yeah," Eddie said sullenly. "I guess that's fair. But crap."

"Not my respectable engineer car," Grandma said. "They'll expect to find that here. You're taking my hobby car."

She pulled the tarp off a hulking shape in the shadows, revealing a red minivan with a dented back bumper.

"Double crap," Eddie said. "No sports car?"

Grandma shook her head. "Did I have this in your world?"

"Nah. You drove the same car for like thirty years. Not a Mercedes."

"Ouch," Grandma said.

"Are you coming?" Rosa asked Grandma.

"No. I need to put those dishes away fast, before they can get in and count them. I'll tell them they were here," she said nodding toward the truckload of people from her world. "I'll think of some reason."

"Let's get out of here," Reg shouted.

Eddie2 started his engine, pulled the truck up to his grandma, and gave her a hug through the window. He cast a glance toward Eddie, riding shotgun in the van, and jerked his chin to him. Grandma leaned in and kissed Eddie2's cheek, then smacked the truck roof and he accelerated away from the farmhouse, bouncing down a dirt road between cornfields.

She came around to Eddie's window and crouched down to look at him. Rosa could see him in the side mirror, and he wore such a look of anguish that she had to turn away. This was why Grandma didn't want him to drive. She knew leaving would gut him and that he would need a minute to recover. A minute they didn't have.

"Eddie," she said softly. "Wherever I am, whichever I am, I'm loving you."

"Yeah," he said thickly, like he'd cut his tongue on the word and had a mouthful of blood. "Love you, Gram."

She grabbed his hand and held his fingers for a moment, then Rosa pulled forward and their hands fell apart and Eddie stared in the side mirror the whole time they drove down the back road, until they turned right and right again to come up on the paved road a mile behind Team 2.

Rosa drove fast, hands loose on the wheel, loving the power, before she remembered it was a minivan. It should have felt like driving a tub of butter.

"I think she modified the engine."

"Yeah," Trevor said from the seat behind Eddie.

Rosa was nearing a stop sign on the highway, so she twisted

to catch Reg's eye. "The others are luring them east. That means we go west?"

"Yeah," Reg said, pointing across the intersection to their road, stretching out before them. "I don't know what we're going to do, but I know where we need to do it. We're heading back to where we landed—to alien NASA."

Rosa pulled smoothly across the intersection and accelerated hard toward Iowa. It was high noon. There were no shadows. It was as though the world was perfectly symmetrical, and you couldn't tell if you were real or just looking in a mirror.

# CHAPTER THIRTY-TWO

Reg met her eyes in the rearview mirror. "I keep visualizing them opening that case in some Johnson County field." He shook his head. "That's not what civilized people do."

"And yet they're so much like us," Rosa said softly.

"Yeah," Trevor said. "Like, exactly like us."

"They'll know their trainees are gone," Reg said, "and they'll guess we went to them for help. It's a logical move."

"I don't think anybody looks at their own face and turns away," Rosa said.

Eddie snorted softly beside her. He had a point—he'd punched his own face. As far as Rosa knew, the only other person who had ever pulled that off was Eddie2.

"Hey," Trevor said. "What did you guys think about the eyeliner on that guy? I mean, was it weird?"

Rosa shrugged. "I don't usually like makeup on guys, but I think it worked. His haircut helped."

"I wonder if I could pull that look off," Trevor said.

She stared at him in the rearview mirror. "Trev—that *was* you. I mean, if he can . . ." She gave up.

"Sorry to turn the conversation from your *eyeliner*," Reg said, "to our *survival*."

Trevor shrugged. "They're probably sending someone to all our homes. They thought Oolitic was a good bet, and I'm guessing they sent the other team to Los Alamos," he said, looking at Rosa. "Your dad has connections. He could have helped us."

"He would have," she said. She was sure of it.

Reg squeezed her headrest like it was one of those balls to calm your nerves. "They'll come up empty. Then they'll start trying to guess our plan."

"Good luck with that," Eddie said. He still wasn't looking at anybody.

"Yeah," Trevor said. "Maybe we should ask them to let us know once they've figured it out. I'm a little fuzzy on the whole going-back thing," Trevor said. "Do we have, say, a plan?"

"I think there's only one thing we can do," Reg said. "We have to destroy their ability to access our world."

"In case they find the bacteria?" Trevor said.

"Yeah. And because I don't trust Sensenbrenner. If he'd do this, what else would he do?"

"That means wrecking their XD craft, right?" Rosa said. She caught his eye in the mirror. "I hear you have some experience with that."

"Damn it, Reginald! You should *not* have told them that."

"Could they just make more bacteria?" Trevor said.

"Wouldn't matter if they can't get it to our world," Reg said. "We're buying time here. And anyway, they can't just build another ship. The other Reg wouldn't tell me much about that coating, but he did say they have to grow it in a lab. All in one piece. Takes years."

Eddie didn't say anything. He stared down the road between the cornfields. A railroad track ran beside them, twin paths stretching before them, mile after mile, across this alien and familiar landscape.

"If we wreck the egg, we'll be stuck here," Trevor said.

Rosa's stomach twisted. How far was she from home? Could it even be calculated?

They drove in silence. When Rosa thought enough miles had rolled under the tires she said, "I liked your grandma."

Eddie glanced at her, then nodded and looked away. She thought he wasn't going to respond, but finally he said, "Almost everything is empty space—from the atom to the universe. Everything is empty." She didn't know what to say to that. "The laws of physics demand separation. Everything is pulled apart."

"Oh, baloney," Rosa said, before she thought about it. "The laws of physics say that we can't observe an electron because all our probes affect the observation. Observing an experiment changes the outcome. They've *proven* that, Eddie."

"I know," he said. "So what?"

"So our interactions *matter*. They *change* things. They actually *change the universe*."

"That's what life *is*," Reg said softly. "Empty space and how we fill it."

Rosa twisted and looked at him, because that was kind of

sensitive for Reg. He looked up from under his lids and swirled his finger, and she turned back to the road.

"There's no empty space around Rosa," Trevor said, "as much luggage as she carries. You're kind of a hoarder," he said to her.

"That's true," she said. "I fill my empty spaces with stuff."

"What do you fill your empty spaces with?" she asked.

He grinned at her in the mirror. "Antibiotics."

"Virtue and erudition for me," Reg said. She took a swipe at him over her shoulder, but he ducked.

"He's actually full of crap," Eddie said. He was a little perkier. Getting to insult people seemed to do that for him.

"You ever think about the fact that you're from Oolitic?" Reg said.

"Um?"

"Oolitic limestone is full of fossils—tiny shell fragments coated in carbonate. They look like little eggs."

"Yeah," Eddie said. "So?"

"You can see Oolitic as the past, or the future—as a fossil, or as an egg. You gotta decide which it is—if you're going to hatch or not."

"I'm not sure I want to *hatch*. And ooliths aren't actually . . ."

"Don't screw with my analogy. Hatch, damn you."

Rosa braked at a four-way stop, empty except for them, and looked both ways. Then she accelerated down the highway, heading straight for Iowa. In the distance, a train blew its whistle, long and lonely.

# CHAPTER THIRTY-THREE

"Did alien Reg tell you how many craft they have?" Rosa asked. She was still driving, even though Eddie had offered to take over six times.

Reg nodded. "So they've got the egg we flew, and two more in the hangar. He said they're extremely expensive to make—especially that coating on the outside. It's a class of substance we don't even know about yet. I tried to get specifics and he wouldn't give me a straight answer, the handsome bastard."

"So we need to break three eggs," Rosa said, "right?"

"Yeah," Reg said. "Let's go make an omelet."

The IA compound was set on land with very gentle hills—just rises, really. Not enough to hide their approach. Cornfields ended abruptly a few hundred yards from the launch perimeter, but the stench of an adjacent hog farm floated through. They passed the pharmacy where Eddie had gotten his vodka—except it was maybe a trillion miles from the store he'd been in. Reg pointed down the highway and Rosa drove on, taking an access road that skipped the main compound and came up on the launch area. It was a broad, flat road, used for heavy equipment. The light was failing, but the road and the launch area were lit as bright as noonday.

"That's a lot of lumens," Trevor said.

"Yeah," Reg said, squeezing Rosa's headrest again. "Well, we knew they'd see us."

A swarm of security vehicles was racing toward them from the command building, tires squealing. They were going to beat security to the egg hangar—but not by much. Rosa floored the van and it responded, motor humming smoothly. Bless Eddie's alien grandma.

"What are we going to do when we get there?" Rosa shouted. They could hear her, but her adrenaline was pumping.

"You remember the sequence to start the craft?" Reg shouted back.

"Yeah."

"I think we're gonna have to get somebody to pilot each of those eggs."

"How are we going to destroy them?" Eddie said, already unbuckling his seat belt. Rosa wasn't sure he fully understood the concept of safety precautions.

"We just crash them," Reg said, and now he needed to shout because the sound of a half-dozen security cars, pistons firing hard, underscored their conversation.

"They're designed for space travel," Trevor said. "A crash that's bad enough to break one of those shells is going to kill the pilot."

"Affirmative," Reg said.

A cold dread sat cradled in Rosa's hips. She stared straight ahead at the gray wall of the hangar coming at them. It was insanely huge.

"You thinking of ramming it?" Eddie said beside her.

She nodded, hands loose on the wheel.

"Don't. We could die in that crash. And we need to die breaking the eggs."

"If I survive this, I'm going to have a deep-seated fear of breakfast," Trevor said.

"I need to be one of the pilots," Reg said. "I'm the most experienced. Rosa should be one because she's one hell of a good driver. Eddie should be the third, because he responds well to danger."

Meaning he could probably pilot his egg straight into a crash without flinching. Without swerving. Rosa wasn't at all sure she could.

"Um," Trevor said. "And I do what?" His voice was high and tight.

"You're my copilot, Trev," Rosa said. "Remember?" She gave him the best smile she could. Copilot on a suicide mission wasn't much of an offer.

She ripped off the road to cut the angle and save a few yards, then rocked to a stop at the edge of the hangar.

They ran for the hangar doors. Eddie got to the enormous handles first and pulled, his back bunched, but the door didn't budge.

A line of security cars screamed down the tarmac toward them.

"An access panel," Reg said, catching sight of it beside the door frame and letting loose a flood of profanity. Rosa grabbed his hand and pressed his fingertips against the panel. The doors slid smoothly sideways.

They ran through the crack as the doors were still opening. Ahead of them were three white craft, each the size of a building. They split up, Trevor running alongside Rosa.

"I'm not going with you," he said.

"You scared, Trev? I am, too."

"Hell, yes." His voice didn't waiver. "But I'm going to march into their Flight Control Room and explain about the bacteria. I'll bet there's a lot of people here who don't know they were going to experiment on a planet with seven billion people."

"Trevor," she said, heaving on the craft door, "you'll be alone."

"I don't care. Sensenbrenner's *misusing science*. And I'm going to stop him, or die trying." He touched a finger to his forehead and ran off through the back of the hangar. Rosa had never seen courage like that, and she hadn't expected it from Trevor. It about slayed her.

Reg ran over, making a head-smack motion. She didn't know what he wanted, but he hauled himself in and pressed his thumb onto her control panel.

"Trev's staying," she said, and her lips quivered.

He gave Rosa a quick kiss on the cheek, then the craft acknowledged him and gave her access and he jumped out and ran to Eddie's craft. She wondered if he'd kiss Eddie, too. Eddie's cheek was an interesting thing, strangely muscular, the skin still smooth under the stubble—two things at one time, like Eddie himself.

She lowered the locking mechanism and sank into the commander's chair. *Commander Rosa Y. Hayashi of the Alien Eggforce.*

Her first solo flight was likely to be fatal. If not, she'd be captured and killed.

*God, I do not want to do this.*

What she had left was the chance to save the people at home. And not to screw up. What if Reg died ruining his craft, and Eddie in his, with his lips that dimpled at the corners and his blue, blue eyes—and she messed up and they still had a way to get back and kill her Earth?

She strapped in, aware of the irony in the act. Her headset crackled on as she settled it over her ears.

"Rosa? Eddie? Can you hear me?"

It was Reg's voice, with his soft Southern accent. She loved his voice right then, the richness of it, the way he lingered on some words, taking their full measure before moving on.

"Um, yeah," she said.

"Roger that," Eddie said.

*Drat. His sounded better.*

"No preflight check since it's okay to crash," Reg said. "I'm not fully fueled, but I've got enough in the tank for what we're doing."

"Me too," Rosa said.

"Same here." It was good to hear Eddie's voice through her headset. "We got a strategy?"

"No. Just get out there and crash."

"Trevor ran out the back," she said. "Did you see that?"

"Yeah," Eddie said. "He'll tell them what happened. With any luck that will bring Sensenbrenner down."

She could hear Reg's engine roar, then the craft to her right began to move toward the open doors. A line of security guards stood behind the doors of their vehicles, weapons drawn. The guards were between Trevor and Flight Control so he peeled off to the side, running toward the launch tower in an effort to out-flank them.

"Think their freaky alien ray guns can hurt us?" Eddie said.

"Nah," Reg said. "This craft can withstand space conditions. Besides, nobody wants to risk ruining something this expensive. It wouldn't be good for their career. Trust me." He revved his engine in warning and the guards scattered, running across the tarmac, leaving the vehicles parked in their way.

A slice of shadow fell across Reg's craft as he rolled past the gates, then he was again in the full glare of the tarmac lights. The sky beyond him was a darkening blue. Navy, really. Rosa's mother always told her to wear navy when she wasn't sure—you couldn't go wrong. Her eyes prickled, and she wiped her palm on her thigh, then put her craft in gear and followed Reg out the gates.

Eddie always had a third way. He thought so far out of the box that he couldn't even see the lettering on the side. *Time for a third way, Eddie. Because I do not want to do this.* As Rosa passed through the gate, his craft angled in behind her.

Reg took off, soaring into the sky. And maybe it was stupid, but given the circumstances Rosa didn't think it mattered: she pulled up a little slower, so that she snapped the door right off one of the security cars as she went by. She had about thirty seconds to live—but she got her teenage rebellion in.

In the distance a couple of security guards split off from the group by the hangar, blocking Trevor's line on Flight Control, and herded him toward the launch tower. Trevor reached the structure, calculated that he didn't have time for the elevator, and began to climb.

*Poor Trevor.* Rosa wondered if he was afraid of heights. He was afraid of everything else. She pulled back on the throttle and rose, then veered left and came around. The best way to help Trevor was to distract the guards.

Reg was making a spiral loop-de-loop in front of their Flight Control window, just like he'd done on their own Earth—his sign-off. He was singing faintly under his breath while he finished his loop and rose straight up, as though someone were lifting him with pinched fingers. He had much better control of his craft than Rosa had of hers. She was rocking and swaying, trying to maneuver. At least the guards going after Trevor stopped at the foot of the launch tower, confident they had him treed.

"You want to join me up here? We can dive together," Reg said.

"Nah," Eddie's voice came in Rosa's ear. He brought his craft around to face hers, maybe a couple of miles away. "I want Rosa to kill me."

Her heart contracted and she made a little gasp, then covered her mouth. She knew they could hear it. She took a long breath to steady herself. "Roger that," she said. "Air Rosa preparing for crash."

"Air Eddie is ready," he said, then, "Oh, man. Those are terrible last words."

"It's been a privilege," Reg said, and in the corner of her eye Rosa saw him drop toward the Earth.

She kept her eyes on the craft in front of her, perfectly symmetrical, like hers. She could have been looking in a mirror except that she could see Eddie behind the controls.

"'Bye, Rosa."

"'Bye, Eddie."

Then she opened the throttle at the same moment he did, and pushed the speed hard. She wanted to be at eight hundred miles per hour when they hit.

They closed so fast. Too fast. No time to think. No time to pray, or review her life, or even be afraid anymore. She felt . . . courageous. She felt strong. In the last seconds she could see Eddie's eyes. They were fastened on hers, blue and beautiful, and he was smiling faintly. She was glad he was the last thing she would see. Death had Eddie's eyes.

There was a flash of white. And then everything was dark.

# CHAPTER THIRTY-FOUR

Eddie had expected to experience the crash at least for a moment before he died—to hear the crumple of metal, maybe an explosion, to feel glass slice through his skin and tendons and trachea. Even at that speed, a moment of agony. He wanted that moment—to know all of life, even the end. Instead it was a sense of spinning, and everything went hazy gray. The only sound was the hum of the engine and the hammer of his heart.

His heart. Beating.

He blinked himself into full consciousness, trying furiously to focus. Had Rosa pulled away at the last moment? He'd been watching her eyes, brown and calm. She hadn't looked afraid. He glanced down—his torso was still strapped in, still had a limb attached at each corner. Nothing severed.

"Near collision," a woman's calm voice said through his earphones. It wasn't Rosa. "Are you ready to resume command?"

*The freaking control panel? What was this, like a car that won't let you hit the one behind it?* He looked frantically out the window, but Rosa was behind him and the controls wouldn't respond.

"Yes! Yes, I'm resuming command."

"Proceed with caution," the voice said pleasantly. "There are two other vehicles in the area."

He banked hard and saw Rosa's egg ahead of him, where it had angled off. He chased it, and on the way saw Reg rise to his side. Reg's eyes were comically huge, and he took one hand off the controls to make an exaggerated shrug. His craft was in perfect shape—no catastrophic damage. The bottom didn't even look dented.

The spacecraft refused to die.

Rosa's craft had slowed to a cruising speed, and Eddie pulled alongside, maybe thirty yards away. It was closer than he'd get in any other circumstance—but since they were trying to crash, and it was apparently impossible, there didn't seem to be a downside. She was sitting slumped in the chair, her head bobbing slightly, and even from here he could see the way her hair fell over her cheekbone. He wished he could tuck it behind her ear for her.

She was coming back to consciousness. When their crafts swerved to avoid each other, she must have gotten whipped around harder. Or maybe it was just because she didn't have a whole lot in the way of neck muscles to stabilize her head. Eddie always paid attention to his neck when he lifted weights. He figured he needed to—people wanted to rip his head off with some frequency.

"Houston," Reg said, "we haven't had a problem."

"I don't know," Eddie said into his headset mouthpiece, "I'm not sure my pants are still clean."

"Eww," Rosa said.

*Seriously?—that's when she regains consciousness?* Eddie looked over at her, flying beside him.

"Hey," he said.

"Hey."

"I'm glad you're alive."

"I'm glad you're alive, too, Eddie." For some reason that made his eyes prickle. His craft rocked, and he turned his attention back to the controls.

"Nobody's glad I'm alive?" Reg said, zooming up on his other side and waving—honest to god waving—at them.

"We knew you'd survive," Eddie said. "The Earth wouldn't accept you. It's like a blessed river spitting a witch back up."

"Sounds about right," Reg said. He pulled in a little closer and said something, but Eddie didn't catch it because he was shouting.

"Hey, give me some space! I don't know how to fly this thing."

"Yeah," Rosa said. "I just knew enough to crash it."

"Stay calm," Reg said. "You both know how to go up and down, right and left. How to adjust for a steady course."

"How to run out of gas," Eddie said.

"Apparently it won't let you crash it, at least," Reg said.

"But now we have to fly them, and that's kind of nerve-racking," Rosa said.

Eddie nodded. "Dang, Reg. There's a lot of switches on this thing."

"We need a new strategy," Reg said. "There's a whole lot of

faces pressed to the Flight Control Room glass, just watching us. See that?"

They did. It wasn't comforting.

"They knew we couldn't scramble their eggs."

"So they're waiting for us to land and get arrested?" Rosa said.

"That appears to be an affirmative," Reg said. "Guess that's why they didn't go for a shoot-out at the hangar. Probably assumed we were armed, and they could just wait."

"Can we hit other things?" Eddie said. "I mean, could we crash into Flight Control?"

"I took a door off a car," Rosa said. "Just 'cause I'm a hellion."

"I love it when you talk like that," Eddie said.

"So maybe the door was small enough that it didn't register," Reg said.

"I was still on the ground, too," Rosa said. "Maybe that makes a difference?"

"We're overlooking something," Eddie said. "If we just bounce off each other, these are the world's best bumper cars. If arrest and execution are inevitable, I'm getting in a game first."

"Never known you to give up," Reg said. That stung a little, but Eddie wasn't letting him know.

"I'm not giving up," he said. "It's just that the lure of bumper cars is irresistible."

"I could try to fly into Flight Control and see if I bounce off," Reg said. "It may be that the no-crash protection is only with other vehicles—that it requires a sensor on both crafts. If I make it"— meaning if he died in an inferno of twisted metal—"you just follow me in."

"*We* could be in there," Rosa said. "What if our alien selves doubled back and are in the Flight Control Room?"

"If we're here, our asses should be out on the tarmac thinking something up," Eddie groused. They'd flown several miles past the IA compound, past the town where Eddie got his vodka. Reg banked left and they followed, moving back toward the IA base. "Hey, what if we just flew them into the ocean?"

"They could recover them," Reg said. "Even if the craft let us go down." He blew air out sharply, and it amplified in the headset. Eddie jerked his head back from the sound, then made a quick correction. "We need some way to keep Sensenbrenner from getting back to our world, at least for a while. At least till we're ready."

"Rosa, okay if I sideswipe you?" Eddie asked.

"Sure thing," she said.

He was afraid to. Maybe the craft's protection was only for head-ons. And maybe he was about to knock her out of control and send her spiraling to her death. He didn't think so, but he did wait till they'd cleared the town, to protect the innocent civilians and vodka bottles below. Then he bashed into her side.

Her craft repelled him. It was like two magnets with the same pole—you can push them toward each other, but there's a force pushing them apart. He bounced back without touching her, didn't correct in time, and bounced off Reg on the other side. He grinned and did it again.

"Damn, boy!" Reg said. He could grumble all he wanted. Eddie knew he was just pissed that he wasn't the one flying in the middle. "So, about flying into the command building . . ."

"No," Eddie said. "I'm not doing it. I'm not killing anybody." He was not his father.

"Yeah," Reg said. "I was thinking a pass-by first, to signal our intentions. So people could run away."

"Not good enough," Eddie said. "Look, I tried to kill Rosa, and it was less enjoyable than you'd imagine."

"Wow," Rosa said. "You are *such* a flatterer."

"I won't risk killing anybody else." Eddie spread his hands gently over the switches in front of him, careful not to reposition any of them. He had no idea how to fly this thing. Rosa was flying more smoothly than he was. She was a better driver, too, if you liked smooth deceleration. A small difference, but small differences can be decisive.

Especially when your idea is particularly dumbass. "Anybody up for a plan that offers a slim chance of survival?"

"Oh god, yes," Rosa said. "Please, yes."

They had shot over the IA compound and were heading past it.

"Reg, do we have enough fuel in these to break free of Earth's gravity?"

"To get into space?" He was silent for a moment. "Yeah, I think so, but I don't think we could make it home."

"Could we get into extradimensional space?"

"I dunno. But there's no point . . ."

"We don't have to crash these things," Eddie said. "We just have to get them out of their hands, right?"

"Right," Reg said. Then he understood. "You're thinking we just fly into the extra dimensions and run out of fuel there? Just sit and watch each other die?" He massaged the top of his head over his headset, making the skin ripple. "I say we try to crash one more time first. Starvation, freezing, asphyxiation—it would be a gruesome death, Eddie."

"Nah," he said. "We just send the craft off where they can't reclaim them. We get a chance to plead our case—expose Sensenbrenner as a murderous asswipe, which may help this world as well as ours. Maybe we go to jail, but maybe we don't."

"I like this," Rosa said. "I like this a lot."

"Yeah," Reg said, and they could hear the disappointment in his voice. "Problem is, these won't take off on autopilot. We'd have to send them from the air, and there's no way to do that without stranding the pilot."

"Sure there is," Eddie said. "I just open the door and jump."

They were silent. Reg stared at him through the curved side of his windshield.

"It's just the way you'd do it on a highway," Eddie said, "jumping from one car to another with your friends."

"There is so much wrong with what you just said," Reg said.

"Who would be the pilot?" Rosa said. "And who would be the jumper?"

"Rosa, you drive better than me, right?"

"Oh, definitely." She flashed her white grin at him and gave a little finger wave.

"Yeah, you get cheeky when you're in an indestructible spacecraft," he said.

She nodded.

"You fly the egg," Eddie said. "And I'll just open the door and hop in."

# CHAPTER THIRTY-FIVE

"Oh boy," Rosa said. "Couldn't you jump into Reg's craft? He can hold his egg steadier." She already knew what he was going to say. Rosa was smart. She just needed to hear him say it.

"No. Because it should be his ship we land in when you jump, too."

"Oh boy."

"Yeah," Reg said. "We have to scuttle two of these. Then we can bail together when we send the last one off."

"Trevor will have cellmates," Eddie said, then caught Rosa's expression. "What? I'm looking on the bright side." He inspected the ground for a moment. "Should I make the jump over a cornfield? The rows will give Rosa a visual for a steady course."

"Some people use the instrument panel for that," Reg said.

"Those are people who know how to fly," Rosa said.

"Gulp," Eddie said.

"Oh. Sorry."

"Reg," he said, "I checked the glove compartment, but there's no owner's manual, just a bunch of leftover napkins and straws. You got any idea how to unlock that hatch?"

"You can just unlatch it," he said. "There's nothing fancy about it."

"If you're really doing this, we need two things," Rosa said. "First, we need to be lined up with the field, going low and slow."

"What's the second thing?"

"You've got to program the craft to get it out of here. Reg, can we put the navigational instructions on time delay?"

"How should I know?" Reg said. "Don't count on it. But, Eddie, you need it to dump its fuel once it gets into extradimensional space. Otherwise they could just recall it on autopilot."

"Holy crap," he said, because he had not thought of that. "How do I do that?"

Reg talked him through it. "The fuel dump will engage with your new course, when you hit enter."

"Okay," he said. "I'm going."

Eddie banked, pinging off Reg's side until he got the idea and curved with him. They made a big sweep around so that all three of them were lined up, the furrows stretching before them. God bless some farmer who could plow straight. Rosa dropped down low and decreased her speed. Eddie stayed alongside her.

"You're gonna get sucked by the air," Reg shouted. "It's gonna smack you hard."

"It's as though you think I've never stood on a pickup," Eddie said, unstrapping. He climbed out of the seat, took a deep breath, and unlocked the door. "I only regret that I have but one life to lose doing stupid stunts." He was getting better at last words.

He opened the door. The air whipped at his face.

"Taking off my headset," he shouted into the mouthpiece.

"Roger that," Rosa said.

"Hey, Eddie," Reg said. "When you change the destination, it's going to shoot into space. You know that, right?"

"Yeah," he said.

"Don't get caught half out the door," he said.

*Crap.* He didn't really need the reminder.

Eddie flipped his headset onto the seat. He was probably about to die. He wondered if somewhere, some Eddie was about to feel inexplicably lonely.

He entered their Earth as the new destination and requested autopilot. Then he pressed enter, ran a step to the door, and dove headfirst into space.

The wind smacked the side of his face. Rosa had her ship ten feet away and a little lower and a little behind his, and for a moment he was flying and saw a sliver of cornstalks pointed at him, pike-like, on the ground below. Then he fell into Rosa's ship, landing hard on all sorts of unyielding surfaces. He grabbed hold of a seat but his legs hung out. The air dragged on them, wanting to pull him into the sky, luring him with the promise of flight but the certainty of a fall.

"Oh god," Rosa said. "Get in, Eddie. Get in, get in."

He pulled himself forward, biceps straining. When he was in he kicked the door shut, then stood and latched it.

"The Hoosier has landed," Rosa said, and Eddie could hear her smile.

"He's in?" Reg said, faint through her headset.

"Affirmative," Rosa said.

"I can't believe that worked," Reg said.

"That was awesome, Eddie!" Eddie shouted. "You are such a stud, Eddie!" He climbed over to sit next to Rosa. He slipped the headset on and grinned at her. She beamed back at him.

"You want me to call you a stud?" Reg said.

"Okay, now it seems creepy."

He spent a minute just looking at Rosa, watching her pilot the ship. She glanced sideways at him, but he didn't look away.

"You had the ship positioned just right," he finally said.

"That was the idea."

And then she leaned over and kissed him. He put a hand on her back, felt her spine curve under his palm, and returned her kiss. In the corner of his eye he could see his craft shooting off into the upper atmosphere.

"You ready to jump?" Reg said in their headsets.

They didn't answer. Their lips were busy.

"Hey," he said. "You two okay in there?"

"Mm-hmm," Rosa said.

"What am I hearing?" Reg demanded. "Are you *kissing*? Damn it, we have two more ships to scuttle."

"In the movies, romantic scenes have a better sound track," Eddie said. It came out a little muffled, because she was still attached to his lower lip.

"Yeah," she said. "Hey, Reg, you got a violin on board?" Her eyes sparkled.

"*Damn* it," Reg said, and then he was reduced to sputtering.

"You want to jump?" Eddie said.

"No," she said. He reached over and unsnapped her harness, and she unsnapped his.

"Eddie, would you go first?"

He shook his head. "No."

She looked surprised. "I thought maybe you could help pull me into the craft."

"That's not our best option," he said, pointing toward the ground. Security forces were scrambling on the tarmac. They seemed to have figured out that the three were systematically removing the spacecraft from their control. And they were brandishing some sort of weaponry.

"They won't fire at the first one to jump. Their reactions won't be fast enough. They'll shoot at the second one out."

"Oh," she said. "Going first sounds okay." She smiled at him. One thing he knew was that Rosa Hayashi had a great smile, and that was a fact.

"Rosa's going first," he said into the headset. "Remember there will be two of us."

"Rosa, don't hesitate or Eddie will lose his chance," Reg said. "There's two of you jumping, but there won't be more time to make the jump. You understand?"

She nodded seriously, even though he couldn't see her, and angled her purse strap across her chest.

"You're bringing your *purse*?" Eddie said. "We're jumping out of spacecraft here." She shrugged. "That's crazy, Rosa. Just leave it. You can replace your library card later."

"I'm still having my period, you knucklehead. If I survive, I'll need my accessories."

"Audio's on," Reg barked.

"Oh. That . . . process . . . doesn't have, like, an emergency off button?" She stared at him. "I mean, even escalators have those." Eddie shrugged. "Seems like a design flaw."

Rosa swooped the craft back around and lined up with a cornfield.

"Taking headsets off," she said.

"Thank God," Reg said. "As soon as we're over that pig farm, we're good to go."

Rosa tapped in the new destination, but didn't press enter. She got into position by the door and gave Eddie a long look. He knew she didn't want to jump. He figured her odds of landing safely at fifty-fifty; she probably calculated them lower. And the longer she thought about it, the worse it would get. His odds of even getting a chance to jump were slim.

And Eddie figured that calculation showed him for a fool, because this was Rosa Hayashi. She slid the hatch door open, steadied herself against the wind, then flung herself out of the craft.

She did it within a second—she wasn't going to hurt Eddie's chances. If he didn't make it, it would be his own fault.

Eddie pressed enter on the control panel and flung himself out after her. He didn't get a good visual until he was already airborne—Rosa hadn't jumped far enough to stick her landing. She was hanging out the side, holding on to the rubber door seal with her fingers, her body flying alongside the craft, buffeted by the wind, her bag bouncing off her hip. She had no hope of pulling herself in, and that was if nothing disturbed her grip.

He was going to hit her as he flew into the open hatch. He was going to break her grip, and there was nothing he could do about it.

Something whistled past him, bouncing off the egg's side without leaving a mark. The security forces on the ground were shooting at them, but he didn't care, because he was focused on the inside of Reg's craft, and what he could grab onto.

He missed Rosa's body because the slipstream pulled her to the side but hit her arms with his thighs and broke her grip. He grabbed hold of the bottom of the pilot's seat with his right hand and held on like the world depended on it, because it did.

As Rosa flew loose her purse strap caught on his foot and he jacked his toe up to keep hold of it. She reached up, desperate, and clawed at his jeans hem, and pulled herself up until his legs grabbed her like tongs. They hung out the side of the hatch, his legs around her.

Her fingers scrabbled up his pants, caught the front pocket of his jeans, and then she crawled slowly up him until she could reach the hatch.

Reg finally figured out that they weren't inside. He tipped slowly up so that they were on top of the craft and flew the egg on its side, letting them ride on top. Eddie couldn't figure how he'd ever crashed—the guy was a good pilot.

Rosa pulled herself inside and then grabbed Eddie's wrist and hauled him in. She grabbed the door and began to heave it shut, and Eddie put his hand over hers so they would do it together.

Then Reg tipped the egg back upright, and they nearly tumbled out.

"Jeez, Reg!" Eddie shouted. "What even the heck?"

They slammed the hatch shut and locked it down hard.

"Here comes the hard part," Reg said.

"Yeah?" Eddie said, his hands on Rosa's waist, lifting her over the back of the pilot's seat so she could sit beside Reg. "Says the man who didn't just jump—twice."

"Nope," Reg acknowledged. "We need to eject someplace soft when we scuttle the last egg. I've been thinking about it—the softest thing around is the mud at that pig farm."

"No," Rosa said.

"We'll . . ."

"*No*," she repeated. "I am not exiting a spacecraft in flight again, ever. And no way am I going to jump out of a moving craft into *pig slop*."

"It's not slop," Eddie said. "Slop is food."

"Can it, farm boy," Rosa said. "I'm saying, why scuttle the last egg? If we can figure out how to refuel it and pick up Trev, we could just go home."

They stared at her and then at each other. Because that was a good idea.

# CHAPTER THIRTY-SIX

"Reg," Rosa said, "does it mean anything that Eddie and I still have legs?"

"It means something to Eddie," Eddie said.

Reg looked sideways at her, flipped a switch overhead, and then made an adjustment with the throttle. "Huh. It means the egg didn't burn them off. Which means that there was no great gush of fire coming from that craft when it changed its mode of flight."

"It was really hot," Eddie said.

Reg was excited now. "These eggs are capable of flying as airplanes, as spacecraft, and in extradimensional space—and we don't even know what that involves. But they can switch from one to the other seamlessly."

Rosa nodded. "Which might mean they're using the same fuel source for each type of flight."

"No bloom of fire," Reg said.

"It was really hot," Eddie said. "It hurt."

"No rocket boosters fell away," Rosa said. "No mashed Rosa and Eddie."

"Eddie was very uncomfortable," he said. "Eddie would like some acknowledgment of his suffering."

"Psssh," Reg said. "Eddie, what does the fact that you still have legs tell you?"

"That my heroics were successful, if undervalued?"

Rosa looked at him from under her brows. Reg took the craft into a shallow dive, so they could see IA2 spread out before them.

"Their teams just appeared on our runway, right? They didn't do some long descent through the stratosphere. They must just have come . . ."

"Straight from the extra dimensions," Reg said. "They're sewn onto the universe like a batting to a quilt."

"They're everywhere," Rosa said. "Not like a portal you have to fly to."

"Yeah," Eddie said. "You don't have to open a wardrobe and walk through." He looked defensive. "What? I like to read."

"Let's pick up Trevor," Rosa said. "And then get out of here."

"He climbed to the top of the tower," Reg said. "See him?" He pointed to a little guy sitting on top of the launch tower platform, swinging his legs. He looked like a photo Rosa had seen of Depression-era steelworkers having lunch on a beam way over the city they were building.

"Guess he's not afraid of heights," she said.

"This thing won't hover," Reg said. "I can go slow, but he's gonna have to jump."

"That's gonna be hard," Rosa said.

"Hey, just circle for a minute," Eddie said, pulling his cell phone out of his pocket. "I want to make a call."

Sometimes the smallest decisions are the most catastrophic.

"Your cell isn't going to work here," Reg said. "You won't have the same phone number. The worlds don't line up that closely."

"It's from this Earth," he said. "I stole it from myself when we were saying good-bye at Grandma's."

Rosa's eyes popped.

"I thought I might need it. Anyway, he's got a truck."

She narrowed one eye at him.

"What? It's mine."

She rolled her eyes. He opened the hatch and stood beside it, holding the phone out. He pushed "1" on speed dial. She could hear it ring—eight times. A person could climb two stairs in the time each ring took. And a person was.

"Hello?"

Rosa could hear a voice, faint but clear. It made her smile. She wondered what hearing it did to Eddie.

"Grandma? It's Eddie."

"Eddie! Did the Reds win? I haven't seen the score yet."

"Um, I don't know."

She was silent for a moment. "You're not the Eddie who drove to Cincinnati and stayed for a Reds game."

"No. I'm the Eddie currently circling the launch tower at your IA headquarters."

"Well," she said, "I'm well blessed with Eddies. What do you need?"

"How do we fuel up this egg? The spacecraft, I mean."

"Oh, that's hard. But why do you need to?"

"Um. We need to get home."

"I know. But you don't need much fuel. Didn't you notice how small the fuel cell is that's on right now?"

"But we're going *home*. It's . . . a long way."

He could hear the smile when she spoke. "No, it's not. If you go into extradimensional travel immediately, you won't need much fuel. You should make it just fine. It would be even faster, but we've rerouted to avoid junk we left in the extra dimensions from our first attempts at traveling there."

"You littered in the extra dimensions? Oh, Grandma."

She laughed. "Just go straight to XD. And leave your cell phone on the tower, will you? You're gonna be mad about that."

Eddie grinned. She was right. "Yeah. Thanks, Grandma."

"You're welcome, Eddie. Love you." He clicked off. And looked up.

"Aw, crap."

# CHAPTER THIRTY-SEVEN

Trevor was climbing down the gray tubular scaffolding of the launch tower, and he was moving fast. Neither safe nor smart, and so uncharacteristic for Trevor—but he was being trailed by a guy with a gun.

Eddie slammed the hatch shut and climbed back up behind Rosa's seat so he could watch from the front as Reg swung the egg around and circled the tower. The guy was wearing khakis and a polo shirt and athletic shoes. He was middle-aged.

"Sensenbrenner?" Reg said.

"Yeah." Eddie had seen a younger photo of him in the newspaper when he'd died in West Lafayette—when Eddie's old man jacked Sensenbrenner's car, pistol-whipped him when he gave the old man lip, and then ran him over.

Trevor stopped and put one hand in the air. He could only let go with one hand. Sensenbrenner waved the gun at him, directing him to walk along the beam below him. Trevor moved slowly until he was up next to the track for the emergency egress system—the roller coaster.

Sensenbrenner motioned to him. Trevor hesitated, then climbed over the railing and stood with his feet on a tie, holding a higher tie with both hands. There was no railing. It was a clever way to keep Trevor occupied—the emergency egress track fell away from the tower at an almost ninety-degree angle—meaning Trevor was going to hold on with both hands. Sensenbrenner talked into a mic on his shirt, and his voice came through on the control panel. Nice audio system.

"Land that craft right now, and come out with your hands up."

"So you can shoot us?" Reg said, flipping a switch so the man could hear them.

"Not unless you run," Sensenbrenner said.

Reg snorted softly.

"Get out here!" Sensenbrenner snarled.

Eddie waggled a finger at Reg, and he flipped the switch off. "I'm going out," he said. "I can't do anything up here to help Trev."

"You are not getting out of this craft!" Reg said.

"Well what are we going to do, then? Are you seriously going to fly away and just leave him?" Trevor had been willing to stay, but that was when the rest of them were planning to die. Leave him now, when they were just flying home?

Reg was silent. He stared at his hand on the control.

"Is there any possibility that we're not going to try to save him? Reg, he's the man on the tracks."

"I should be the one to go after him," Reg said.

"We need you flying this thing," Rosa said. She unsnapped her restraint and stood. "I'll go. I'm a smaller target."

"No," Eddie said. "I can reach between rows of scaffolding and you can't."

"We both have to go, Eddie. The only way to save him is to get down to where he is. And we're going to have to do it together."

Her dark eyes were sure.

"Do not do this!" Reg shouted, but his attention was on the controls. He was flying in tight circles around the tower. He was going as slowly as he could, but he couldn't risk engaging the no-crash system. Then the egg would bounce away while they were jumping.

"Hayashi and Toivonen," Eddie said. "Team 3." Then he flicked his finger again, and Reg flipped the audio back on.

"We're coming out!" Eddie shouted, even though Sensenbrenner could probably hear him okay. "If you treat us right, Reg will surrender himself and the craft." That was a lie, too. But with any luck, it would keep him from shooting them as they jumped.

Reg fine-tuned his course as he started a pass in front of the launch tower. He dipped his head in acknowledgment. Eddie squeezed Rosa's hand and threw the door open. Then they jumped.

Reg had them about twelve feet from the top platform, which was incredibly close when you were flying a space egg, and probably as close as its crash-prevention system would allow. But it was awfully far when you were jumping. If they hadn't started above the platform, they wouldn't have made it. As it was, Rosa

landed close enough to the edge that the railing scraped her butt
as she fell. They lay sprawled on the platform.

"You okay?" Eddie asked.

She nodded, but rubbed her backside and stood, walking a couple
of steps in place. Then she nodded again, sure this time.

"You?" she said.

"I think my adrenal glands exploded."

"Get down here!" Sensenbrenner shouted.

A few IA security guys were gathered at the bottom of the
tower, unsure whether to go up or control access from the ground.
Sensenbrenner stood on a beam ten feet below Rosa and Eddie,
right above Trevor. He was going to want them to climb down
where he could see them. Eddie didn't want to, not because they'd
be so vulnerable scrambling down the outside of the tower, their
arms and brains all occupied with not falling. He didn't want to
go down because once they got to where Sensenbrenner wanted
them, they'd be stuck on the tracks with Trevor. And then he'd yell
for Reg to surrender. And what could Reg do?

"Can you see them?" Eddie whispered. Rosa was standing, and
he was still sitting on the platform.

She shook her head. "They're too close. I've got a visual on
the guards at the bottom of the tower. Two of them are missing—
heading for the elevator, probably."

Eddie nodded. If they didn't hurry, they'd have company
up there.

"Get moving!" Sensenbrenner shouted. "Go to the left post
and start climbing down. Eddie first."

"Aw, you know my name. I'm touched."

Rosa made why-are-you-so-stupid eyes at him. Eddie thought maybe she was right—he shouldn't piss Sensenbrenner off, given what he was going to do next. "Don't shoot," he yelled down. "I'm just gonna peek over to get my bearings."

He did, and saw something so unexpected and beautiful that he wanted to smile. Sensenbrenner stood on the first beam below the platform, right beside the roller coaster track, his gun pointed at where they'd landed. He wasn't paying attention to Trevor at all. People underestimated Trevor. That wasn't a smart thing to do.

Trevor was standing on the track below Sensenbrenner, and had reached his right arm between the ties. While the IA director was glowering at Eddie and waving his gun around, Trevor was very gently untying his shoes.

Once he got them untied, Trevor tied them together, looped around one of the narrow pipes Sensenbrenner was standing on. The lowest possible tech solution.

Eddie wanted to laugh. He pulled his head back and laid alien Eddie's phone above Sensenbrenner so they couldn't misjudge the spot, then in a rushed whisper told Rosa what Trevor had done. They argued for a moment about who should do what came next, but she was so much smaller that Eddie had to concede. Besides, Sensenbrenner wanted Eddie where he could see him. He was underestimating Rosa, too.

Eddie moved to the left of the tower platform, making sure his footfalls were plenty loud.

"Okay, I'm on my way," he called.

"I can't believe you came down here," Sensenbrenner called. "You can't get any stupider than that."

"You underestimate me," he said. "Hey, Trevor? How good was your kindergarten teacher?"

"Spectacular," Trevor shouted up. "Mrs. Hufford was the best."

"Good to know," Eddie said, and scrambled faster, keeping Sensenbrenner's attention focused on him. He tried not to look into the gun pointed at him like all the emptiness in the world concentrated into one hollow point.

Rosa swung off the edge of the platform and landed on Sensenbrenner.

The beam he was on was made of two long, thin pipes with short pipes angled between them, like the corrugation in a cardboard box. It provided strength, and still let the wind blow through. Good design, unless you found yourself having to move backward on one of the beams.

Sensenbrenner tried to move his feet, couldn't, and teetered off the edge of the beam right as Rosa grabbed his torso and swung off with him. Trevor's knots held. A long moment later the gun made a tiny *plink* on the concrete below.

Rosa swung around so she was headed back up. She wiggled free of Sensenbrenner's flailing arms, used his crotch as a step, and pulled herself onto the beam. He swung helplessly by his feet. She crawled toward Trevor.

Eddie stepped off the column he had been climbing down and out onto the beam, then followed her example, because it was really high, and there was a bit of a breeze, and he was getting tired of this crap.

Sensenbrenner tried to pull himself up. He hooked his left fingers over the piping, but Eddie pried them off, letting him swing back down. Sensenbrenner screamed as he dropped backward, and tried a couple more times to pull himself up, but didn't have the abs for it.

Rosa grabbed the ties above Trevor and pulled herself onto the almost vertical track. Eddie crawled over Sensenbrenner's feet. He could have untied his shoelaces. It might have done the world a favor—two worlds. But he wasn't his father.

"You magnificent bastard!" Eddie said to Trevor when he reached them.

Trevor grinned at him. "Let's take a roller coaster ride."

Rosa led the way. Trevor crawled up the track after her, and Eddie followed him, trying not to look down because they were seriously high, and not to look up because that was Trevor's ass.

# CHAPTER THIRTY-EIGHT

"You want a front seat?" Rosa asked Trevor, slipping into one herself.

"Back's good," Trevor said.

Eddie climbed in next to Rosa, and she pulled the lever up and they shot forward and then down, riding the emergency egress coaster away from the control tower. They threw their arms over their heads and screamed. They'd needed to scream for a while.

They zoomed right past the security guards at the bottom of the structure, rode to the end of the line, and ran for it. Reg swooped past the Flight Control Room and hit the runway, heading away from IA instead of toward it. He braked as fast as he could, but still ended up a half mile beyond where the roller coaster track ended.

The IA2 security forces were chasing them, but they had a head start and were going to make it. One of the security guys was headed in the other direction—going for a car, probably—but the time he'd lose going back for it canceled the speed advantage he'd have later.

They reached the egg, breathless and grinning, and hauled each other up into it. Reg slammed the door shut behind them and vaulted back into the commander's seat.

"Holy crap, Hayashi!" he said. "You have a future in the circus."

Rosa grinned, then gave both of the younger guys a kiss on the cheek. Trevor blushed, and Eddie waggled an eyebrow at her. She climbed into the pilot's seat beside Reg, and he took off.

"Damn it, Reginald."

"Oh," Rosa said. "We started halfway down the runway."

He nodded, concentrating furiously, trying to get the lift he needed. The pig farm was coming at them, fast, and just at the last moment the animals seemed to notice them. They started to run away, squealing, and as the egg clipped the fence and rose, just clearing the first line of trees around the farm buildings, the hogs rushed in the other direction and spilled out onto the runway.

"He looks like Mussolini hanging off the meat hook," Trevor said, looking back at Sensenbrenner, already tiny in the distance, as his security guys scrambled toward him.

Rosa leaned back to give Eddie a high five.

"It's a good thing you came," he said. "I'm too heavy—I'd have broken the shoelaces."

"Yeah," she said. "You would have."

"It was hard to let somebody else rush in and do the stupid stuff, though." He grinned at her. "I'm working on it. I'm trying not to die on every hill."

"We should put up a plaque," Trevor said. "Eddie Toivonen didn't die here."

"Going into XD flight," Reg said. "Everybody shut up, 'cause this gives me the willies."

They shut up. It gave them the willies, too.

They went from normal airplane altitude to the encompassing blackness of the extra dimensions, and Rosa's hair floated up around her head.

# CHAPTER THIRTY-NINE

They sang railroad songs on the way home, and that was Trevor's fault. Rosa was looking out the window into the nothing and said, "I think this is Nietzsche's abyss."

"When you gaze long into the abyss, the abyss gazes also into you," Eddie said.

She nodded.

Then Trevor started singing about being five hundred miles away from home and they all joined in. And it was crazy, because they were probably five trillion miles from home. And also right next to it. This was stuff none of them understood, which made them kind of crack up. Hence the railroad songs.

They were working on the railroad all the livelong day when Reg said, "Hang on," and the control panel voice said, "Leaving extradimensional space." Suddenly they were in sunlight and everything sparkled, and their world was low and green and beautiful before them.

"I'll be damned," Reg said. "We still have gas." It wasn't gas, it was nitrogen tetroxide and monomethylhydrazine, but that wasn't his point. "Going straight from airplane height to XD saves a ton of fuel. Gotta remember that."

"They're okay, don't you think?" Rosa said. "The people who were in our Flight Control Room?"

"Yeah," Reg said. "It sounded like the alien teams were just disabling our people so they could go get their bacteria."

"They couldn't have just blasted the room with a ray gun or something, and got everybody?" Trevor said.

Rosa turned and stared at him.

"Yeah, Trev," Eddie said. "Maybe they could have. But who could imagine an explosion of violence like that toward innocent people?" He leaned in a little and Trevor pulled back.

"Oh. Right. Sorry."

"Should we let them know we're coming?" Rosa said.

"They'll see us," Reg said.

"Besides, the egg is linked to their communications system," Eddie said. "I don't think we *could* contact our people with it."

Reg brought them in lower.

Home. But not for Eddie. Because he was kicked out, and even if they reinstated him for boosting the aliens' ride, there'd still be his father to take him away.

"Identify yourself," the control panel said. They all looked at Reg. What was that about?

"What?" he said.

"You identify biometrically as Reginald Davis," the voice said pleasantly. "Reginald Davis's access has been revoked."

They stared at one another, eyes huge.

"Wow," Trevor said. "It's about time they thought of that."

"If there is a person on board with permission to fly, please identify yourself now."

"Damn it, Reginald," Reg said, and put the craft into a dive.

"Identify yourself," the panel said.

Eddie unsnapped and stood up. "I am Spartacus," he said.

"Access denied, Spartacus," the panel said. "If access is not confirmed within sixty seconds, I will assume command of the vehicle and return to base."

"That's *their* base," Rosa said. "We won't make it."

"We'll get stuck in XD space," Trevor said.

"Kill the panel!" Rosa yelled. "Reg, kill it before it can take over."

Reg began frantically flipping switches. "I can't land in the next minute."

"Could we bail?" Rosa said.

"Too high," Trevor said.

He was right. They needed more than a minute.

"If we can cut power to the panel, we can at least crash and keep them from getting the egg back," Reg said.

"We can't crash," Eddie shouted. "Remember?"

"We can here," Reg said. "Their sensor isn't going to work on our world."

"Hooray?" Trevor said.

Reg concentrated on flying. Eddie vaulted forward between them and yanked at the control panel cover that fit over the switches and hid the wiring. Rosa tugged on it, too, but it was screwed onto the console. No point pulling out his pocketknife—there just wasn't time to unscrew the whole thing.

"Which switch?" Eddie yelled. "Reg, exactly what do we have to kill?"

He pointed to a red switch at the top of the panel. Eddie leaned back, planted his left foot, and came forward with his right, smashing the switch with his heel. He could feel it shatter. The console bent and there was a hole where the switch had been. He leaped onto the arms of Reg and Rosa's chairs, one foot on each, crouching. He could see wires, but they were too deep to reach.

"It's still in command," Reg said, bashing switches on and off with the side of his fist.

Through the windshield, Iowa was rushing up at them.

"Get some water!" Eddie shouted to Trevor.

"Where? Where?"

"You have ten seconds to confirm access," the control panel said.

Eddie unzipped his jeans and grabbed Edward the Great and started peeing into the hole in the console. "See, if we'd had root beer, this would be easier." *Now those are good last words. Practice makes perfect.*

"Eww," Rosa said, turning toward the side window. Edward was a little offended.

A tiny trail of smoke came from the control panel, mixing with the urine odor. It wasn't really an improvement.

"Access . . . access . . ." The panel voice cut off. Eddie did, too. He stuffed Edward back in his boxers and zipped up.

"I still have control!" Reg shouted.

Eddie climbed back down, sat in his seat, and buckled up. Rosa was still sitting with her hand over her eyes. This would probably always be an awkward moment between them.

"Okay, *now* I don't have control," Reg said.

"What?" Eddie said. "I drowned their ability to take over!"

"Yeah," he said, keeping his focus on the ground below them. "You drowned the whole panel. Everybody strapped? We're gonna crash."

# CHAPTER FORTY

Reg flipped switches and pulled levers with speed and precision, and Rosa had no idea how to help him. She wasn't anyplace close to trained enough to copilot in an emergency.

Iowa rushed toward them. She was going to die in a pee-soaked alien egg. She hoped that didn't go in her obituary. Her father would be mortified.

"We saved them," Trevor whispered, gesturing vaguely below them. "And we prevented alien NASA from being able to return."

And then a second later the ground and the sky and the craft met. Rosa gripped her armrests hard, and she didn't know how much of the shaking was the egg and how much was her. They rocked and bounced and scraped and sparked, but they didn't spin and they didn't roll. And then the egg shuddered and there was no motion, just a low hiss. The cabin filled with a high, acrid stench.

Eddie was up and heaved the door open before Rosa unbuckled.

"Who's injured?" Trevor shouted.

"I'm okay," Rosa shouted back, climbing over the console between the seats and staggering to the door. She'd lost her balance with the craft's pitching.

Eddie was outside, and reached a hand up to help Rosa out. She let him, and then Trevor climbed down.

"Reg?" Eddie said.

"Reg?" Trevor echoed.

"I don't know," Rosa said.

And then Reg was at the doorway, holding one arm, trying to step down. He was shaking. Eddie ran to him, grabbed him, and carried him like a baby for twenty yards, trotting away from the egg.

"Put me down," Reg snapped. "This is a terrible visual."

"Hero trainee rescues bald pickle-snapper?" Eddie said.

"Let me look at your arm," Trevor said.

"It's broken, and it's not compound," Reg said. "Nothing to look at. Besides, I think we smashed up the fuel tanks when we landed."

Rosa's eyes flared. "Um, when you mix nitrogen tetroxide and monomethylhydrazine . . ."

"Things go boom," Reg barked. "Run."

They ran for the launch pad, and beyond it, the Flight Control Room.

"I always wanted to do that cool walk away from an explosion," Eddie shouted. "This is our best chance, but we're running, and we've got no explosion."

With that, a giant fireball erupted from the egg, and ragged fragments of metal snagged the sky. Rosa ran straight, because in three-dimensional space the shortest distance between Rosa Hayashi and the cover of the launch tower was a straight line.

Debris fell around them, a bloom of fire and shrapnel and deafening sound. It was like being inside a firecracker. It was like riding the sun. A bit of shrapnel streaked past and scraped the side of Trevor's calf. He glanced at it but kept running.

They were halfway to the launch tower when Eddie fell.

# CHAPTER FORTY-ONE

Eddie didn't see the egg explode, but it rattled his bones, trying to separate them. The way everything separates. They were halfway to the launch tower when he pitched forward.

He didn't know why. Nothing hurt. Adrenaline killed pain better than the stuff in the brown paper bag.

He was on his face, tasting blood. It felt like the old man was punching him in the back, punch, punch, punch. He twisted his arm behind him, and his fingers found something thin sticking out. Metal, because it cut them. He pulled his hand back and it was full of blood.

His lungs couldn't draw enough air. It felt like the time he almost drowned in a river saving a choir. Only that couldn't be right. His vision was closing in at the sides, like the water was winning.

Then he stretched his arm out in front of him and pressed his hand down, leaving a bloody handprint to show he was here. He'd tried. God, he'd tried to make it.

*What goes up must come down.*

# CHAPTER FORTY-TWO

Rosa screamed. Reg was behind her. He let go of his arm, and he grabbed her and pulled her forward. There was a slender piece of silver sticking six inches out of Eddie's back, and bright blood was burbling out from the base like it was a fountain. She would never forget that.

Reg pulled her past Eddie's body, and they ran for the cover of the launch tower. The ground stopped vibrating and shrapnel stopped hurtling through the sky before they got there.

"Don't touch any debris," Reg shouted. The explosion had blasted their ears and he sounded muffled, even though he was right in their faces. "We don't know what this stuff is."

Rosa ran back the way they'd just come, and it felt like a dream where you can't move your legs. She ran and ran and didn't seem to get closer to Eddie, lying on his face with one hand pressed onto the tarmac. She was crying.

Vehicles came from the Flight Control building. Rosa knew

there were sirens and shouting and the dull thrum of engines, but she didn't hear any of it. She just saw Eddie's red shirt getting bigger, spreading out beside him. But it wasn't his shirt, it was his blood.

So much blood.

And then Trevor passed her, pounding along the tarmac, leaping over smoking bits of debris from the alien craft. He got to Eddie first and knelt there, fingers on his neck.

"Help me roll him!" he shouted as Rosa reached them. "Easy."

They rolled him up so Trevor could assess his chest and belly, and Eddie's head sagged, his eyes pointed toward the earth. Then they laid him gently back on his face. The IA vehicles roared in then, a whole fleet of them. They stopped fifty yards back because of the debris field. Two medics ran up, pulling a stretcher. They knelt by Eddie.

"Pulse one hundred eighteen and thready," Trevor said. "Respirations twenty-one. He's tachypneic from hypovolemic shock, secondary to a small deep puncture wound to the right dorsal torso. That's all I've found so far."

The medics raised their eyebrows at him and did their own quick assessment.

"I think it hit his kidney," Trevor said.

"Yeah," one of the medics said. They lifted Eddie and put him on his side on the stretcher, and his arm flopped. Then they rolled him away at a run.

Rosa and Trevor stood by the pool of blood and hugged. It was a big pool.

"I cannot believe," Trevor finally said, "that of all the crazy-ass stunts Eddie Toivonen pulled today—or in his whole life, for that matter—the thing that got him was running away."

Rosa gave a small, sobby laugh. "He's not good at running away."

And then she thought of their joke of putting up a plaque that said "Eddie Toivonen didn't die here." Except maybe he did.

They trudged past his red handprint and back to the IA officials walking toward them. Rosa could see Stanford Smithson and John Taylor Templeton and Friesta Bauer among them. So they were safe. It had worked. They'd gotten the bacteria off their world and drawn the alien teams away and saved them.

Rosa started to cry again.

Some other medics checked them out and put them in hospital beds with giant sheets of clear plastic between them—Reg, then Trevor, then Rosa. They were in quarantine in case they had space germs. Rosa got a window. It looked out over the back of the building they'd done the simulation in. She had a view of fields of low green corn. She couldn't see the red handprint, but she knew exactly where it was.

Rosa rang for a nurse. He came in wearing all sorts of protective clothing.

"Do you know," she said, "that I flew through the extra dimensions twice, wearing a pair of shorts?" He shifted uncomfortably and started an explanation about precautions. Rosa looked him in his plastic eyeshield and interrupted. "Can I call my parents?"

He smiled. "They're here, Miss Hayashi. They've been waiting here for three days."

He left, and a couple of minutes later her mom and dad came in, all suited up. Her mother lay in the bed with her and held her, and her dad pulled the chair up next to the bed and stroked her hair. She told them everything, even about kissing Eddie. Then she fell asleep.

# CHAPTER FORTY-THREE

They kept the trio in quarantine for two weeks. Reg's arm was in a cast, but it didn't prevent him from forcing them to play Monopoly with him. Trevor passed the time by checking the scrape on his calf for signs of infection. Rosa showed him how to put on eyeliner, and they both experimented with it. They agreed that she looked fabulous with a smoky eye, but he was better off with a simple black rim. She kept asking Reg to let them try it on him. He was going to owe NASA's swear jar a lot of quarters.

None of them showed signs of anything but boredom and irritability, so the doctors finally discharged them. Rosa and Trevor both flew home with their parents. Interworlds Agency Director Smithson saw them off at the airport.

"We're hanging your mission plaque in two weeks," he said. "You'll be back for that, right?"

"You bet," Rosa said. They hung a plaque on the Flight Control Room wall after every mission. It was a big deal. Their names
would be on it, together, forever: Davis, Hayashi, Toivonen, and
Clayborn. Eddie got his name on a plaque after all.

# CHAPTER FORTY-FOUR

Two Weeks Later

The ceremony was at two o'clock, to be followed by hors d'oeuvres. Rosa wore a red dress and didn't straighten when she passed the paparazzi stationed along the road to the compound, and the news vans from all over the world parked inside. Trevor looked handsome in a suit. Their parents were there, and everybody at IA who'd been in the Flight Control Room when the alien teams had landed. There was a full contingent of NASA brass, too, including John Taylor Templeton—the head of NASA, there to honor them.

Rosa and Trevor and Reg stood together at the front of the Flight Control Room. Their families stayed off to the side. There was a long table covered with fruit and cheese slices and gourmet crackers for snacking when the ceremony was done. Reg's wife, Jennifer, squeezed his good arm and slipped out of the room.

When she came back a minute later, Eddie was with her.

He was pale and had shadows under his eyes, and although he

walked slowly he was steady on his feet. He saw Rosa and grinned. She smiled back at him and did a little finger wave by her thigh. They hadn't let her see him before she went home. She hadn't seen him since the explosion.

The crowd broke into a low clap, and Jennifer Davis walked down the long aisle with him. She knew better than to try to hold his arm to help him. When he got to the front Rosa grabbed his face and gave him a kiss right on the lips, and everybody clapped harder, even her dad.

"I'll settle for a handshake," Trevor said, smiling and grabbing Eddie's hand. Reg gripped his shoulder and gave it a squeeze.

"Glad to see you," Reg said.

"Likewise," Eddie said. "Your arm okay?"

"Yeah."

Rosa slipped her hand around Eddie's arm, and he squeezed it against his side.

Smithson cleared his throat. "I don't want to keep Eddie on his feet for too long, so let's get started. It is the greatest honor of my career to welcome IA's Team 3 and their instructor. They saved the lives of probably everybody on this planet . . ." Here he was interrupted by thunderous applause and a couple of whistles. "They commandeered an alien spacecraft, figured out how to fly it through the extra dimensions, evaluated a new world, made contact with friendly locals, ditched that bacteria, scuttled two craft, and flew the third home. I'm just sorry we weren't able to salvage more of that craft so we could examine its control panel."

"Yeah, they probably don't want to do that," Eddie whispered. Trevor snorked.

Smithson shook his head. "You have courage, tenacity, and the ability to work together. And now you have a place on the wall."

He nodded, and the camera flew in and blinked green, ready for them. They each pinched the edge of the black silk covering an easel, looked at each other, and gave it a little tug. The fabric slid off and there was their mission plaque: a solid black field with their last names, and below them two identical blue Earths.

Everyone clapped, and then a couple of guys propped a ladder against the wall and one climbed up and hung their mission plaque. Eventually there would be another to its right, and then another, and another. But this one would always be theirs.

Most people pulled out their phones and took hover selfies with them, and the trainees shook a lot of hands and smiled, and then made their way to the refreshment table. Jennifer Davis went with them, but their parents hung back.

"I figured out why you lost a kidney," Trevor said. "It was the egg's revenge for you peeing on it."

"Hey, that makes sense," Eddie said. He grinned.

John Taylor Templeton came by and flashed his green card at Eddie. "May I access the hors d'oeuvres table?" he asked, smiling.

Eddie made a show of looking at the card. "Yeah, but stay away from the bacon-wrapped shrimp. They're mine."

Templeton patted his shoulder, took a little paper plate, and moved past them. Rosa took a plate, too, and dropped some grapes on it.

When they'd had a few minutes to eat, Smithson got their attention and said, "We have a few small things we'd like to give these people." Which meant that everybody was quiet and watching when Eddie's old man walked into the room.

Eddie set down his plate, then stood perfectly still. Watchful. Ready.

Rosa and Trevor exchanged a glance. They couldn't let him get in a fight, considering the size of the scar he must have on his back.

"Any reason I wasn't invited?" Mr. Toivonen said as he sauntered up the aisle, picking food off the table as he went. "Hey, Eddie," he said as he breezed past them. Reg was breathing hard and had his head down, and looked like a bull ready to charge.

"You haven't been answering my phone calls," Mr. Toivonen said to Director Smithson. "So I thought I'd just stop by." John Taylor Templeton walked over to stand next to Smithson.

"God," Eddie said. "Now? This is when he shows up?" He pulled his mouth in tight, like he was in pain.

*I guess he is*, Rosa thought.

"You damaged my son, and I'm going to need reimbursement for that damage," Mr. Toivonen said, as though Eddie were a *thing*. "Or I'll have to sue you and this joker . . ." He poked the NASA director in the chest. "And everybody in this goddamn place."

"I'm glad you're here," Smithson said smoothly. He pulled a folded set of papers from his jacket pocket. "If you're Eddie's legal guardian, you're responsible for his hospital bills. Which have been considerable."

"Hell, I am!" Mr. Toivonen said. "You said you have insurance."

"We do," Smithson said. "But the deductibles are in the thousands, once it's all added together. Here, take a look." He held the papers out to Mr. Toivonen.

"That's not my responsibility!" he said.

"Actually, it is. As long as you have parental rights." Smithson pulled another set of papers from his jacket pocket. "You can give me a check, or you can give up your parental rights."

"Which you would lose in a few months, anyway," Templeton said. "About the time he's well enough to work again."

"This is a con," Mr. Toivonen said.

"You would know," Smithson said.

Mr. Toivonen bunched his shoulders and worked his jaw, but Smithson didn't flinch.

"Whatever," he finally said, grabbing the second set of papers. "Little asswipe isn't worth the money." He took the pen Templeton proffered, signed the paper, and left it on a console. "Hey, Eddie," he shouted across the room as he left. "You're a fucking emancipated minor. Good luck with that." He picked up a tray of smoked salmon on crackers and walked out with it. The whole tray.

"Sorry," Eddie whispered. "I ruined you guys' ceremony."

"Oh, Eddie. Not your fault," Rosa said. "Anyway, it's your ceremony, too."

He shook his head. "I'm kicked out, remember? I'm only here because I was on the . . . well, it wasn't even a mission. I just boosted a ride. Like him." He turned to go and Reg grabbed his arm, but when Eddie spoke again it was to Rosa. "See my clothes?" He was wearing khakis and a dress shirt that still had windowpane folds in it. He tilted his head toward Reg's wife. "She got them for me this morning when she found out I was gonna wear jeans and a T-shirt. 'Cause that's what I had."

"That was nice," Rosa said.

"I'm a frickin embarrassment," he said. "I should go." He blinked hard. "I have the worst luck in the entire universe. There's no other Eddie out there with worse luck."

Rosa hooked her pinkie around his, down low at their sides. "Knock knock."

He blinked at her, then finally said, "Who's there?"

"Me, okay? I'm here." She gave his pinkie a squeeze before she let it go.

Templeton called to them. "This would be a good time for some remarks, I think," he said. "Can Team 3 come over here?" He motioned them back to the easel.

Rosa tilted her head toward Templeton, inviting Eddie to walk with her. He hesitated, then hooked his pinkie back around hers and let her lead him over.

"For all of Earth's history we have spun alone in the dark, one planet, gazing at the stars and wondering," Templeton said. "Now we have traversed the farthest reaches of space only to see our own faces. We stand at the brink of a new age: we are not alone. In a real and demonstrable way, what is out there," he said, sweeping his hand upward, "is what is in here." He tapped his chest. "We sent four people into space—not authorized, mind you." Everyone laughed. "But I can think of no better ambassadors to extend their hands across that vast divide."

He nodded to Smithson, and the IA director stepped forward.

"We have some gifts," he said. "First, Team 3's trainer, Commander Reginald Davis," Smithson said. "Reg, you wanted a little time away from flying after a tragic crash. During that 'time off' you flew through extradimensional space and made one of the most impressive landings in aviation history. We're not falling for your excuses anymore." Smithson smiled. "You're reinstated. Fly at will."

John Taylor Templeton pinned an eagle medal on Reg's chest. Reg puffed out a little, and shook their hands.

"Thank you," he said softly. "I'd like to stay on as Team 3's instructor, if I may."

Smithson and Templeton exchanged a glance. "That's not typical," Smithson finally said.

"Anything about any of this strike you as typical?" Reg said.

"Commander Davis has a point," Smithson said, and shook his hand again.

"We got you something, too," Rosa said. Trevor grinned and trotted up behind a console in the front, and came back rolling a barrel on its rim.

"Pickles!" Trevor said.

Rosa added, "We thought you should have a full week's supply." Everybody laughed. The mood was lightening after Mr. Toivonen's scene.

"We've learned that when we gaze into the sky, someone is looking back," Smithson went on. "One of the people out there is another Rosa Hayashi, which is comforting when you think of her remarkable intellect, courage, and leadership. It's disconcerting when you realize she might launch herself through space at you."

Eddie grinned at her.

"For Rosa," Smithson said, reaching behind him, "a cape." Everyone laughed again. It wasn't a cheap Halloween prop—this was made of heavy taffeta and had a crystal clasp at the neck. Rosa dropped it over her shoulders and made superhero arms. She would have loved this when she played dress-up as a little girl. "That'll help you the next time you jump off a launch tower."

Her dad put his hands over his face and groaned. He hadn't liked hearing that part of the story.

"Did you see the clasp?" John Taylor Templeton said.

Rosa hadn't really looked, so she took the cape off to examine it. It was the NASA logo worked in crystals.

"It detaches so you can wear it as a pin."

"Oh," she said. "It's gorgeous." And she meant it.

"Trevor," John Taylor Templeton said, "you ran off to take on a planet by yourself. I need a word beyond courage." Templeton shook his head. "In addition to your extraordinary heart, you paid close attention in kindergarten. Thank you for that." Trevor grinned.

Templeton held out a first aid kit. Looking at the crowd he said, "We had them engrave something on it. It says, 'Does this look infected?'"

Rosa and Eddie sagged into each other with laughter. Trevor clasped his hands together and shook them over his head, then reached for the kit, but Templeton kept hold of the handle. When he spoke again, his voice was serious.

"Trevor, you know we normally just have two team members."

"Um, okay," Trevor said uncertainly.

"You would be great on an IA team, but we think you'd be even better on our medical staff. If you want it, the contents of the first aid kit are yours."

Trevor took the kit, glanced nervously at Rosa and Eddie, then flipped it open. "Gauze!" he said. "Just what I've always wanted!"

"I think that's true," Eddie whispered.

"Oh. Oh. And, um," he held up a piece of paper, "a certificate that says it's redeemable for an education at Harvard Medical School."

The room rustled, and Dr. and Dr. Clayborn squeezed each other's hands.

"Just to be clear, we don't expect you to start with med school," Smithson said. "It includes four years for a BS first—and you'll have your final year of high school here."

"Thank you so much," Trevor said. "I do want this. But I wonder if I could trade it for going to the University of Iowa."

Smithson and Templeton looked at each other. "I think our donor would agree to that," Templeton said.

"Good," Trevor said. "I have a couple of friends I want to keep up with."

Rosa kissed his cheek and Eddie bounced his fist gently on Trev's head.

Smithson looked out at the crowd. "I'm always going to be the guy who cut Eddie Toivonen from IA. At least let me also be the guy who welcomes him back. Eddie, will you accept my apology—and a position on Team 3?"

"Yeah," Eddie said. His voice was thick.

"Good! We were aware that you know math and that you

know physics. But we didn't realize what a fluid thinker you are."
He handed Eddie a gold-plated urinal, and the place roared with
laughter.

Eddie took it. "Jeez, it's heavy." He shook it over his head. His
post-op instructions probably didn't allow that, but then Eddie
never was a rules follower.

"We have something else for you, too," Smithson said, holding out a small wooden box.

Eddie put down the urinal, took the box, and flipped up the lid.
"A compass?"

"Because your moral compass points north, Eddie. We believe
in you. You believe in you, too, okay?"

Eddie nodded and blinked and slipped the compass into his
pocket.

"Trev and I got you something!" Rosa said. They dragged a big
box out from behind a console where they'd hidden it.

"It's a train set," Trevor said.

"A train set?" Eddie said, clearly mystified.

"It's because we solved trolleyology," Rosa said. "The unsolv-
able problem. When Trevor was trapped on the tracks, you didn't
push the person next to you."

"That's 'cause you're not fat enough," Eddie said. She smacked
him on the arm.

"Shush. We're having a moment."

"Okay."

"We jumped *together*. Nobody pushing anybody." She looked at
him, willing him to understand.

"I tied his shoestrings," Trevor said, "you kept the gun pointed

at you, and Rosa went flying squirrel on him. So we got you a
train set, to remind you that you don't always have to do it alone."

"Huh," Eddie said. Then he put his arms around both of them.
"I always wanted a train set. Are there little trees and stuff?"

"Yeah!" Trevor said. "And hoboes! We got you hoboes."

# CHAPTER FORTY-FIVE

The room began to clear, which was fine with Eddie because he needed to sit down and he had no plans to admit it. He snagged a piece of licorice off the table, and Reg motioned him to the windows. Eddie thought Reg wanted to show him something, but it seemed he just wanted to talk. Jennifer Davis was there, too. They both looked serious.

"Eddie, you're still recovering," Reg said.

*Well, duh.* That's why he wanted to sit down. Reg glanced at Mrs. Reg, and she waved a hand at him.

"Jennifer makes a fine tuna casserole. She puts those fried onions on top."

"Um . . ."

"Reg," she said.

"I'm telling you, a good tuna casserole is the foundation of domestic bliss." He took a deep breath. "We want you to live with us while you're recovering."

Eddie stared at him. He did not see that coming.

"And after. Once you get settled, it would be inefficient to move out again."

"What Reg is so eloquently saying is that we'd like it if you'd make our place home," Jennifer said. "For as long as you want. You should have a place to come home to once you do leave."

"At Christmas," Reg said. "And to have someone to call if you blow a tire, or forget how to calculate the cosmological constant."

"Huh," Eddie said. "Would you stop throwing Ping-Pong balls at me?"

"Not a chance," Reg said.

"You got root beer?"

"A whole fridge full," Jennifer said.

"Huh," Eddie said. "I guess we can give it a try."

He went over and told Rosa and Trevor. He had to recover more before he came back to continue training, but he'd see them again.

Eddie carried his gold-plated urinal with pride, and felt the weight of the compass in his pocket. Reg dragged the train set out to the car with one arm.

"You know I get to play with this, too," he said.

"Yeah," Eddie said. "You can't play with a train by yourself."

He was on Team 3.

He was going to have a train set in the basement of Reg and Jennifer Davis's house, which was also his house.

And he was going to kiss Rosa Hayashi every chance he got.

That's what he knew.

# ACKNOWLEDGMENTS

So many people helped with this book in some way, and I'm grateful to them all.

Daniel McMahon, M. D. and Adam Ryan, M. D. checked medical scenes and language for me. Kristy Ryan put up with a discussion of mitochondria at her dinner table. Thanks to Christine "Vole-Flinger" McMahon for the walks and conversations in the park.

Dr. Thomas Kroc explained the difficulties of observing electrons. Dr. Jonathan Green and Rose Green discussed the appropriateness of "Friesta" as a first name; it's not their fault I went ahead and used it. Dr. Richard Kaae shared his knowledge of scorpions. Tom Billings, Tom Cone, and Mary Anne Siurek helped with Indiana criminal sentences. Additional expertise was provided by Robin Prehn, Bruce Nesmith, NASA, Johnson Space Center, and Kelly Humphries at JSC. Any errors are entirely my own.

Anne Bingham, Vonna Carter, Marcia Hoehne, Ena Jones, Cyndi Marko, and Laurel Strong read or provided support. :bigkiss

Thanks also to Mrs. Edith Hufford, my first grade teacher. Mrs. Hufford got her degree at age sixty and only taught a few years, but what a world of difference she made.

The Sweet Sixteens were a terrific debut group, and I'm honored to have been included. We still need to get those T-shirts, guys. The SCBWI Blueboard has been a wonderful place to hang out. Thanks for sharing the journey.

Tim Jarboe talked railroad songs with me. If Tim, John Robert McFarland, and Joseph Kennedy help Eddie set up his toy train, he's going to have a fabulous layout.

I wanted Eddie to have a good best friend so I gave his hometown buddy Heather Jarboe's last name. Heath, I am always available for a three a.m. game of Go Fish.

Thanks to Brigid Kennedy and Joseph Kennedy for brainstorming with me and for their many insights, and to Joe for letting me try to throw him down a flight of stairs to clarify the action in one scene. No children were harmed in the making of this book.

Thanks to John Robert McFarland and Helen McFarland for their encouraging breakfast messages, and also for driving around Oolitic, Indiana, and sending maps and photos. Mary Beth McFarland displays my books on her desk at work. Patrick Kennedy washed a lot of dishes while I wrote, and never once complained. Thanks for always being there.

I had to be completely out of touch for a few days right when my agent, Kate McKean, was negotiating the deal for this book. I told her that I trusted her and to do whatever she wanted to. Kate, thanks for your skill and caring. If there's another Earth out there, I hope it has a Kate McKean.

My editor, Sarah Shumway, championed Rosa and Eddie and strengthened their story in so many ways. She also put up with my sassy margin notes and sent me chocolate and baby pictures—that pretty much makes her perfect.

Thanks to the rest of the team at Bloomsbury for their expertise and support, especially Patricia McHugh, Claire Stetzer—who came up with the title, Diane Aronson, Lizzy Mason, Anna Bernard, Donna Mark, Melissa Kavonic, Kerry Johnson, Catherine Onder, Cindy Loh, Colleen Andrews, and Oona Patrick.

I'm glad that all of you are on my Earth.

One more thing . . .

When I was just starting this book, Kira Vermond challenged me to put licorice in the last scene as a tip of the hat to her. Did it, Kira. Now I get to issue a challenge to you for your next book. Game on!

Because there's no air in space, the asteroid hurtled toward Earth in absolute silence. Of the two objects headed toward North America— the BR1019 asteroid and Yuri Strelnikov's flight from Moscow— only his plane made a sound. The thought made Yuri smile faintly as the American military plane descended, engines roaring.

The aircraft touched down and taxied, and a moment later the pilot opened the door for its lone passenger. Yuri stepped to the top of the airstair and surveyed the sun-drenched airport. Then he trotted down, carrying a single suitcase and a book bag looped over his shoulder, and headed to a waiting helicopter.

Yuri dragged his suitcase with one hand, felt the bite of the book bag's strap and the heat of the sun on his shoulders. He rolled up the sleeves of his dress shirt with his free hand as he walked. He'd grown an inch in the past six months, and while the sleeves were long enough now, they might not be in a couple of weeks.

How would he get a new shirt here? Better to roll the sleeves up from the start, so people were used to it.

An American officer stepped forward to open the helicopter door. He got in after Yuri and nodded to the pilot. Yuri took the headphones he offered, and a moment later the man's voice crackled through. "NASA's Near Earth Object Program is housed at the Jet Propulsion Laboratory in Pasadena. I'll point it out as we get close."

Then the pilot lifted off, and once again the ground fell away below Yuri. The pilot threw the throttle open and the craft shuddered and then responded. Yuri laid his cheek against the glass and gazed into the blue arcing over America. He wouldn't see the asteroid. He knew that. By the time you could see it, it was too late. Because, although it was still in the dark reaches of space, the asteroid was traveling at 159,000 miles per hour.

Yuri sat in the back of the helicopter, his headphones muting the *whomp* of the rotors, and looked down at this dry city, lower and brighter than Moscow. He didn't know what he thought of it yet. It was just . . . different. Yuri glanced at the officer and tried not to fidget. He could see people in white-and-glass buildings watching their descent as the pilot banked and landed. As they climbed out, the officer shouted at Yuri to keep his head down, and put a heavy hand on his neck to make sure he avoided the slowing rotor blades. He ushered Yuri inside one of the buildings and said, "Good luck."

Yuri started to say, "You, too," but realized it wasn't appropriate, and was still searching for a response as the man left. Yuri stood for a moment, fingering the strap of his book bag, wishing he didn't have the suitcase with him. Who brings a suitcase to an office building? An air-conditioning vent blasted ripples through his blond hair.

A security guard walked over to him and said, "Follow me," then turned and led Yuri to a door off a large conference room. "You're supposed to wait in here." He jerked his head toward the door and walked off, and Yuri went in. The room was very small. It had two chairs on the right wall, two on the left, a tiny table with a pile of old magazines against the far wall. A boy of maybe five or six sat in a chair to the left. Yuri unslung his book bag and sat down opposite him.

The boy fingered the handle of a plastic tote bag as though Yuri might steal it. "Who are you?"

"Yuri Strelnikov. Who are you?"

"I'm not supposed to talk to strangers."

"Oh."

They were quiet for a moment.

"I'm Tim." The kid flopped across both chairs, with his head hanging off the end. He rolled to his side and pointed at Yuri's bags.

"What's in there?"

"Clothes mostly."

"I've got blocks in mine."

Tim opened his bag and dumped a pile of blocks on the floor. He began to build a tower, one block on top of another.

"Your base needs to be wider. See how it leans?" Yuri pointed. "It's already maybe eight degrees off vertical."

Yuri got on the floor beside him and snapped two long blocks onto the bottom of the tower. "See? This will increase your structural integrity."

Tim grabbed more blocks and widened the base of his tower again, so that it was four blocks wide at the bottom.

The door opened. A tall man peered in at them. He was bald and had piercing blue eyes below a forehead that rose like a crown. "Dr. Strelnikov?"

Yuri rose. "Yes?"

The man flushed, then stepped forward and threw out his hand. "I'm Karl Fletcher, director of NASA's Near Earth Object Program. Nice to have you aboard."

He led Yuri out of the room. "Sorry about the confusion. The boy is the grandson of one of our support people. He's waiting for her."

"Oh."

Fletcher cleared his throat. "You're seventeen, right?"

"Yes."

Fletcher shrugged apologetically, and then Yuri got it. *Oh.* The security guard thought Yuri was the grandson. And the director had walked in to see two kids on the floor playing with blocks. It could not be more humiliating. Yuri felt his face flame and knew that just made it worse. Fletcher pulled him into a large conference room, mostly open, with tables holding coffee decanters and doughnuts pushed against a far wall. The suitcase still embarrassed Yuri, and he pushed it under a table with his foot. The director introduced him to a half-dozen people—the local caffeine addicts, probably—and Yuri slowly relaxed. They wore name tags emblazoned with "NASA" and the agency's symbol, an orbit and wing in mid-century style.

Fletcher handed him a name tag, and Yuri looked at it and smiled. He had seen his name spelled in English before, but it still looked funny, English requiring a *y* and a *u* to make one Russian letter. He pinned the name tag on his shirt.

"I don't know what you've heard about this rock," Fletcher said. "Since you're gonna help us stop it, let me bring you up to speed. BR1019"—he said it like "Bee Are Ten Nineteen"—"isn't from the asteroid belt—it came from way out. We don't know if it's swung close by Earth before—it could have an orbit in the thousands of years. Or it might have hit some piece of space junk that altered its orbit."

Yuri nodded. Happened all the time.

"It's dim, so we were late picking it up—and of course it's coming out of the sun. Makes it harder." Fletcher snagged a doughnut off the table. "It was an amateur who found it."

Yuri shrugged. "Not so embarrassing as it sounds. You were looking at places where asteroids come from, yes? And this one is in retrograde orbit."

"Not what we were expecting," Fletcher admitted. "We haven't had a chance to do everything yet. Shape, spectral analysis—we had to concentrate first on calculating the orbit, and once we realized it'll be a direct hit, we've had to calculate speed . . ."

"So we know how long we've got," Yuri said.

"Right."

Against the wall, the coffee decanter was doing steady business as people filtered in and out of the room, feet soundless on the light blue carpet.

"So what exactly do you want me to do?"

A man with rimless glasses and thinning hair approached the table, but he wasn't looking at the decanters. There was something in his stride that made Yuri stiffen, and he shifted to conceal his suitcase. The man cocked his head to the side and as Fletcher gestured toward Yuri, starting an introduction, he spoke. "Russia's boy wonder. Huh." Yuri wasn't sure how to answer that, or even if it was a question, but he felt the room stir around him. People were watching. "I'm Zach Simons."

"Zach is your team leader," Fletcher said. "Zach, this is . . ."

"Yeah, I know who he is, I just don't know why he's here. I got a question for you, Dr. Strelnikov. Do you shave yet?"

"On formal occasions," Yuri said, keeping his eyes on Simons. "I shaved for night I accepted Wolf Prize, for example."

Simons reddened as an appreciative murmur rose from the other scientists in the conference room.

"Okay," Fletcher said. "Nice that you guys met." He led Yuri to the far side of the conference room, away from Simons. "Obviously nudging it off course would be the first choice," Fletcher said, getting back on topic. "It's too late for that, so we're going to try to shoot it down. Send weapons into it, try to blow it into several pieces, and hope they're small enough to burn up in our atmosphere. We already know our best window will come when the 1019 is very close."

Yuri shifted impatiently. He already knew this. Everyone already knew this.

"Essentially we're making one giant mathematical computer model. I've divided it into twenty-three different sections." Fletcher finished off the doughnut and licked his fingers. "We have that many teams, each working on one part of the problem."

Fletcher motioned him back to the other side of the room, and Yuri sheepishly retrieved his suitcase and lugged it over to Fletcher. Because being a third the age of everyone else didn't make him stick out enough.

"You're Team Eleven, working with the charming Zach Simons and Bruce Pirkola, who's the sonofabitch over there swallowing a bottle of Tylenol. See, in the corner? Because he chose this particular week to get a goddamn kidney stone." Fletcher stared into Yuri's eyes. "I trust you're too young to have a kidney stone?"

"Yes, sir."

"Good." He thrust a thick printout with a black binder clip at Yuri. "This is an overview of the model. Your section is highlighted. You and Simons and Pirkola figure out what goes in it."

"What weapons are we using? We'll need to know mass, speed . . ."

"Yeah." Fletcher rolled his jaw side to side. "We've got people working on that. You don't need access to the weapons list."

Yuri stared at him. "This is critical information. To calculate our section . . ."

"Your team doesn't have to know this," Fletcher said.

Yuri picked at his bag strap with his thumbnail. "How can you possibly keep information from some of people working . . ."

"Not some people," Fletcher said, smiling tightly. "Just you. Look, if you really need something, if you think weapon specs will change your calculations, ask Simons. He's your group leader. He can talk to me, and I'll figure it out."

He led the way upstairs and to a small office off a hall to the right, brushing powdered sugar from his shirt as he walked. "This is yours for the duration. And we got you a hotel room. A car service will take you over there tonight. There's a cafeteria downstairs. You don't need money, just take what you want. We've . . ."

"But won't we be working all night? I mean, is critical situation."

"Of course not," Fletcher said. "This is going to take days. You know impact is June ninth, right?"

Yuri nodded.

"We're all going to work our asses off, but we'll get it done. The last thing I want is a bunch of sleep-deprived zombies making critical decisions."

He opened the door to Yuri's office. Yuri unslung his book bag from his shoulder and rested it on his foot.

"If you need something, just hit '1' on your phone. The person who answers isn't a secretary; she's one of us. You can talk physics to her, explain what you need, who you have to get hold of."

Yuri ran a hand through his hair and looked at this pale blue office half a world from home.

"We have to avoid group think," Fletcher said. "Make your

own calculations, and then the three of you hash it out. Pray you come up with the same damn thing. You have to agree, because whatever your group comes up with is what we're going to enter. Then we'll embed the equations in the computer model they'll use to program the weapons. Got it?"

Yuri nodded.

"Now get the hell to work. You're already behind everybody else." Fletcher started back down the corridor.

"Sir? Dr. Fletcher?"

He turned. "Yeah?"

"Am I the only one who's not American?"

"No, we got a Chinese guy, too. He arrived four hours ago." He stared for a moment at Yuri's blue eyes, his tousle of blond hair. "Your work on antimatter? Blew us away. If we survive this, you're gonna be the youngest person to win a Nobel." He shook his head, then waved his hand toward the office as though sweeping Yuri inside, and started back toward the conference room.

Yuri licked his lips and called after him. "Dr. Fletcher? What they're saying, that if this doesn't work, asteroid will explode over Los Angeles with enough force to devastate whole city? Is that true?"

Fletcher took a breath, then answered flatly.

"That's what Moscow's saying? It isn't true. If we have impact, it'll lay waste to the whole region. A tsunami may take out Japan."

Yuri stared at him.

"But," Fletcher said, "I guess they didn't see any need to panic people."

Yuri walked into the pale blue office, found a roll of masking tape, and wrote his name on it in marker, copying from his name tag so he couldn't misspell it. He ripped the piece of tape off, enjoying the faint rubbery scent, and smoothed it on the wall outside his door: *Strelnikov, Y.A.*

Then he sat at the desk and pulled his calculator out of his book bag, and a hockey puck signed by Moscow Team Dynamo's captain. When he left Russia, the authorities had given him twenty minutes to pack. He'd thrown clothes in his suitcase, tossed in a couple of reference books, but was stumped when it came to keepsakes. He didn't get where he was, as young as he was, without giving up a lot of things—that meant he didn't have a shoe box stuffed with ticket stubs and photos with friends.

So with a driver standing at the door, tapping his foot, Yuri had tucked in a photo of his dissertation advisor—Dr. Kryukov, a wonderful old man with extravagant eyebrows—and the puck, his one true keepsake. The photo wasn't framed, so he kept it in his bag. It was enough knowing it was there. He rolled the puck under his palm, released it, and let it clatter to a rest. Then he spread the printout of the work and scanned it, trying to get his bearings. He should get some idea of what he was doing, and then talk to his team members.

But Fletcher's words ran in an endless loop inside his skull, like a bird he'd once seen trapped in a library dome. It flew in faster and faster circles and finally dropped, dead before it hit the floor. *If we survive this.* Because Yuri had just put himself in the path of the asteroid.

There was time to do the math, to make the computer model to guide the missiles. It would be hard work, but there was time, enough that Fletcher wanted them to sleep well, even unwind a little. Yuri would do his work; Simons and Pirkola would calculate their solutions. They would compare, and because they all knew what they were doing, they would get the same result. They would give Fletcher their part, and the Americans would shoot down the asteroid. He would go home, exaggerate his role, and maybe get laid.

And if it didn't work?

He was seventeen and he would be dead in three weeks.

Who would mourn him? Gregor Kryukov. And his mother, of course. They'd probably put a memo on her desk, and she'd read it when she had time. But he wouldn't be like all those regular dead kids who had a park bench with their name on a plaque. He wouldn't get a bench, but he didn't want one, either. He wanted a Nobel.

No—after his group worked out their part of the math, he was just going to have to fly home to Moscow. It would be painful explaining to Fletcher that he was leaving them, that he'd done his best, and if it didn't work, well, Yuri didn't want to be in Pasadena when it hit. But it wouldn't be the *most* socially awkward moment he'd ever had.

He flexed his hands, stood his puck on its edge for luck, and started reading. An elevator down the hall rumbled, or maybe it was a drink cart going past. Did they do that? And then the puck rolled to the end of his desk, paused, and rolled the other direction.  He stared at it. Yuri had studied with brilliant people at one of the best institutions in the world. He understood laws of motion. He didn't understand this. A body at rest . . . flew off the edge of the desk. And then the books were shaking, inching forward on the shelves, and falling off, splaying open on the carpet, and he could feel the vibration through his feet, all the way up to his knees. *Earthquake.*

He ran from the room. The hall was filled with people standing calmly in their doorways. "Is earthquake, I think!" he shouted, running down the hall. A few doors were closed and he beat on them as he ran by. "Earthquake!" He paused at the elevator and imagined the car swaying on its cable, and he plunged into the east stairwell.

The shuddering stopped, but he grabbed the railing with both hands and crabbed down sideways, not convinced that the ground wouldn't move beneath him again. It looked ridiculous to hold on like that, but it beat being buried in rubble for three days and having to drink his own urine. At the bottom he looked up and saw a dozen faces on each of the stairwells above, looking down at him. Idiots. They were all going to die, and he was going to have to stop the asteroid by himself. The ground gave another jolt. He threw his arms up and shook his hands and shouted, "Earthquake!" over the rumble. Then he ran out the stairwell doors and into the lobby.

He could see the coffee decanters in the conference room bouncing across the table, as though containing that much caffeine had finally gotten to them. A lamp swung overhead, reminding him of Galileo's pendulum experiments, but, with the unsteady rippling of the earth, the time the light took to complete its arc was not constant. And that was so, so wrong.

"Help me, Galileo," he muttered. It was as close to praying as he was going to come. He started for the front door, but it was glass, and he should stay away from glass, right? So he stood in the lobby, hands out at his sides, palms down, as though to calm the earth.

"Hey." It was Karl Fletcher, the director. The ground quieted.

"Is earthquake, I think."

"Yeah, we get these."

"We need to evacuate building. I banged on doors upstairs and shouted to people, but maybe nobody heard."

"Seriously? Okay, let's get you outside." He gripped Yuri's upper arm and pulled him through the plate glass door, down the steps, and into the middle of the street. "Better?"

Yuri watched the street suspiciously. The rumbling was over, and the pavement was still. Inside, the lamp would be describing normal arcs again, and then be stationary. He took a breath. "Nobody else came out."

"Nah, this wasn't too bad. Enough to get your attention, though, right?"

Yuri flushed and glanced up. The windows were lined with people looking out into the street. "Perhaps I overreacted?" The director laughed and slapped him between his shoulder blades. "I didn't want to have to drink my urine," Yuri said.

Fletcher was silent for a moment. "We do have beverage alternatives. There's a vending machine downstairs."

Yuri barked a laugh.

Fletcher led him back upstairs to his office, one hand on Yuri's arm, the other angrily waving gawkers away.

"We have asteroid coming in very fast. Would be nice if Earth stayed in same place for little while."

"It would be nicer if it moved the hell out of the way," Fletcher said. He smacked Yuri on the back. "Show's over. Get to work." He shut the door and left.

Katie Kennedy is a college history instructor and the author of *What Goes Up* and *Learning to Swear in America*. She has a son in high school and a daughter in college. She lives in Iowa—where the Interworlds Agency might be—and has a cornfield in her backyard. She hopes Rosa and Eddie land in it someday.

www.katiekennedybooks.com
@KatieWritesBks